THE CUBAN CONNECTION

A Novel

By

M.L. Malcolm

A Good Read Publishing
Washington, DC

Print ISBN: 978-0-9815726-3-5
ePUB ISBN: 978-0-9815726-2-8
MOBI ISBN: 978-0-9815726-4-2

Print layout by eBooks By Barb for booknook.biz

Praise for M.L. Malcolm's Previous Work:

"*Heart of Lies* takes the reader on a thrill ride that spans continents and decades, but at heart it's an enduring love story."
Melanie Benjamin, New York Times bestselling author of *The Aviator's Wife* and *Mrs. Tom Thumb*.

"A deeply compelling and extraordinary debut novel. It has everything you want: suspense, adventure, and romance across several continents."
Dorothea Benton Frank, New York Times bestselling author of *Return to Sullivan's Island* and *The First Original Wife*.

"A sweeping saga reminiscent of Jeffrey Archer and Susan Howatch... brilliantly researched and beautifully written. I could not put this book down."
Karen White, New York Times bestselling author of *On Folly Beach* and *The House on Tradd Street*.

"Malcolm spins a mesmerizing tale of love, deceit, and betrayal as father and daughter are torn apart by a world increasingly spinning out of control."
Booklist

"Ambitious, captivating... The expansive plot and rapid-fire pacing are underscored by brilliant depictions of post–World War I Europe and Asia."
Atlanta Magazine

"A superbly crafted story, creatively capturing a slice of history with eloquence and realism."
In the Library Reviews

"Malcolm is a fabulous writer with an astonishing romantic clarity and captivating narrative style."
International Herald Daily News

PREFACE

I am writing this book because I miss my mother.

I can almost hear the wisecracks my former colleagues would've made if they'd ever heard me, Katherine O'Connor, say something that sentimental. One would say he'd always thought that I'd been born fully grown: spit out by a dragon, maybe. Another would say yes, the idea seemed incredible, but it could be true—even crocodiles have mothers, don't they?

Those jibes would've reflected their opinion of me, not my mother. Let's just say I wasn't known for my ladylike qualities among my fellow Members of the Press. When I started working as a reporter back in 1953, there were no Ladies of the Press. If you were a reporter, not a gossipmonger or the editor of the society page or an announcer reading a script but a *real* reporter, then you were by definition not a lady.

But I was a born storyteller, and as a reporter I used that gift to unweave tales. I followed fragile threads of information, stalked loose ends, and checked under rugs for bits of truth swept there by people in positions of power. I unraveled spider webs. I've written stories about war, natural disasters, near-miracles, and horrible tragedies. I've written about corruption and altruism, about men and women who faced adversity and rose above it, and about those who were crushed by it.

The one story I've never made public is my own. I'll settle for a decent obituary when the time comes, which won't be too long from now.

But there is one chapter in my life that has become more vivid as I age, not less, as if it wants to be shared. It was then that my mother dipped her hand into the waters of my life and changed the course of it. For that I owe her something. An offering of gratitude. And what can a storyteller offer, other than the gift of a story?

I will tell my part from my perspective, and relate the story of the other person who played a pivotal role in this tale the way he told his story to me, with the understanding that as one ages the events of the past shift around in one's memory like bits of colored glass in a kaleidoscope. All you can do is try and capture the image the way it appears at the precise moment the pieces stop spinning. And old age does have its privileges; there are few people alive who know enough about these events to contradict me.

This story is for you, Margaret Mary O'Connor.

CHAPTER ONE

I should have known something was up when I got the call telling me that I'd been reassigned to the New York office.

It was June of 1960, and I'd been working as a staff reporter for Reuters for nearly five years. Like the Associated Press and United Press International, Reuters was a subscription news service. Reporters "on the ground" sent their stories to their division editors, who reviewed them and then sent the best ones "over the wire" to Reuters' subscribers. Some of the world's largest newspapers bought stories from Reuters, but the service was invaluable to hundreds of minor ones—small papers that couldn't afford to send reporters roving around the globe in search of the latest news.

Staff reporters at the big subscription news services were usually anonymous creatures. Unless you were a lead correspondent, or managed to scoop a really big story, your copy was tagged with the originating location and date, but without a "byline"—your name—on it. My ultimate goal was to become Reuters' lead correspondent in South America and leave anonymity behind.

To become a lead correspondent is a rare achievement for any staff reporter, but I was tenacious. Rather than beg for a job after graduating from journalism school I'd worked freelance, persistently excavating and following up interesting leads. After six months, I beat the *New York Times* to a story about a hardware company that was making under-the-counter payments to officials at the Parks and Recreation Department, in hopes of securing city contracts for playground equipment. That small coup led to my job at Reuters, where I continued my constant — some might say relentless — search for my next big lead.

I'd started at Reuters New York, but in early 1959 I was sent to Reuters' home office in London. Given my desire to work internationally, I viewed this as a real step up — so my sudden transfer back to the States was a move in the wrong direction. Rather than meekly accept my fate, the day after my return to New York I decided to convince my boss to send me to Cuba.

I knew the man pretty well, having worked under him before going to London. After careful consideration, I concluded that the best time to bring up the subject would be right after he returned from his daily Three Martini Lunch.

Given our managing editor's choice of midday sustenance, post-lunch permission to enter his office was seldom given until he'd been back for at least thirty minutes. My hope was that his secretary would leave to powder her nose after diligently manning her post during the lunch hour. Sure enough, as soon as my portly, middle-aged quarry returned, she dashed away from her desk, and I slipped in, unnoticed.

"What the hell?" he said when he looked up to discover it was me and not his secretary who'd stepped into the room. "I thought we did our welcome back thing yesterday. You know, with the donuts."

"You should assign me to Cuba," I began, and without waiting for him to reply I outlined my reasons. My Spanish was excellent. I'd studied Latin American history, knew the culture, and I'd read everything that had ever been printed about Fidel Castro. And — as he already knew — I'd earned two international bylines while I was working in London: no easy feat for a staff reporter. I was ready for tougher territory.

"Reuters hasn't sent out anything from Cuba that the *New York Times* didn't get first. Why not give me a chance?"

He looked as though he regretted not having had a Four Martini Lunch. "O'Connor, I can't in good conscience send a woman down there. Castro's thrown half a dozen journalists into jail this year. It's too dangerous."

"Ruby Hart Phillips reports for the *Times*."

"But she lives in Cuba, and she's lived there for years. She's like an institution. She's not threatening. You'd get into trouble."

Before I could respond his desk speaker beeped. "Robert Bentley to see you," a disembodied voice announced.

Relief replaced my boss' beleaguered expression as he hit the response button. "Send him in."

Robert Bentley had started at Reuters a few months before I'd left for London. He was tall, handsome (in an intensely white-bread way) and also a bit of a dandy. He dressed better and drank better liquor than most newspapermen, who were not above a little class warfare, as most of us came from less-than-privileged backgrounds.

9

Bentley had been hired away from some small paper in the Midwest to work as part of Reuters' United Nations press core, where, in my opinion, he'd done pretty mediocre work. Despite my adamant objections, he insisted on calling me "Red" whenever he saw me. This was allegedly because of my hair color, but I knew from the patronizing way he said it that it was also meant as a put-down—all women are moody, redheads even more so, therefore I lacked the self-control to be a top-notch reporter, etc., etc. My attempts to retaliate by calling him "Bobby" only seemed to amuse him.

"Hiya, Red," he said as he entered the room. "Are you going to keep the boss busy all afternoon?"

The words were innocent enough, but his tone implied that I was both wasting *his* time and keeping the boss "busy" with some activity that had nothing to do with reporting.

That did it.

I gave him my best Betty Davis smile and walked toward him. His eyes widened as I placed my right hand around his forearm and seductively stroked the top of it with my thumb.

"Well, Bobby," I said, my voice low and sultry, "if I'd known you were free, I'd have made room for both of you on my schedule."

Before he could respond I gripped his arm like a vice and pushed my thumb down hard on his median nerve. He emitted a squawk and his knees buckled as I dropped his arm, shifted my weight, and delivered a karate-style front kick into the middle of his chest. Bentley toppled backward onto the floor.

The boss was on his feet now, staring at Bentley, who was staring up at me, more stunned than hurt. "As you can see, I am very capable of getting myself *out* of trouble," I said. "Send me to Cuba. You have nothing to worry about." I glanced down at Bentley and added, "And I've asked you before. Don't call me 'Red.'" With that, I stalked out of the room.

I was pretty sure my demonstration of physical prowess wouldn't change my editor's mind, but it made me feel better. I was also pretty sure that I wouldn't hear Bentley calling me "Red" again anytime soon.

* * * * *

I owed my ability to execute that little party trick to the teachings of my brother, Timothy. Tim was the only one of my three brothers to survive the war. I should clarify; I mean World War II. It was many years after 1945 before the phrase "the war," meant anything other than World War II, and for those of us who lived through it, it was, and always will be, simply, the war.

Tim and my oldest brother, Mark, were "Irish twins," meaning they'd been born almost exactly a year apart. They were incredibly close, and shared everything from their marble collection to their underwear. Had my mother not drawn his teacher's attention to his obvious ploy, Mark would have happily failed first grade in order to spend every day in the same classroom as his younger brother.

After Tim finished high school he and Mark joined the merchant marines, not having found any other productive employment during the height of the Great Depression.

Their ship was hit by a German torpedo in 1943. They both made it ashore, but Mark's wounds were more severe than Tim's. He died on the beach in his brother's arms.

Tim didn't come home until January of 1946, and no one could get a solid story from him about where he went or what he did after their ship went down. I did come across one clue that should have given me some insight into how Tim spent the remainder of the war, although I didn't make the connection at the time.

I found a slim paperback book in the glove compartment of his car a few months after he came home. On the cover was an illustration of a man in a business suit, aggressively poking his fingers into the eyes of a German soldier while kneeing him in the groin. The title, "GET TOUGH!" blazed across the cover with the exaggerated bravado of a Marvel comic book. The subtitle read, "You don't need brute strength: with your bare hands you can beat the man who wants to kill you."

I was sixteen, incorrigibly curious, and not very respectful of other people's privacy, so I snatched the book and read the thing from cover to cover. It was exactly what it claimed to be: a detailed manual on how to kill people, and how to keep from being killed, written by an Englishman who looked more like an accountant than an assassin.

Tim looked furious when I showed him the book and asked him about it. Then an aura of uncanny calm settled over him, which I found much more terrifying.

"Okay, you little snoop," he said, "there are some things in here that'd be helpful for you to know if you plan to spend the rest of your life sticking your nose in places where it doesn't belong." And so he taught me a few moves, several lifted from the Asian martial arts, which were not very well known at the time, and they did prove remarkably handy.

It wasn't until years later that I learned Tim knew how to kill with his bare hands because he'd spent the last three years of the war in a special forces unit, risking his life behind enemy lines in an effort to expurgate the sin he'd committed by surviving when his two brothers had not.

* * * * *

Until I knew which way my career was headed I didn't want to lease an apartment, so I went home to Ma's. She lived on the Upper West Side, in the same house where she'd raised all five of us: my brothers Mark, Timothy, and Jamie, my sister Maureen, and me. I was the caboose of the family, five years younger than Maureen and fourteen years younger than Mark. That's an unusual gap today, but not unheard of back when good Catholics still let the Pope make up the rules for a game he didn't play.

Ma had paid off the mortgage with the life insurance money she'd received when my father died, which is why we had a place to live after the Depression hit. Having life insurance in those days was a pretty rare thing, but Dad bought a generous policy from the nephew of a second cousin who'd loaned my dad money when he'd first arrived in America. That was how things worked in the Irish immigrant community. Once you had your feet on the ground you paid the favor forward to help out the next family members coming over. I'm sure my father had no intention of making payments on the policy for long. He was trying to help the kid get started as a salesman, but with a bit of typical Irish luck he died unexpectedly while the policy was still in full force, thereby providing for his family in a way he'd never have been able to do had he lived.

I was barely two when my father passed away, so I never knew him well enough to miss him. And by then the house was already full, sheltering all of us, plus various visiting aunts, uncles, cousins, and others more ambiguously related, who rolled in and out of the house from down the street or across the ocean. The memories I have of my father still play in my head like old black-and-white movies, fashioned from bits of stories that others told about him back when our whole extended family still had reasons to get together.

But as a child all I needed to do to see what my father looked like was gaze upon the face of my youngest brother, Jamie.

I'd like to think that most parents try hard not to have a favorite child, and try even harder not to show it if they do happen to keep one of their offspring closer to the heart; but as fair-minded a person as my mother was, there was just no way for her to hide her partiality. Her love for Jamie slipped out in subtle ways: the slightly bigger slice of pie, the warmest pair of gloves, her willingness to let him get his way after a bit more cajoling. It wasn't something the rest of us talked about, if for no other reason than Jamie made her laugh. While she was normally a pleasant person, our mother didn't laugh often.

But none of us were prepared for how badly it broke her when we lost him.

* * * * *

When I walked in Ma was standing over the kitchen table, vigorously wiping away a dribble of some substance only she could see. I had to say hello twice before she looked up.

"Why Mary Kate, you're back."

She sounded so surprised I wasn't sure if she meant back from London or back from the office. And I didn't really want to know. If she meant London, it would be because she didn't remember my having come home, suitcase in hand, asking if she could put me up for a while. So I just nodded.

She smiled and went back to wiping up the nonexistent stain. "Will you being staying long?"

"I don't know, Ma. I'm waiting on my next assignment."

"You should visit your brother and sister while you're here."

"I'll try."

At last she seemed satisfied that the table was clean. Turning to the sink, she rinsed out the rag she'd been using and hung it neatly over the faucet. "Will you be wanting some dinner, then?"

"No, thanks. I grabbed a hot dog on the way home."

She didn't answer, and I wondered if she'd heard me, or if her mind had already drifted away. "So, I'll see you in the morning, I guess," I said as I inched out of the room.

"Before ya dash off, can ya tell me, have ya heard from Jamie?"

My heart froze. "No, I haven't," I mumbled.

"It's terrible, the post these days. His letters never get through anymore."

"I'm sorry, Ma," I said, and then, like a small child caught in a nightmare, I fled.

CHAPTER TWO

"Comrade Turgenev, you wish to see me?"

Raul Garcia entered his supervisor's office expecting to see the older man waving a mechanical pencil across a massive blueprint, anxious to point out some problem, assuming that Raul could offer a solution. Raul always cooperated, never complained about the extra work, and never sought any of the credit when a project's prospects for on-time completion suddenly improved. He'd learned long ago that life in the Soviet Union was easier—and likely to last longer—if one managed to spend as much time as possible out of the limelight.

This time he saw no blueprints. Two unfamiliar men were seated in the small room. One wore the military uniform of an East German intelligence officer. The other was dressed in a dark gray suit, the color and cut of which signaled, "possible KGB."

"Yes, Comrade Garcia. Come in. I wish to introduce Colonel Leopold Koehler, a liaison officer with German intelligence, and Comrade Alexander Mestrovic. They've asked to meet with you privately." Then Turgenev straightened an already neat stack of papers, nodded to the man in the gray suit, and left.

As soon as the door closed the man called Mestrovic stood up and propped his considerable bulk on the corner of the desk, one foot rooted to the ground. He held a manila folder in one hand, and used it to gesture for Raul to take the seat he'd just vacated.

Raul sat down and glanced over at the German. The man gazed back at him, his face expressionless, and Raul was struck by the vibrant blue color of his eyes. Eyes that had seen what? Piles of Jewish corpses? The bloated bodies of starving children? The incendiary bombing of unarmed villages in Spain? He knew that the East Germans served as useful lackeys to the Soviets, but the sight of a German uniform brought too many grisly memories out of their hiding places.

Why do these men want to speak to me? He lived an orderly, unspectacular life. He wasn't an enthusiastic party member, but he participated as required. He was a civil engineer. What could the Stasi or the KGB want with him?

"Your parents sent you and your sister to the Soviet Union when you were very young," Mestrovic began.

"Yes, 1937. I was ten."

"And I see you worked in a factory in Saratov during the Great Patriotic War. Airplanes, was it?"

"First tanks. Then aircraft." *For sixteen hours a day. With no shoes, and my feet have the scars to prove it.*

Mestrovic tossed the folder onto the desk. "You have excellent work evaluations, Comrade Garcia."

"Thank you, Comrade Mestrovic."

The German spoke up. Unlike Raul, whose Spanish roots poked through his speech, the man spoke Russian with a flawless accent. "Have you kept up with the events in Cuba over the past eighteen months?" he asked.

Raul addressed his answer to Mestrovic. "Only by reading *Pravda* and watching the newsreels."

"And do you have an opinion about the situation?" the German inquired further.

An opinion? Did the man think he was an idiot? It was never safe to have an independent opinion about anything. Raul kept his answer vague.

"I'm not sure what you mean. I'm glad that Castro succeeded in ousting Batista."

Mestrovic resumed control of the conversation. "How is your Spanish? A bit rusty, I would think."

"No, comrade. All of our classes before the war were in Spanish, and we—some of us keep in touch with each other. Those of us who survived." He managed to keep himself from glaring at the German as he said this.

"You did not try to go back to Spain when you were permitted to do so?"

After Stalin died, was the unstated part of that question. Thousands of unaccompanied Spanish children had been sent by their parents to safety in France, Britain, Belgium, and the Scandinavian countries during the Spanish Civil War. They'd all been sent home when Franco finally prevailed—except for the four thousand children sent to the USSR. Stalin was not going to let four thousand communist children grow up to be fascists. He'd kept them, all the "Spanish Children of Russia," in Moscow and Leningrad, where they were treated extremely well—while being used as propaganda, as poster children and newsreel stars, advertising the generosity and prosperity of the Soviet Union. Until the Germans invaded.

But Mestrovic must know all of this already.

"I saw no reason to go back to Spain. I'd had no communication with my family during my many years in the Soviet Union, and have no reason to believe that any of them survived Franco's victory. I'm a Soviet citizen, and my life is here."

In truth, Raul hadn't even been tempted to go back. His last image of his mother was the one he wanted to preserve in his mind: her long waves of dark brown hair falling over his face as she wept, promising that he and his sister would be gone for just a short while, until the war was over, until they could be safe again.

He wanted to continue to believe his mother's long silence was the result of her death, and not because she'd abandoned them. Dead like his father, whose demise had been dramatically reported in a Soviet newsreel a year after Raul and his sister arrived in Leningrad. "A brave, bold leader of men: a true communist hero," the announcer had declared in a language Raul barely understood at the time. His sister was four years old, and did not recognize the man on the screen as their father. Raul did not explain.

But this was an old wound, almost forgotten. He needed to focus on what was happening right now, in this room.

Mestrovic continued with his questions. "You're divorced, correct?"

"Yes. I was married for three years, after university. We parted amicably."

"Convenient, given the opportunity we have for you. We're asking some of our Spanish-Soviet citizens to go to Cuba, to assist Castro as part of a program of cooperation between the USSR and the new Cuban regime. You'd work there both as a structural engineer and a translator."

"To Cuba?" *What risks would be involved in going, and what would be the consequences for refusing to go?* "I would — could I think about it?"

"If necessary. We'll send around twenty or so of you — our *Hispanic-Sovieticos* — to Cuba. There will also be several citizens of the East German Democratic Republic in the delegation, people whose parents were communist party members living in Germany before the war, who managed to escape to South America when Hitler turned against us."

That explains the German. They must be fishing everywhere for communists who can speak Russian and Spanish, and I've been scooped up in their net. Well, he'd heard that Cuba was a beautiful place. It could be that or prison; it was never wise to say, "No," to the KGB.

"It would be my honor to go. I understand how I could be useful."

"Very good." Mestrovic stood. "Do not discuss this assignment with anyone."

"As you wish."

Raul took his leave and walked through the sterile corridors back to his own claustrophobic office. *Cuba.* Would it be anything like southern Spain? The thought unleashed an avalanche of long-suppressed images, each one drenched in vivid colors and suffused with pleasant smells: the azure blue of the Mediterranean; russet and gold sunsets; freshly caught fish frying in olive oil; the sensuous warmth of the sun on wet skin. Briny tide pools full of sea urchins and small, agile crabs. The silvery green leaves of the olive trees. Fresh oranges. Flamenco music playing on the radio while his grandmother cooked the evening meal. His mother, happy and relaxed in her parents' home, resplendent as a goddess in a bright red sarong tied casually around her waist. At the beach she always smelled like baby oil mixed with sherry and roses.

All so long ago.

Cuba. His fate was now linked to a small island that had come to the center of the world's attention through the charismatic audacity of its new leader. Another journey. He could only hope that this one would prove less eventful than his last.

CHAPTER THREE

The day after I'd flipped Bentley I was back in the newsroom, hoping to shake an assignment out of someone before I had to start doing man-in-the-street interviews to come up with copy. Everyone fell silent as I entered: never a good sign. But I wasn't the type to sit around and wait for a bomb to drop, so after making some stilted small talk with a couple of my colleagues I headed up to my editor's office and planted myself in the chair across from his desk.

I sat back and crossed my ankles, very nonchalant. "Why is everyone so unnerved by my appearance here today?"

He just looked at me.

"Well?" I demanded.

"You're… that is… you're being let go. In a fashion," he stammered.

I felt my mouth fall open and had to snap my jaw back into place. "What? Is this some kind of joke? I get brought back to New York so you can fire me? Hang on—is this because I laid Bentley out?"

Getting his announcement out seemed to have helped the man find his spine. "No, it has nothing to do with yesterday," he answered in his best Newsroom Editor

Voice. "I knew this was coming. I just didn't know when. And I didn't have a choice."

I stood up and moved toward his desk. "If you didn't, then who did? I've been a good producer."

"Very true. That's why we'd welcome a look at anything you send us freelance."

"Freelance? That's demeaning, after I've been a staff reporter."

"But it gives you a lot more freedom to go wherever you want."

"With what money? There's a reason Reuters keeps people on the payroll, you know."

"I know that," he said, now all fatherly and sympathetic, "but the company's cutting back. We're having to rely more and more on stringers. And people just don't care about international news like they used to. There's no big war on, and Europe's pretty well patched up. The guys who are hip-deep in Cold War coverage aren't gonna budge, especially not to let a wo—ah, a young hotshot try and scoop 'em. There aren't that many newsworthy places where we can send a female reporter, not even one of your caliber."

I sucked in my breath.

His courage failed him. "Don't kick me," he said, looking like he'd duck under his desk if I moved.

I glared at him, too angry to speak. *Don't you dare cry.* I knew this level of rage could erupt into involuntary tears, like steam pouring out of the safety valve on a pressure cooker, and that crying would be interpreted as a demonstration of feminine frailty. I had to leave before *that* happened.

"I'll pick up my stuff tomorrow," I muttered through clenched teeth. Then I turned and stormed out, slamming the door behind me with all the force I could muster. To my intense satisfaction, the glass—whereupon was etched my now-former editor's name and title—cracked, right down the middle.

* * * * *

I walked two blocks to Wally's, a bar and grill frequented by many of the newsmen headquartered in that part of town. My first stop was the ladies' room, where I did let a few tears escape; it had always bothered me that women were somehow wired to use tears as an anger management tool, but as good as I was at dealing with anger in other ways, sometimes that tear-duct reflex did kick in, and this was one of those times.

I managed to cut off the waterworks, washed my face, and put on some powder and lipstick. This was all the makeup I carried: the powder to hide a few of my freckles, and the lipstick because it added at least a touch of femininity to my face. Luckily my eyelashes were darker than those of many redheads, so I didn't bother with mascara. Back then, wearing mascara required a cake of the stuff, access to water, and the skill of an artist. Plus, it started to run at the mere hint of moisture, making it, in my view, completely useless.

With a deep breath I left my womanly sanctuary and reentered the bar.

It was headed toward two-thirty in the afternoon, so most of the lunchtime patrons were gone. There were a few faces I recognized, but no one likely to strike up a conversation. I slipped into a booth and ordered a whiskey and soda, then waved the waitress back and added an order of fries. No good drinking on an empty stomach, and I was pretty sure I wasn't going to stop at one.

I was halfway through the fries and waiting on my second whiskey when an unwelcome presence slipped into the booth across from me. *Damn. I should've sat facing the door*, I chastised myself, annoyed that I'd been so distraught that I'd forgotten this basic rule.

"I had to sit down immediately lest you decide to kick me over again," said Robert Bentley. "Mind if I join you?"

"Since you already know the answer to that question, a verbal response seems redundant," I replied, sounding as irritated as I felt.

He ignored this and looked down at my food. "Fries and whiskey. Add a glass of milk and I think you have all the basic food groups covered."

"Now that you've voiced your opinion concerning my dietary habits, do you have something worthwhile to say? Or should I start kicking you under the table until you withdraw?"

I heard him slide his feet away and had to suppress a smile. *Maybe I should use my combat skills more often. How could they have hired this model of mediocrity to handle the UN beat, but let me go?* I thought. *The UN was the one show in town I'd have been interested in, if that was my only choice. Maybe I could ask about replacing him....*

"So word's spreading around that you've lost your post," he was saying.

"And you've come to gloat. That certainly reinforces

my opinion of you," I said, wondering if that second whiskey and soda was worth putting up with Bentley for another ten minutes.

He feigned surprise. "A nice guy like me? I wouldn't do anything like that. I had a hunch this might be where you'd come to lick your wounds, and thought I might be able to offer some assistance."

"With the licking? I don't think so. But you *can* kiss my ass."

The waitress appeared at the table with my second drink, causing Bentley to hold back whatever retort he may have had in mind. "I'll have a beer," he said, without waiting for her to ask.

"No, he won't. He's not staying," I responded.

"And put her whole order on my tab," he said.

"No, thank you," I said in a steely voice.

"Why not let the guy buy you a drink?" the waitress asked. "You richer than Rockefeller?"

"Bring me my beer and we'll fight over the check later," Bentley said. The waitress gave me a smug look and headed back to the bar.

"Listen Robert," I began, "tell me whatever it is you're here to say and let me go back to drowning my sorrows. Alone." To emphasize the sincerity of my intentions, I drained most of my second drink. Bentley watched this performance, then gallantly handed me a napkin. I took it and wiped my mouth, more out of reflex than necessity.

"How would you like to go to Cuba?" he asked as I put down the napkin.

"Can't you pick a different topic with which to taunt me?"

The waitress came back with a beer and a basket of pretzels for Bentley, and another whiskey and soda, which she plopped down in front of me.

"I didn't order this," I told her, and attempted to hand the drink back to her. My dislike of Bentley aside, I almost never let a man buy me a drink unless I was part of a group trading rounds. Back then, there was still too much innuendo attached to letting a man pay for your alcohol.

"It's on the gentleman's tab," the waitress replied a touch too sweetly before she walked away, leaving the drink in my hand and an aggravated look on my face.

"Relax and have another drink while I tell you what I have in mind," Bentley said, "and you know better than to think I'm trying to get you drunk. I've seen you drink. Three whiskey and sodas don't even constitute a warm-up."

I put the drink down on the table, untouched. "Okay, what do you want?"

"I know we got off to a bad start." He paused for a swig of beer. "I had no business calling you 'Red,' though God knows you got the last laugh on that one. I haven't seen anyone use a move like that since—well, for a long time."

"You've been flattened before, eh? Why does that not surprise me?"

"Are you always this sarcastic?"

"Are you always this annoying?"

I finished my second whiskey and eyed the third, but did not pick it up. "I think it's time for me to leave," I said, "as much as I've enjoyed your company—"

"I'm serious about Cuba," he interjected. "I agree with

28

you; for this assignment, you're the most qualified reporter Reuters has

"Had," I corrected him.

"Right. The point is, I think you'll be able to connect with some credible sources of the kind that a man couldn't even approach." He held up his hand. "And before you launch another verbal assault, I'm not talking about any Mata Hari methods. You're clever, resourceful, and you'll be able to fly under the radar more easily than a man. Especially if no one knows that you're a reporter, which you don't have to announce since you're not on the payroll anymore."

"And the minute a story appears in the US with my byline I'll be thrown in a Cuban jail for not disclosing that —surprise!—I really *am* a journalist. No, thanks."

"Okay, I admit that's a problem. So you'd have to save it all for one big piece, and come back home to write it. Sell it freelance to the highest bidder, and if it's big enough, you'll have every major paper in the country pounding on your door."

I had to admit that I was intrigued. It was the perfect time to be stroking my ego given the bruising it had just received, and I did have enough faith in my own abilities to believe that I could get the story that other more complacent, Castro-worshipping reporters had missed.

The truth was that the American news media, beginning with Herbert Mathews of the *New York Times*, had "made" Fidel Castro by giving him all the supportive, glamorized coverage they could convince their editors to print. And after he'd beaten Batista, in January of 1959, the American news media elite had hosted Castro at the

National Press Club in Washington, DC. That gave him a high-profile stage from which he could woo the public, and woo he did; he leveraged his invitation from the National Press Club into an appearance at the United Nations, an interview on *The Ed Sullivan Show,* and a meeting with Vice President Richard Nixon, among other coups.

After his first US trip Castro was the subject of near-universal adoration: a modern David, slayer of Goliath; the defender of the people. He'd waged war against a tyrannical ruler and, against all odds, had succeeded. But the news media's Golden Boy kept making moves that seemed distressingly dictatorial in nature, such as executing hundreds of his supposed enemies after trials that were so transparently phony they made the Soviet legal system look like a model of impartial jurisprudence.

It was probably true that many of those killed had been responsible for carrying out the brutal repression that had helped keep Batista in power, but the capriciousness of the whole process raised many a wary eyebrow in the US After that, Castro made several suspicious political turns to the left, but few journalists were willing to admit that they might have erred. "Have patience while he sorts things out," was the message that Mathews and other venerated reporters continued to send to the American public.

Ruby Hart Phillips was the exception. She'd been living in Cuba for years, and served as the *New York Times* correspondent after the *Times'* previous part-time correspondent had passed away—an American businessman who also happened to be her husband. Phillips was the only one brave enough to suggest that Mathews had been wrong. That we'd all been wrong. Castro was in bed with the communists, she maintained; and that was the least of his shortcomings.

By the summer of 1960 even reporters like Phillips had to be careful not to say anything that could give Castro a reason to throw her out. The voices of the people in Cuba were being silenced. And after being persuaded that Castro was a modern hero, most Americans did not want to believe that he would engage in the torture and murder of dissidents, wide-spread extortion, and ruthless repression. Cuba was only ninety miles away from Florida, after all. How could all that be happening so close to home?

I wanted to get at the truth. Badly. However, one of the many lessons my mother had taught me was that if something sounds too good to be true it probably is, and Bentley's offer sounded way too good. I needed more information.

"So who's going to pay for this venture? I don't have much of a bankroll, and at the moment exactly zero money coming in."

"Well, I thought I would. Finance you, I mean."

"Oh, heaven help me. See what comes from lettin' a man buy you a drink?" I could hear a tinge of my mother's Irish brogue creeping into my speech, as sometimes happened when I was very angry. "And what other services would you be expectin' to get fer yer money? Do you pay extra for redheads?"

"Now hold on," he replied, putting his hands up in front of his face as if to protect himself from whatever object I might throw at him, "it's nothing like that. I'm proposing a partnership. An honest partnership."

He looked sincere, and a little scared, which helped reinforce his sincerity. I sat back with a sigh. Cuba was too big a temptation for me not to at least hear him out.

"What did you have in mind?" I asked.

"A shared byline, that's all."

"*What?*"

"Look, I won't take any credit, except for a co-byline like, "with the assistance of Robert Bentley," or something like that. Everyone will know that you were the one on the ground."

"And everyone will assume we're sleeping together."

"Why? You'll be in Cuba, I'll be here. I can give you the names of a few people to talk to when you get there, maybe open a couple of doors. And I might be able to help you place the piece faster, and for more money. I move in some of those circles."

"Where? Places like your illustrious former employer, the *Illinois State Journal*?"

I could tell he was starting to build up some steam under that Brooks Brother collar of his. "I should think that with your educational background you'd appreciate the value of personal connections—"

"Because they make up for a lack of talent?"

Bentley kept his facial expression pretty well under control, but some rapid eyebrow movement let me know that I'd hit my target. "As worldly as you make yourself out to be, I'm surprised to discover you're that naïve," he said.

I let this pass. He was a Yale grad, and those guys were

the worst — or the best, depending on how you look at it — at overlooking mild incompetence in order to give a fellow Yalie a lift. I'd always thought that Barnard, my alma mater, and even Columbia, where I'd gone to journalism school, were both more attuned to meritocracy: maybe because they were in New York, one of the few cities where immigrants occasionally won the who's-on-top game. But Bentley was, in fact, correct. Connections could help, and the diplomatic skills that helped to establish those sorts of connections were not my strong suit.

"I'll think about it," I said.

"Don't think too long," he replied, slipping me a card with his contact information printed on it. I picked it up and stuck it in my pocket.

"So you're picking up the tab?" I asked.

At this he smiled. "I said I would."

"Good," I said, and shouted out to the waitress, "I'll have a Rueben to go. Extra sauerkraut."

* * * * *

A short while later, I was sitting on a park bench, pondering Bentley's offer as I bit into my sandwich. I hadn't been totally honest with him. I wasn't flat broke. I did have a small nest egg. Being a gainfully employed, unattached woman with very simple taste in food, clothes, and men, I'd been able to stash away a little money for a rainy day.

But was now the time to break into my savings? *No,* I scolded myself. *Start looking for another real job.* I was sufficiently well-credentialed to get my foot in the door somewhere, wasn't I?

But the truth was I'd been lucky to land a job that sent me overseas; few women worked as foreign correspondents, and my position with Reuters was one that many male reporters had envied. And I really wanted to work in Latin America.

I'd been fascinated by the goings-on in that part of the world since elementary school. I guess it started with the huge influx of Puerto Ricans into New York during the war. When two groups are competing economically, it doesn't make for friendly relations, and after the Great Depression the Irish workingmen of New York weren't too happy about competing for jobs with what they viewed as the latest group of upstart immigrants.

But I was a contrarian by nature. I didn't want to hate these new people just because someone told me I should. So I started to learn something about Latin American culture and history, which led to a desire to learn the language. I took classes at school, and then spent one summer as a nanny for a Panamanian diplomat who was stationed at the UN. I was not a very good nanny, but I was very good at picking up new languages; none of the kids died, and my Spanish improved dramatically.

After that I worked in a Puerto Rican restaurant during college, which led to a summer job in San Juan. Ultimately it seemed to me that the Irish Catholics and the Islanders had a lot in common: our religion, our love of music, a history of exploitation by an imperial power—and quick tempers.

This would be my first opportunity to go to a Latin American country to work as a journalist. I should be jumping at the opportunity.

Yet something about Bentley's scheme wasn't sitting right. Even if my antics in our editor's office had changed his opinion of me, I still didn't trust him. If I went to Cuba, I'd go on my own dime.

Maybe Bentley and his connections could help if I managed to get myself arrested. That would be the best reason to team up with him. And a few leads wouldn't hurt.

Undercover reporting, right under Castro's nose. What a challenge. What an opportunity.

CHAPTER FOUR

R aul was astonished by the amount of blood on his hand. He'd approached his attacker with the utmost stealth, delivered one definitive, lethal blow, and now his palm was smeared with an incredible quantity of his own blood.

He wiped his hand on his pants leg. If, as some claimed, Cuba had been the original Garden of Eden, then its mosquitoes must be creatures from hell, deposited on the island after the Fall of Man to discourage any mortals who might dare to try and retake the territory. They were bigger, hungrier, bolder, and more plentiful than any other biting insect he'd ever encountered, and every fatality he inflicted upon a member of their population brought him intense satisfaction.

He'd also noticed that humans seemed to possess an individual sensitivity to mosquito venom. While he found the creatures irksome, some of the white-skinned Russians he'd come with were so covered with bite marks they looked as if they'd contracted some tropical disease. They moaned aloud at night and clawed themselves until they bled, tormented by the incessant itching caused by previous attacks, and the tyrannical buzzing that signaled another foe was about to feast.

Raul examined the squashed carcass on the windowsill. He'd heard that the natives of Cuba had been killed off by the contagious diseases the Spaniards had brought with them from Europe. Could mosquitoes be the Russians' strategic weakness? He imagined the international head lines: US DROPS MOSQUITO LARVAE ON MOSCOW: PARALYZES USSR.

Smiling to himself, he left his room.

He couldn't complain about his accommodations. Most of the Soviet advisors were housed in enormous mansions in the most elegant residential district of Havana: some seized from Batista's supporters as soon as the dictator and his major cronies fled during the early days of 1959, others appropriated as the forfeited property of "traitors to the Revolution" when their owners emigrated after Castro had consolidated his power.

Raul's own room was bigger than his entire efficiency apartment in Moscow. A trio of large windows yielded a generous view of the garden's exotic vegetation: hibiscus, bougainvillea, and birds of paradise, all flowers that Raul hadn't seen since he was a child in Spain. Large shutters defended the interior from the afternoon heat, creating a cool environment for an afternoon *siesta*, a ritual most modern Cubans no longer practiced despite living in the type of climate in which the *siesta* was adopted in order to keep man's activities in harmony with those of nature. Raul had lived in Russia for so long he'd forgotten what it was like to live in a place governed by the moods of the sun.

And the caprice of the sea.

As a young child Raul had loved the ocean, but on the journey from Spain to the Soviet Union it had become his enemy. The Northern Atlantic was not blue like the welcoming Mediterranean of southern Spain; it was a dour gray, the color of an old spinster's hair, all covered with foamy spit. During the journey from Spain to France she'd behaved decently, but as soon as they left France for the Soviet Union the Atlantic had begun harassing them, rolling and battering their ship like a hapless piece of driftwood, causing those children who could still eat to vomit all over the deck, their thin mattresses, and themselves.

The young refugees huddled together in the hold, all twelve hundred of them, wondering what they had done wrong to deserve such punishment, begging God's forgiveness for every transgression they could think of: sticking out their tongue behind a teacher's back, making fun of a man who lisped, giving a morsel of precious meat to the cat. Around them dark-skinned Indonesian crew-members scurried like furtive serfs, unable to speak any language that would enable them to explain to their terrified charges what was happening or how long it would last.

But in Cuba Raul met the Caribbean, and her sister sea, the Gulf of Mexico. Together they beguiled him with qualities even more captivating than his memories of the Mediterranean; their waters were clearer, warmer, and even more enticing. The ocean was the real coquette of Cuba: so beautiful and seductive that one could fall deeply in love with her in one day, or during one sunset—or at the very least become temporarily infatuated.

When Raul emerged into the bright sunlight of that glorious Cuban morning, the driver of a battle-worn jeep was waiting for him in front of the house, ready to bring Raul to a breakfast meeting with Che Guevara. *Hopefully this time he'll bathe,* Raul thought. Guevara's negligent approach to basic hygiene mystified him. The man was a trained physician, after all; surely he understood the health benefits of cleanliness. Was it some sort of protest against the norms of the middle class? If so, Raul was grateful that the Russian communists had never adopted this particular method of defiance: the equalitarian value of body odor.

A few minutes later the jeep pulled up at the entrance to the seaside mansion Che used as one of his head-quarters. The official line was that he lived in a small apartment and used this villa as a place to conduct business on behalf of the Cuban people. Raul suspected otherwise, but that charade was no different from those practiced by the leaders of the communist party in the Soviet Union; he'd worked on the engineering plans for several extravagant homes occupied by members of the Politburo. One did not live long if one made it one's business to publicize hypocrisy among the ruling elite in the USSR, and, Raul suspected, the same would be true in Cuba.

He was given a quick pat-down before a sentry brought him through the house, into the garden, and out onto a large stone patio overlooking the ocean. A small table rested beneath an elegantly placed group of palm trees. Raul double-checked his watch. He was right on time. Where were the others? He'd expected this to be a group meeting—ten or twelve people at least.

"He'll meet you here," said the young man who'd

shown him to the table, "but it's not uncommon to have to wait."

Raul balked. "But the table is set for two people."

"You should be honored."

Raul watched as the man stopped to say something to one of three guards who stood around the edge of patio, then went back inside. Two more members of the Revolutionary Army graced the upper balconies, armed with machine guns. Everyone on the grounds wore the olive fatigues and brimmed caps adopted as the uniform of Castro's forces. They also sported scruffy beards. While battling in the wilderness Castro had declared that he wouldn't shave until he'd beaten Batista, and the men who fought with him did the same. Now their unkempt facial hair set these men apart as soldiers of the Glorious Revolution. So, despite their victory, none of them shaved—not even Castro—and they were universally referred to as *los barbudos*, "the bearded ones."

An attractive young woman wearing a similar outfit (minus the beard) soon appeared. She invited Raul to take a seat, and offered him some coffee. He waited until she'd retreated before picking up his cup, trying to look as if he were totally at ease. He was more alarmed than honored to be meeting alone with Che. Raul had never even spoken directly to the man.

And then there he was, walking toward Raul with a hand raised in greeting, an unlit cigar planted in the corner of his mouth accenting his smile like a bloated exclamation point. Che was no longer the lean, gaunt-faced guerilla warrior that Raul had seen in the newsreels celebrating

Castro's victory; he wore his shirt untucked, and the fabric pulled across a well-fed belly.

Raul rose as Che approached, but his host gestured for him to retake his seat. Before Che had lowered himself into his own chair Raul could tell that the man had *not* bathed.

Che addressed the woman who'd brought Raul coffee. "Rosita, bring toast, fruit, and some eggs." She headed back into the house, a look of such intense pleasure on her face that Raul could not help but wonder what other services she provided for *El Che*.

Che took the cigar out of his mouth and balanced it on the edge of an expensive-looking silver ashtray in the center of the table. "I've been to Russia twice," he informed Raul. "The food there is shit. Cubans have fertile soil and abundant sun; they should be eating fresh fruit and vegetables, beef, chicken—all the bounty of the earth—but they grow only tobacco, sugarcane, and fruit, mostly for export. That will change soon. Within a few months the rape of Cuba by the Yankee imperialists will come to an end."

"I'm afraid I'm the wrong person to advise you on farming techniques," Raul responded. "I'm—"

Che didn't let him finish his sentence. "You know it was my idea to bring you over—all of the *Hispanic-Sovieticos*. Such a valuable resource. Like you. You've done quite well for yourself in your adopted homeland."

"I'm not sure what you mean, Señor Guevara—"

"No honorifics. All men are equal in the eyes of the Revolution. What I mean is that you received an excellent education, and you've used it to become a man of accomplishment. You're an expert in your field, and you move

41

among men of power, although you're not powerful yourself. More like a helpful ferret—the rat catcher—scurrying underneath them and around them, close but unnoticed, doing their bidding. In your case, building the things they want built. But do you know how lucky you are?"

Raul said nothing, hoping the question was meant to be rhetorical. He was correct about this at least, because Che did not wait for an answer.

"You were born a Spanish communist. You and your family have made admirable sacrifices in support of the cause. This is your reward: to be at this place, at this time, to witness the birth of a global revolution. We will feed off of our hosts—the Americans, and the Soviets—until we have the strength to spread revolution across South America."

Raul tried to mask the shock he felt at hearing the Soviets openly maligned, but he must have revealed a hint of his reaction, because Che smiled at him with the benevolent grin of an adult amused by the incomprehension of the young.

"Come now," Che chided him. "It's no secret that the Russian Revolution was corrupted by Stalin, and that the Soviet Union has unfortunate imperialist tendencies of its own. Now we need our Soviet friends, but someday soon we won't. Cuba must not trade one master for another."

Rosita came back with their food, sparing Raul from having to come up with an immediate response. He took a bite of egg but his mouth was so dry he couldn't swallow, so he reached for his coffee and tried to gulp everything down together.

Che was plowing through his breakfast. He looked cheerful, relaxed, and confident.

"I'm sorry, but I believe you have me confused with someone else," Raul said. "I'm no philosopher, and no politician. I'm just an engineer."

At this Che laughed, shooting several crumbs of coffee-soaked bread from his mouth to the table. "I know exactly who you are," he replied before swallowing his food. "I know where you came from, who your father was, everything you've done since you arrived in the Soviet Union, and why you were chosen to come here."

"Señor Che, I'm flattered that you've taken such a personal interest in me, but—"

Che did not let him finish. "Do you have any idea how many hundreds of people want to see me every day? And how many of them I will never see? Yet here I am, having breakfast alone with you. That should tell you that you are here on important business, my friend. Very important business."

Raul fought the urge to recoil as Guevara leaned closer. "Even though he does his work underground," he said, "a ferret hears things. They are, as I said, useful creatures. You will pass on to me anything your ferret ears hear about what the Soviets have planned for Cuba."

"But I don't know anything. I can't—"

"But you can. And you will, so that the sacrifices made by you, your father—your whole family—will not have been in vain."

"I mean no disrespect, but I must decline—"

Che's tone of voice remained amiable, his expression almost jovial. "You've heard about the executions that took

43

place when we liberated Cuba, of course. Hundreds of enemies of the Revolution, all quickly eliminated. We do what we have to do to ensure that the Revolution will succeed."

Raul just stared at him. Che reclaimed his cigar and continued, still speaking casually. "I have no doubt that when you realize what you can help us accomplish, you'll be proud to be part of it. But make no mistake—friends in high places can be an advantage; enemies in high places can be just as inconvenient."

He rose and looked down at Raul. "Do we understand each other?" Raul nodded. He did not try to stand. He wasn't sure that his legs would hold him.

"Good," Che responded. "Now you will go back into the foyer; the other Soviet advisors I invited will arrive soon. You will say that you confused the time and arrived early. Sadly, I will not be able to keep this morning's appointment, and one of my colleagues will run the meeting. The agenda is rather dull, I'm afraid." He took out a lighter and held it to the end of his cigar. After it was lit, he said, "A woman—Tamara—will be contacting you." As Rosita rushed over to clear his dishes, Guevara walked back into the villa.

CHAPTER FIVE

Although the closest sand-swept beaches were a twenty-minute drive from the city's center, in Havana one was never far from the sea: the Atlantic to the east, the Bay of Havana in the center of the city, and, to the west, the Gulf of Mexico. There were several spots not far from the house in which Raul was billeted where one could hike along paths broken up by patches of sand, shallow water and coral shoals, or jump from the rocks into the gulf for a swim. He headed that way.

He walked in relative solitude for almost an hour — too lost in thought to notice what colors the sea was wearing that day — to a point where yards of scrub brush and bleached rock separated the shoreline from the main road. There he found a fairly dry patch of rock and sat down. How the hell was he going to come up with any information that would satisfy Che Guevara, without getting shot by the Russians?

I'm just an engineer. He helped build big, noticeable things: bridges, buildings, dams. Once he'd been called in to assist the team developing the engineering plans for some missile silos Stalin wanted built, but that was the only strategic project with which he'd been involved, and he'd never known more about it than the small puzzle piece he'd been asked to address.

Missiles? *In Cuba?*

Surely Khrushchev, the Soviet Premier, wouldn't dare —not this close to Florida. *And even if he were insane enough to try it,* Raul thought, *I'm not high enough on anyone's list to be privy to that sort of plan.*

He would call Guevara's bluff. He was probably issuing similar "invitations" to all the other *Hispanic-Sovieticos* in Cuba. *Maybe one of them would come up with something,* he thought, *and Guevara will get bored with me and leave me alone.*

He closed his eyes. The sound of the waves was soothing, the open expanse of ocean so peaceful.

"Has the patrol come by yet?" asked a small voice from behind him.

Raul turned to see a boy crouched a few feet behind him, clinging to a rock with his fingers and bare toes like some amphibious creature. He was dressed in a worn-out pair of khaki shorts and a shirt that was too small for him across the shoulders. A faded baseball cap covered his curly brown hair.

"I haven't seen anyone," Raul said, treating the question with the utmost seriousness.

The boy stuck out his lower lip while he pondered this, which made him look even more like a large frog. "You're not Cuban."

"No. I'm from—Spain."

"Thought so. Your accent isn't Cuban. My great-grandfather was from Spain. From Madrid. Do you know it?"

"No," Raul answered. "I've never been there."

The boy looked surprised. "How could you be Spanish and not know Madrid?" he asked.

"I left Spain when I was young."

This seemed to satisfy him. "So did my great-grand-father." He stood up, put his hand over his eyes to block out the glare of the afternoon sun, and then looked up and behind them toward the road. "I don't see them yet."

"What patrol are you talking about?"

The boy shrugged. "The militia. You know, the *Fidel-istas.* They come by in their jeeps, waving their guns, very macho, to see if anyone is lurking about or trying to leave."

"To leave?"

The child shrugged again, which this time seemed to mean that no elaboration would be forthcoming. "Would you like to see a dragon?"

Raul tried not to smile. "A real one?"

"Of course, a real one. I bet you don't have them in Spain. But I know where to find one."

"Is it close by?"

Yet another shrug. "Close enough. Do you have any money with you?"

"It costs money to see this dragon?"

The child looked incredulous. "I know where they live. I can't share that secret for nothing."

Such is the difference between capitalism and communism, thought Raul as he checked his pocket, *at least in theory.* He knew he was about to get taken, but the boy was so capti-vatingly precocious—and it was just a few coins. "Will this be enough?" he asked, all seriousness.

The boy gazed thoughtfully at the money in Raul's outstretched hand. "Well," he said, "I usually get more, but seeing as how you're a visitor from Spain, this will do."

He started to take the money, but Raul closed his fist around the coins. "Oh, no you don't. I'll pay you when I see the dragon," he replied, more amused by the moment.

The boy stepped back, looking insulted. "You don't trust me? Then why should I trust you? How do I know you won't take a look and then run off without paying me?"

What a little operator. "Well, what if I give you half now, and the other half when we see it?"

The putative dragon guide considered this option. "Okay," he agreed, holding out his hand, "but if the patrol comes before I find the dragon, we'll have to make a run for it, and I'll keep the half I've been paid."

The sly pup has probably timed the arrival of the patrol so that he can dash off with my money, thought Raul, but the boy was so engaging he felt as if he'd already gotten his money's worth, so he stood up and handed over the first half of his payment.

The boy took it, pulled out a none-too-clean handkerchief, wrapped the coins up carefully, and put the bundle back in his pocket. "Follow me."

"What's your name?" Raul asked as they set off.

"Emilio."

"How old are you?"

"Ten."

"Do you live around here?"

At this the boy stopped and asked brusquely, "Are you here to see a dragon, or to spy on me?"

"Why on earth would I be spying on you?"

Emilio put his hands on his hips and gave Raul a look

that communicated his opinion that this Spaniard was an idiot. "How long have you been in Cuba?"

Once again Raul had to squelch his amusement. "Not long."

"I didn't think so," Emilio replied as he turned back around and marched ahead with a decidedly more defiant stride.

They turned inland when they reached the next rock outcropping, walked for a few yards, and then made a sharp turn that led them through a row of palm trees into a thick clump of scrub. Raul had to bend low to make it through some of the twisted branches, and a wave of concern swept over him. Maybe the rascal was being paid to lead him to where robbers were waiting.

"I don't think—" Raul began.

"Shh," Emilio whispered as they emerged again onto the sand. Across a narrow canal Raul saw another sandy spot and several large boulders.

"There they are. Don't scare them," Emilio cautioned as he squatted and pointed.

Raul looked around. He didn't see any confederates lurking around waiting to pounce, so he dropped down beside Emilio.

"Them? Where? Behind that big rock?" Raul squinted as his eyes readjusted to the bright sunlight. The boulder was rough textured, like lava rock, except the color was a sandy brown, dappled with some sort of black lichen. Suddenly a portion of the rock shifted, and Raul realized that it was not covered with plant life; it was covered with iguanas.

They were hideous, malevolent-looking beasts, with

muscular legs, long claws, massive, spiked jowls, and a ridge of prehistoric-looking spines that ran along the length of their backs and halfway down their thick tails. And they were enormous. Several of them were easily a meter and a half long—nothing like the diminutive, nimble, sun-loving reptiles he'd chased through the bushes at his grandmother's beach house in southern Spain. Raul could imagine the reaction of a Spanish Conquistador coming across a horde of the monsters; of course he'd think he'd stumbled upon a nest of dragons.

One of the beasts opened its eyes and yawned; his eyes were a devilish red. A mischievous grin broke out on Emilio's face as he turned to Raul. "What did I tell you? Dragons."

"That is a magnificent sight," Raul said, meaning it. "Thank you for sharing it with me." He looked back at the mass of reptiles curled up on the large rock. The late afternoon sun set everything to glowing—sky, water, sand, skin, leaves, and even these ugly creatures. "The magic hour. God's attempt to perfect the imperfect," his grandmother used to say.

"Magnificent," he repeated.

Emilio tugged on his shirt sleeve, and they backed up through the brush. When they reached the other side of the thicket, Emilio held out his hand. "That was well worth the price," Raul said gravely as he handed over the remainder of his payment.

The child pulled out his handkerchief and added the additional coins to his pile. "I can show you other amazing things," he said, sounding ridiculously mature as he tucked his earnings back into his pocket. "I can show you beautiful places, too."

"I'm not sure I can afford all that," Raul answered.

"Oh, well, if you're a repeat customer, you know, you'll get a discount," Emilio said as he reached down and tugged at his drawers. "We should go this way; the patrol will be on the beach road by now."

"And what would this patrol do if they were to see us?"

Emilio gave him a somber look. "They'd do whatever they want to do, and only the sharks would know the truth."

"And how do you know all this?"

"Come on," Emilio said, ignoring this question. He walked away from the direction of the water, Raul close on his heels. They came to what looked like a path, although it was fast losing its battle with the voracious vegetation.

"Go that way," said Emilio, pointing. "You'll come to the road. There are a lot of houses, and you won't be bothered, at least not until after it's dark," he advised.

"And where are you going?"

Emilio grinned at him. "To buy some ice cream."

He turned and dashed back into the bushes, leaving Raul to wonder who cared for this young ruffian, where he lived, and what he really knew about what happened on the beach in the evening when the patrols came around.

CHAPTER SIX

"She's getting worse," I told Tim as I slumped into the opposite side of the booth.

We were at Hooligan's, our favorite pub. It was a small, dark retreat in the basement of an old brownstone, in a neighborhood that had yet to be rediscovered by people with money.

Gracie, the waitress who'd been there for as long as I could remember (and had been wearing the same wig and the same shade of lipstick for just as long) looked over and caught my eye as soon as I sat down. I nodded at her. Tim was halfway through what I assumed was his first pint, although it could've been his second; I was a good fifteen minutes late.

"And a fine hello to you, too, Miss Mary Katherine Anne O'Connor," he said wryly as I turned back to him. I hated being called by my complete Christian name, and Tim knew it.

"Hello-dear-Timothy-how're-you-this-lovely-afternoon-well-I-hope-it's-surely-a-grand-pleasure-to-be-seeing-you," I fired back in a thick Irish brogue.

"That's more like it," Tim replied. Gracie brought me my beer. I took a very long gulp.

"Easy now. It's a bit early for that, isn't it?" Tim admonished. Once a big brother, always a big brother.

"It's been a tough week." I pushed the mug several inches away from me, as if a slight distance would keep me from downing the whole thing at once. "But things are looking up. I'm going on a special assignment."

"Where to?"

"Can't tell you. Not yet, anyway. And I don't know how long I'll be gone, so I wanted to see you while I'm in town... and, you know, talk about Ma." I inched the beer closer. "She's getting worse, Tim." I repeated.

"What's your basis for comparison?" he responded, instantly defensive. "You're never there. You go globe-trotting and leave her all alone in that big house."

I bristled. "Don't start with that. I have to travel. It's my job. You could move in with her, you know. It's not like the house isn't big enough."

"Oh, and wouldn't that be pretty — a forty-three-year-old bachelor moving back in with his mother. I'd never get another woman to look at me."

I made a face at this handsome brother of mine. "Getting women to look at you has never been the problem, Tim. It's getting *you* to marry one of *them* that's always the issue."

"Well if that isn't the pot calling the kettle black. Where's your own lovely wedding ring, I'd like to know?"

I sighed. There was no use in continuing this topic of conversation, and we both knew it. "What about Maureen?"

"What about her? Do you think she's going to give up her country club on Long Island or her kids' fancy school to move back into that old dump? Or that Ma will leave her home in the city and plop down in suburbia, when she can't drive and she doesn't know anyone? C'mon,

Katherine. Maureen doesn't even have the guts to bring it up with her, even though our materially-minded sister knows that we'd all come into a pile of money if she could get Ma to sell the house."

"I can't believe you said that."

"How is it helping her to let her rattle about that big empty place by herself? She could fall or have a heart attack and no one would know."

"So move in with her."

"Well, it's been nice having this chat with you. Be sure to drop a line from wherever you're off to next." He started to rise.

"Okay, I'm sorry. We'll figure something out."

But our mother did not make it easy to come up with a solution. Ever since the last two boarders had been spirited away by their families to live out their days in an old folks' home, she'd lived in the big house by herself, waving away the many offers from developers who salivated at the thought of building another multi-family building on that valuable piece of land. "I'll let you and Tim do the selling for me when I pass," she'd say to me on the very rare occasions when I brought up that subject. "Then you can do what you want and split it up between—between the three of ya."

There was always that small hesitation, a verbal ellipsis to gloss over what she was thinking. *There should have been five.*

I picked up my mug and polished off most of the second half of my beer as Tim settled back into the booth. He looked at me with a mix of admiration and irritation. "Jesus, girlie. Where do you put it?"

"Hollow leg. Lots of practice." I waved at Gracie, who waved back and headed to the bar to get me a refill.

"At least Ma's still pretty fit," I commented, grasping for something positive to add to our conversation. "It's not like her health is failing."

"Not that we know of, anyway. Do you know when she last went to a real doctor?" He didn't wait for me to respond. "When you were born. Over thirty years ago."

"So why don't you take her for a check-up?"

"Why don't you?"

I let that pass. Taking Ma to the doctor would be tougher than pulling a bear out of its cave to go greet some hunters. There was a reason she never went, which was probably fear, but she would never admit to that. "Going to the doctor when you're healthy is a waste of his time and your money," was her excuse. And her commitment to old wives' tales — like sleeping with a bowl of chopped onions next to the bed to get rid of a cold — seemed to have kept her healthy enough.

"Look, we can argue all day, but that won't help Ma," I pointed out.

"Does she need help? She's happy enough, isn't she?"

It always came back to this. We should do *something*, but making Ma do anything she didn't want to do was like moving the Rock of Gibraltar. It couldn't be done, and it wasn't pleasant to try. She would give you that look — the one that made you feel like you were eight years old and in big, big trouble — and neither Tim nor I were brave enough to face that more than once every other year or so. Maureen had never been brave enough.

Before the war, Ma was the neighbor everyone turned

to when they had a problem that required some serious thought. She would offer a sympathetic ear, but never stop working; Ma could listen attentively while drying dishes, shelling peas, or folding clothes. And by the time the visitor left, he or she would feel better, having received a cup of tea, perhaps a bite to eat, and some sound advice from Maggie O'Connor.

She was the mother who could scold anyone's child, with the only response from the parent being, "You must've deserved it." She wasn't overly affectionate, but she made all five of us feel loved, and her calm sensibility made us feel safe.

That all changed when Jamie died. And now she was crumbling away like the foundation of an ancient fortress, while we pretended not to notice.

"We're related to half of New York. Isn't there someone who wants a nice roof over his or her head who could look after Ma for us?" I asked Tim plaintively, hoping he could come up with someone.

"Do you have someone in mind?"

I shook my head. And even if we could think of someone, Ma would have to approve, and that was unlikely. After living in an overcrowded house all her life she seemed to relish her solitude. "Gives me more time to pray," she'd say when one of us asked if she ever felt lonely, "God is with me every minute of the day."

Of course this was another troubling sign. Ma had always been religious, but not quite so vocal about it.

Gracie delivered my second beer. I started to take another large swig, thought better of it, and settled for a sip. There was one more thing I wanted to know, and I didn't want to give Tim an excuse to change the subject after I'd broached it.

"Does she... does she ever talk about Jamie when you're with her?"

Tim looked guarded. "What do you mean?"

"Well, like he's still here. As if he weren't... you know, dead."

"I have no idea what you're talking about," Tim replied in a tone of voice that let me know he knew exactly what I was talking about, and had no intention of discussing it.

I shrugged. "Okay," I said, "then she's not as bad as all that." And I reached again for my beer.

CHAPTER SEVEN

I n the early summer of 1960 Cuba was still a vacation destination, although few Americans went there after Castro closed the casinos and kicked out the mob guys who ran them. Castro's nationalization of some major business assets owned by American companies didn't help, either. But despite the rapidly deteriorating relations between the two countries, when I left New York for Miami in the summer of 1960, Fidel Castro was still welcoming American visitors and their dollars with open arms.

I was hoping that if I could break a good story from Cuba, I could use it to win my way onto the staff of an outfit big enough to send me to places like Brazil and Chile, with the blessings of a supportive editor, the convenience of a generous expense account, and a guaranteed byline. Politically, the whole continent was coiled as tight as a spring. I wanted to be there when things started to pop.

But when I began working as a reporter in the early 1950s there was just one way to succeed in a newsroom: you had to scoop a story. And you didn't get leads if you weren't respected, and you weren't respected unless you could play in the male world by male rules.

This was first explained to me in 1952 by one of the few

American women who'd had a spectacular career as a foreign correspondent prior to the war in Vietnam. I've never been the type to go all gushy over celebrities (although I'll confess I did have a few lustful twinges in my loins the first time I met Robert Kennedy) but this woman was my idol. She made her name in the late 1930s reporting from Spain during the civil war, and since then had sent stories over the wire from war zones in every corner of the world. When she came to speak at Columbia, I was disappointed by what she had to say. Nothing but anecdotes—no advice.

So after her speech I followed her to a bar in Midtown. She must have hit the place regularly; the bartender greeted her with a drink as soon as she sat down, without waiting for her to order. At first it struck me as rather odd that she'd go out for a drink by herself. She must have known hundreds of people in New York. But you make as many enemies as you do friends in this business, and I understood the need for restorative solitude.

Sitting at the bar she looked every minute of her sixty-plus years. Her skin had the texture of a worn tire, and the bright red capillaries visible on both sides of her nose announced that she was no stranger to the bottom of a bottle. Her one enviable trait was her hair; it was that unique blonde color that somehow merges smoothly into gray as you age. Still thick and wavy, she wore it short, Amelia-Earhart style.

It didn't take long for her to polish off her first drink, and I asked the bartender to send her a refill on me. My generosity meant I'd be eating nothing but macaroni and cheese for a week, but I figured it was worth it if she'd talk to me. When the bartender identified me as her benefactor she shot me a look that was anything but welcoming. Despite her grimace I moved over and planted myself on the empty stool next to her.

"And you are?" she asked, without changing one millimeter of the sour look on her face.

"Katherine O'Connor. I'm a student at the Columbia School of Journalism."

"Oh, bloody hell," she responded, and took a long pull on her scotch. She lit a cigarette. I waited, fighting an atypical urge to dash out the door.

"Do you smoke?" she asked.

I shook my head. "No."

"Well, you'd better start," she replied, without offering me a cigarette. "Having a cigarette gives you a reason to step outside and have a private conversation when you need one. Giving a cigarette to a man who hasn't had one in days can be like finding a key to a locked door. And if you're hanging around, waiting for a story to break, and everyone else is smoking, you better be smoking too, or you'll choke to death."

"Thanks. I'll keep that in mind," I replied, then mentally kicked myself. Not exactly a riveting response.

She stared at me, and I wondered what silent test I had to pass in order to continue our conversation. Then she asked me an unexpected question.

"Why do you want to be a reporter? And don't give me any of that journalism school bullshit about shedding light on the truth and the public's right to know."

Mine is not the unexamined soul. I knew that my ambition wasn't entirely fueled by the universally acceptable motivations she'd dismissed with such derision, so I blurted out the truth.

"I'm a prisoner of my own curiosity. I want to be a reporter—no, a foreign correspondent—because I want to know what's happening all over the world. And when I discover something worth knowing, I have an insatiable desire to share it."

"Why?"

"I just have to. It's like—digging for gold. And I want people to know that I'm good at finding it, so unearthing a treasure trove doesn't mean as much as it should unless I can let everyone else know what I've found."

She considered this as she blew out more smoke. "That's not a bad answer. Don't let any of those First Amendment philosophers fool you. Ours is not a noble profession. Hell, it's not even a profession. You don't need a license to be a reporter. All you have to do is convince someone who runs a newspaper to hire you."

"So why are you in it?"

"God knows it's not for the money." She scowled down at her glass as if she were surprised to find it empty. I waited. I didn't have the money to buy her another drink. Either she'd talk to me or she wouldn't. To my relief, she went on.

"Not everyone gets this speech, and if I see any of it printed anywhere I'll make sure no one ever hires you. Is that clear? And no notes."

I hastily shoved my notepad and pen back into my jacket pocket. "Sure."

"There are three things you need if you hope to have even a small chance of success in this business: persistence, persuasion, and luck. The first you're born with, the second you can develop, but the third is beyond your control. The best you can do is try to put yourself in a place where Lady Luck can find you if she's feeling generous. That takes planning. And guts."

I nodded. She stubbed out her cigarette, lit another one, then continued. "Reporting is about winning. It's about getting there first. To find a good story look for hypocrisy. Compare what people say they believe with the facts contradicting them, and you'll find at least a kernel of truth somewhere in the middle. But don't kid yourself — truth is a flexible commodity."

I wasn't prepared for such full-blown cynicism from my childhood hero, and my face must have communicated as much, because she started to laugh. Hard. The laughter turned into coughing and the bartender rushed over with a glass of water.

"I started out like you," she continued after she'd caught her breath, "thinking the truth was something static and discoverable, like, well, the gold you mentioned. But it isn't. Try hard to get close to it, though. Protect your reputation above everything else. That's your stock in trade. That's why people will talk to you, because they think they can trust you. And you'll get breaks because you're an attractive woman. Take them. They'll never make up for all the walls thrown up in front of you for the same reason. You'll have to drink like a man, smoke like a man, and cuss like a man to join the club, but don't ever get caught fucking like one. You'll get crucified." And with that she walked out, leaving me with the entire bill.

That night I thought I'd made a very expensive mistake. I didn't. Her advice paid for itself many times over, and I capitalized on it when I made my first trip to Cuba.

* * * * *

Having "Mary Katherine Anne O'Connor" on my passport made it unlikely that an official at the Havana airport would connect me to Katherine O'Connor, journalist. Women weren't expected to have a career, so I didn't think I'd be quizzed all that carefully about what I was doing in Cuba. But I made sure that I'd be noticed: I wore the shortest, tightest skirt I could pour myself into, the highest heels I could walk in without falling on my face, and a blouse that exposed more of my meager décolletage than had ever before seen the light of day. The center attractions were propped up and out with the most obscene item of clothing I'd ever worn: a padded, push-up bra imported from Canada, recommended to me by the friend who'd loaned me the clothes. An aspiring actress, she swore by the effectiveness of this instrument of not-so-subtle subterfuge.

I'd even gone to the beauty parlor the day before and had my long, curly-cue mass of hair straightened, which involved sitting for an interminable amount of time under the dome of a gargantuan hair dryer, sporting curlers as big as coffee cans all over my head. After that, I'd told the beautician to swoop my mane up into one of those fancy French twists, and asked her to paste on some low-key false eyelashes. To complete my ensemble I wore red lipstick, white gloves, and a small, stylish hat.

I looked, in short, like a vixen.

There was a full planeload of people waiting for the Pan Am flight from Miami to Havana. A few seemed recreation-minded, explaining loudly that they wanted to get to Havana "before it was too late," but most of the passengers were men in suits, probably going to Cuba to try and sort out some problem caused by Castro's rampant nationalization of formerly foreign-owned assets.

I zeroed in on a mildly handsome middle-aged man, and made sure that he wore a wedding ring before I struck up a conversation. I learned that he was going to Cuba to see if he could help an old friend sell his interest in a canning factory. "Not many potential buyers now," he explained, "but the guy did me a good turn once, and I might be able to put him in touch with someone. Assuming Castro lets anyone own anything by the time he's through."

I pretended to be riveted by this, and continued by asking if he'd been to Cuba before this trip. Oh, to fish? Deep sea fishing? How exciting. Like Hemingway. Would he be able to do some fishing while he was in Cuba this time around?

Once I felt the gentleman relaxing into the cordial intimacy of our conversation I asked him to do me a favor. "I'm an artist," I began, "at least I'd like to be, and I've always wanted to go to Cuba. I hear the light there is fabulous, so I decided to make the trip before things get any worse."

I leaned closer to him, allowing my Canadian co-conspirator to help me make my case. As he fixed his eyes on my artificially enhanced cleavage, I continued in a whisper, "But I've heard those Latin men can be somewhat forward, and I don't want to get into an awkward situation. So I was wondering—if you wouldn't mind, could you escort me through the airport when we get there? That way if any of those Cuban men get any fresh ideas, they'll know I'm not alone."

"Say no more," my new-found protector responded enthusiastically, "I'll take your arm as soon as we get off the plane, and won't let go until you give me the green light."

"Thank you so much," I said, gazing at him with wide-eyed gratitude. I had to get the hang of this flirting thing if I wanted to add it to my bag of tricks.

I'd flown over the Northern Atlantic several times, but I'd never seen the Gulf of Mexico. On the day I flew to Cuba the sea was so clear I could see dolphins playing on the surface and seaweed growing on the bottom. Anything that clear should have been colorless, but it wasn't. The sea shifted from bright turquoise to aquamarine, then teal, then a deep azure. And, as a native New Yorker, I was seldom impressed by modern feats of engineering—what could anyone build that we hadn't built first? But the slim ribbon of highway that stretched from the edge of Florida down to Key West amazed me.

Forty-five minutes after takeoff we arrived in Havana. My new friend was waiting on the tarmac for me. He hooked his arm protectively through mine as we headed into the terminal. To my dismay—and his—we were sent to different tables for a baggage inspection.

The khaki-clad young man looking through my things made quite a show of pulling out several rather daring undergarments (which I had no intention of wearing; I'd piled those on top as a distraction, to hide the dowdier clothes beneath them). Holding a miniscule pair of lace panties in his hand, he asked in perfect English, "Is that fat guy your boyfriend?"

I snatched the panties out of his hand and tossed them back into the suitcase. "I'm not sure how that concerns you."

He gave me a nasty grin. "You can do better than him."

I glanced over at my chivalrous protector. He looked as if he were about to break out of line and come to my rescue. The insolent inspector was now going through my second, smaller suitcase, which contained several different sized sketch pads, some charcoal pencils, and a large set of pastels.

"What's all this?" he asked, now looking more suspicious than lecherous.

"I draw. As a hobby, not professionally. I was hoping to do some sketching while I was here."

"Oh, yeah? Do you need a model?" He adopted an exaggerated pose, his right profile facing me. "This is my best side."

"I don't think now is an appropriate time."

He turned to face me again and his eyes narrowed. He picked up a pencil, one of the drawing pads, and thrust them at me.

"Draw."

"Here? Now?"

"Draw."

I'm no artist, but thanks to a couple of art classes in college I do know the basics, and managed to come up with something that at least resembled a human face.

"There," I said, handing him my masterpiece.

He looked at it and grunted. "I hope your boyfriend is rich. You'll never make a living at *this*."

"I'm a student," I said, holding out my hand.

Instead of giving my sketchpad back to me he dropped it into my suitcase. "Enjoy your stay in Cuba."

I closed my bag and straightened my shoulders: haughty, not angry. "Thank you," I replied, and walked through the exit, shoulders back, head held high, hips swinging as aggressively as my heels allowed.

My new gentleman friend was waiting for me. He took my arm again, his face colored with apprehension. "Well, my dear, it seems as if your concern was well-founded. I can't believe the Cuban government allows that sort of thing to go on in the airport. That impudent fool should be fired, if not arrested. I think I should escort you to your hotel."

"Oh, please, I wouldn't dream of putting you to that much trouble," I said earnestly.

He gave my arm a reassuring squeeze. "No trouble at all."

But I don't want you to know where I'm staying, I thought. The whole point of the floozy outfit and picking up a willing escort was so that I would look like any other mistress coming to Havana for a couple of weeks with her paramour. The sketch pads allowed me to bring in pencil and paper without looking as if I were prepared to take notes, and being an "artist" of sorts I'd have an excuse to wander around a bit—assuming it was still possible to do so without running afoul of the police. My escort had played his part, and now I was done with him.

67

"No, thank you, I'll be fine," I said again, trying to dislodge myself. "And you're a married man. Why, you wouldn't want anyone to think—"

He dropped my arm as if I had some contagious disease, and his expression shifted from chivalrous to scared so fast I had to assume that fidelity had been an issue between him and his wife—at least once.

"Why... if you're sure," he stammered.

"Yes, but thanks again." I gave him a slightly-less-than-chaste kiss on cheek, so that anyone watching would assume that I was getting into my own cab just to be discreet, and throwing a look that promised more over my shoulder, walked away.

CHAPTER EIGHT

A city has a unique personality. Its people move with a certain rhythm, a collective attitude. It's impossible to find reflected within each individual, but readily apparent when examining the whole. On the surface Havana felt like Manhattan on a tropical vacation: focused on business, but willing to stop for a drink, a dance, a nap, or a chat.

And, like New York, the capital of Cuba was very international. Its foundation was Spanish, but the slaves forcibly imported from Africa during colonial times had brought their own culture with them, which altered the mix (although power and wealth were always concentrated in the hands of light-skinned Cubans—and still are). In Havana, prosperity had fueled a thirst for those things humans can only enjoy at leisure, like art, music, fine food, and fast cars. But unlike New York, in Havana the optimism that had nurtured the city's growth was rapidly fading.

The famous hotels, like the former Hilton, Tropicana, the National and the Riviera, were already under government control, and would therefore contain too many employees with too much time on their hands for me to come and go unnoticed. My hotel was in Old Havana, where the streets were narrow and the alleys abundant; easier, I thought, to get lost in a crowd if necessary.

Before long I was sitting in my room pondering my next move. First I had to finish establishing my adopted persona, so that I could shed it and start moving around the island more anonymously. I donned my swimsuit (a clingy one-piece; I was not prepared to wear a bikini— ever). I slipped a blousy cover-up over it, put on yet another pair of potentially deadly shoes, and sashayed down to the lobby.

The ruse seemed to be working. The concierge spent an excessive amount of time explaining the advantages and disadvantages of every beach within a thirty-mile radius; the bellman raced out to flag down a cab; a porter, unasked, brought me a glass of water with a sprig of mint; and when I arrived at the beach my cab driver offered to accompany me down to the water. I declined with what I hoped was a mysterious smile, saying that I was to meet a "friend," and asked him to come back in an hour.

It was around three o'clock when I arrived on the beach outside Havana. The wide swath of sand was nearly empty. I saw a few men fishing, patiently casting lines out into the surf and reeling them back in; their comfortable silence and sun-scarred faces told me they'd probably been fishing together for years. Further along, a young couple lay on a blanket, he napping, she reading. I plopped my towel, sandals, and cover-up down on the sand and headed for the water.

I love the ocean, and I love to swim, even though I'm not very good at it. I can, however, hold my breath under-water for a very long time. In fact, I think I developed this talent because I never got the knack of swimming across the surface, where I'd always felt as if I were imitating the spasmodic death dance of a large fish. Underwater I could glide with what I imagined to be mermaid-like prowess.

Of course my determination to stay underwater as long as possible caused my older siblings more than one anxious moment, but I gloried in this, too; I was the baby, but I was *not* spoiled. If I ran and fell, I was told to stand up, shut up, and stop crying. If I tripped on the stairs and landed on my rump, I was the subject of jokes for days. But when we were at the beach, one of my siblings was always "in charge of Mary Kate," and when I went underwater and stayed there, and then stayed there a little longer, it invariably caused a bit of panic.

And for some reason salt water has never bothered my eyes very much, so I could do fun things like sneak up on one of them and pinch a leg. To watch someone who'd been making fun of you all your life shout in terror and race to shore — well, it was almost worth drowning for.

The water was warm and amazingly clear: the sand underneath my feet smooth and free of anything sharp or off-putting, like broken shells or decomposing seaweed. I hadn't swum for years, but as soon as I dove under that wondrous feeling came back to me, as if I'd crossed over into an underwater Narnia, a place where my physical movements were no longer graceless but as elegant as those of a fairy.

I came to the surface and then dove again, this time headed toward a buoy about forty yards out. Given the remarkable clarity I could see the large shadow it cast under the water, so I aimed in that direction, determined to make it all the way there in one breath.

When I emerged I could see that the underwater portion of the buoy was covered by colorful marine flora and fauna. Spotting a patch on one of the supports that looked relatively barnacle free, I grabbed it with both hands and lifted my head and torso out of the water. I wiped my eyes with one hand and glanced back at the shore to check on my things. A young boy was standing almost motionless at the edge of the water, gaping at me.

I gave him a friendly wave, then pushed myself back from the buoy, spread my arms, and stretched out onto on my back. The salty water made it very easy to float. I focused on the feel of the sun on my skin, enjoying the blissful feeling of weightlessness. An unfamiliar sense of peace wafted through every part of my body, including the interior of my head.

I rolled over and started swimming toward the shore. When I rose to take a breath I was able to catch an incoming wave, so I half-swam, half-bodysurfed back in.

The boy was still there, still staring at me. He looked to be nine or ten years old, and his lean, tanned legs were covered with the scratches and bruises typically acquired by an intrepid explorer of the Great Outdoors.

"*Buenos días,*" I said, sitting up as I wiped the water from my eyes. I collected the long, tangled mess that was my hair and wrung out some of the seawater.

"Are you a mermaid?" the boy asked in Spanish. His dark eyes were enormous, and his lashes so thick he looked as if he were wearing mascara. They stared down at me from his round, pecan-colored face with such a solemn expression I couldn't resist teasing him.

"Of course I am," I answered, smiling up at him.

"I thought so. What did you do with your tail?"

Children's games, imaginary or otherwise, were never my style, so I was surprised to hear myself say, "I had to slip it off before I could come back on land, of course."

"Where did you hide it?"

I laughed as I stood up. "Now, you know I'm not a mermaid and there is no tail."

"So you won't tell me," he said, looking thoughtful. "Well, that's okay. You don't know me well enough yet, and that way you'll be sure it's there when you need it."

"Right again," I said as I headed up to collect my things. He trotted after me.

"I'm Emilio," the boy said as I dried off and wrapped my hair up in a towel turban. "This is my beach. Well, sort of mine. I know all its secrets. Except where you've hidden your tail."

I took his hand and shook it, gently but with great dignity. "It's a pleasure to meet you, Emilio. My name is Maria."

His eyes lit up with the thrill of possibility. "That's the name of this beach. Is that why you came here, Miss Maria? Is this *your* beach?"

I shook my head. "It's been nice talking to you, Emilio, but you'll have to excuse me. I have to get back."

"Back where?"

"Back to Mermaid Land."

He made a face. "You're making fun of me."

"A little." I slipped my cover-up back over my head.

"Will you come back here?" Emilio asked, his scowl shifting into a look of longing so profoundly expressive I didn't have the heart to say no.

"Maybe."

"When?"

"Well, you must know I can only stay on land until the next full moon. So, sometime before then."

"I *knew* it," he exclaimed, punching a fist into a grubby palm.

"You're a real clever kid," I said, then left to see if my cab driver was still there, waiting to take me back to Havana.

CHAPTER NINE

Raul walked out onto *Plaza Vieja*, the most elegant town square in the oldest section of Havana, and paused to admire the architecture. Old Havana had been built around a series of public gathering places, in the style of many old Spanish cities. This plaza was not large but it was beautiful. The gray cobblestone street was surrounded by narrow, stucco houses all painted in soft pastel colors. Many were adorned with stained-glass windows. Every building had a second-story terrace guarded by intricate wrought-iron railings, below which rows of connected colonnades and arches helped to form a continuous shaded walkway all around the plaza's perimeter.

Havana was full of green parks, fountains, and shaded streets, where people strolled and stopped to chat every time they ran across an acquaintance. So unlike Moscow. Raul couldn't think of a single public plaza in the Soviet capital that was not dedicated to some military or communist hero.

He was at the plaza to have breakfast with Tito Rodriguez, a talkative man with hair as wiry as a scrub brush, pock-marked skin, and a belly that betrayed his fondness for beer and pierogies. Tito was an old acquaintance of Raul's, and now one of his *Hispanic-Sovietico* colleagues in Cuba. His family had sent him to the Soviet

Union around the same time that Raul and his sister arrived there, but they didn't meet until they'd been evacuated from Leningrad in 1941.

On that day Raul had been standing in a line of people, waiting for bread, when he'd felt the icy wallop of a snowball on his shoulder. Turning, he saw a boy about his own age standing twenty feet away, his broad grin inviting retribution.

"Defend yourself," the boy shouted in Spanish, and Raul had tried, scooping up a mound of snow and giving chase for a good thirty yards, determined to shove it down his unknown attacker's neck even if it meant missing out on whatever stale excuse for bread they were supposed to receive that day.

Without warning, a huge blast wave sent them both flying forward into a deep snow bank. They emerged flapping and spitting, like young walruses exiting a snowy cave. The small storehouse and the line of people who'd been waiting in front of it had disappeared, replaced by a white crater streaked with abstract splotches of red, brown, and black, sprinkled with shards of wood and bits of what had been several dozen, grumpy, hungry human beings.

"I saved your life," Tito uttered with stunned awe.

"May—maybe," Raul stammered as he managed to gain control of his trembling limbs and stand up.

He shook away that memory as he approached the café where he and Tito were to meet. There he was, at an outdoor table. "Every time I see you, if you're not in the process of smoking a cigar, you're chewing on one until you get a chance to light it," Raul said in lieu of a greeting as he sat down. "You haven't even had breakfast yet."

Tito took the cigar out of his mouth and admired it fondly. "My friend, smoking a cigar is like making love to a beautiful woman, and compared to the ones I usually smoke—when I can get one, which is rare—these Cuban beauties are sublime. It's like the difference between being with a Castilian princess or a Bulgarian whore. Castro may be sending boatloads of these to Russia, but you know they won't be available to the likes of us. So until I have to go back to sucking on Soviet Shit Sticks, I'm smoking Cubans, and as many of them as I can."

"Well, that sounds reasonable." Raul knew that he couldn't rush headlong into his real reason for meeting without giving too much away, so after the waitress had taken their order and they'd engaged in a few pleasantries, he started grousing about the interminable number of meetings—badly organized and of limited purpose—that they were forced to attend.

Tito agreed. "We may be building good Soviet-Cuban relations, but we certainly aren't getting much done."

"And you know these Cubans often use American words in place of Spanish ones when they're talking about any sort of technology," Raul continued. "Makes it tougher for someone like me, who is not good with English."

"Don't I know it," said Tito. "So much of what I learned at university regarding agriculture, I never learned the Spanish for, so I have to sort of puzzle words together, sometimes even pantomime to make my point. And when comprehension dawns, the Cubans laugh and give me the word in Spanish, as if I can't speak my own language."

Raul deemed it time to raise the subject he'd come to discuss. "So, Tito," he began, "what do you think of *El Che*?" He made sure to ask this in Russian, and although it was unlikely that anyone else in the café knew that language, he spoke quietly.

Tito's eyebrows lifted in surprise and he took the cigar out of his mouth. "Why ask me?"

Raul shrugged. "You've been in meetings with him on some of the agricultural issues, isn't that right? He speaks in passionate generalities, which might work with politics, but in my line of work that's not helpful. If he does end up asking me for something specific, I'd like a better sense of how to handle it."

Tito cocked his head as he assessed this explanation. "I've heard some of his more practical proposals," he said slowly, "imperialist crops like sugar and tobacco that have enslaved the Cuban economy must be phased out; the workers of the Revolution will build Cuban cars, Cuban sewing machines, even radios — so that no one will have an excuse to miss one of Castro's verbal marathons, no doubt." Then he grinned. "I guess next it will be Cuban spaceships, so Che can export revolution to the whole solar system. But I don't know that I have any helpful insight about what makes Guevara tick. He reminds me of what I've read and heard about Lenin: brilliant, inspirational, manipulative, and ruthless. And a true communist."

Raul smiled at this. "I don't believe I've ever heard Comrade Lenin described so succinctly. Who'd ever believe that you could be so eloquent?"

Tito planted his unlit cigar back in his mouth.

"Thanks," he muttered as he searched his pockets for his lighter, "for that, you can buy breakfast."

Their good-natured argument was interrupted by a young voice. "Hey, mister," it said, "you dropped this."

Raul turned to see Emilio standing right behind him, hand outstretched, offering Raul a Cuban peso.

"I did?" Raul was startled to see the boy in town, at least ten kilometers from where they'd met.

"Pretty sure you did," Emilio replied, using this inter-action as an excuse to walk up to the table. He looked down at the coin, then back up at Raul. "But I can keep it if you don't need it."

Raul glanced at Tito, who was smiling at him, waiting for his answer. He was pretty sure he hadn't dropped anything, but he didn't know what Emilio was up to, so he played along. "I guess it's mine, then," he said, and took the peso from the child's hand. Emilio sighed deeply, but rather insincerely, as if he'd expected that to happen.

"How about you give me a chance to earn it back?" he asked. "I can show you something—"

"I don't have time right now."

"How about tomorrow?"

"I don't think so."

"But you don't know what you're missing."

"Well, he's a persistent little bastard," Tito commented in Russian as he reached to dump his cigar ashes into his empty coffee cup, "but kind of young to be pimping for his mother, isn't he?"

His tone was not lost on Emilio, who glared at him, correctly assuming that he was the butt of Tito's joke. Raul got the feeling that if the boy had understood Russian he'd have done something to defend his mother's honor—something that would have landed him in a whole lot of trouble.

"Listen, kid, I have things to do," Raul said.

"Don't you have any time off?" Emilio asked in a tone that was one part plea, one part accusation.

"And if I did, why would I spend it with you?" Raul replied.

At this, all the boy's buoyant energy dissolved. He gazed silently at Raul, oozing disappointment from every millimeter of his scrawny frame.

"Oh, cheer up. I might be able to get to the beach later today."

The boy brightened immediately. "Meet me at Playa Maria. Don't come before four o'clock," he said, "or later than five-thirty. It has to be low tide."

"Fine," Raul agreed gruffly. "I'll be there if I can. But don't count on it."

"Okay! But remember, don't come before four o'clock." Without waiting for another of Raul's hedges, Emilio scampered away.

"I didn't know you were such a soft touch," Tito said, his eyes still following the retreating child.

"Oh, shove it," Raul responded, none-too-politely, "I don't have time to go to the beach. And I have no idea what the kid wants, but he'll have to get it somewhere else." He turned and signaled for the waitress to bring their check.

Tito still gazed across the square, as if trying to memorize the exact spot where Emilio had disappeared into the mid-morning crowd. "What is he, nine, maybe ten years old?"

"Sounds about right."

"About the same age we were when we left Spain."

Raul stayed silent. Since the end of the war he and Tito had run into each other a few times, before they'd met again in Cuba. They'd always been happy to see each other; they'd quaff some vodka, retell some war stories, and share what gossip they knew about their mutual acquaintances. But neither of them ever reminisced about the circumstances surrounding their exile.

They'd all come to the Soviet Union from Spain as brave young heroes: courageous little communist soldiers. Official parades were given in their honor, songs sung, flowers and gifts presented by a cheering public. Stalin himself had visited some of the houses where large groups of homesick Spaniards struggled with their grief, the strange food, the cold climate, and a new language—but none of that appeared in the newsreels. The children were always happy up on the movie screen, where Uncle Joe read them stories, watched them play sports, or nodded his approval of their academic efforts as he supervised the taking of an exam.

Somewhere along the way, his young guests became his prisoners.

To analyze the past was a perilous endeavor. Easier and safer to stay silent, which suited Raul perfectly. No, they'd never talked about their exile from Spain, and Raul was not going to start now.

"Doesn't this place remind you of Spain?" Tito asked him.

"Not the part I came from." *Cuba is like Southern Spain, the home of my mother's people: a land of good food, laughter and music. So completely different from Russia.*

Tito sighed. "For me, it's like being back home again. The sun, the food, the women, the pace of life. The openness."

"That may change."

"I hope not. I tell you, I could see myself living here. Permanently."

"Do you think that will be an option for any of us?"

"Why not? Khrushchev is taking Cuba under his wing. Can you imagine how it would aggravate the Americans to have a Soviet ally sitting right under their noses?"

"Of course."

"Well then, I don't see us losing our usefulness so quickly."

"Perhaps not."

"You know, old friend, I'm trying to remember if I've ever heard you offer a firm opinion about anything that didn't involve cement or steel."

"Tito, I'm an engineer. That's all I think about."

* * * * *

It was easy to catch a bus out to the beach. Cars were relatively cheap in Cuba, coming as they did from the United States, but not every family could afford one. The bus service in and around Havana was inexpensive and reliable, and group travel seemed to suit the Cuban personality. Raul had come to believe that Cubans never did anything quietly.

As he broke through the scrub brush out onto the sand, Raul wondered how on earth he was supposed to find Emilio. He walked down to the water and looked up and down the beach, hoping to catch a glimpse of him. Then suddenly there he was, about fifty meters away, racing closer.

"I knew you'd come," he said cheerfully when he was within a few feet of Raul. "I wish you'd come earlier. I met a mermaid."

The uneasiness that had been wafting around his innards evaporated as soon as Raul saw the excitement in Emilio's eyes. "A mermaid? Well then, why did you tell me not to come before four? Can you go find her and tell her that I'd love to meet her?"

"I don't know where she is now. But she has to come back here sometime before the next full moon to get her tail back from where she's hidden it, so I'm keeping an eye out for her," Emilio answered with unabashed confidence.

"And if she doesn't come back for her tail?"

Raul could almost hear the gears spinning in the boy's head as he considered this. "She has to stay on land, I guess," he finally said, "or maybe she dies." The prospect of the mermaid's death seem to disturb him, but then Emilio shook his head and upper body vigorously, the way a dog shudders to shake off water, and changed the subject.

"Come on. We have to hurry before the tide starts coming back in."

"So you've said. And what are you going to show me today?"

Emilio turned and headed back up the beach, gesturing

for Raul to follow him. As soon as Raul caught up to him the boy began to elaborate on the object of their quest. "We're going to see a special kind of fish. But they weren't always fish. An Orisha put a spell on a whole village for eating the food her worshippers left for her on her altar. She turned all those greedy people into tiny gray fish, who can only eat once a day and have to hide in holes because they are so ashamed."

"What's an 'Orisha?' A kind of witch?"

"Not a witch. A powerful spirit. From Africa."

"Why would an African spirit be causing problems in Cuba?"

Emilio stopped and gave Raul a condescending look before saying, "You don't know anything, do you?"

Raul grinned. "No, I guess I don't."

Emilio rolled his eyes, turned on his heel, and resumed his quick pace. "The African spirits came to Cuba with the slave people, to protect them and answer their prayers," he said as he strode along. "You know, like praying to the Holy-Virgin-Mary-Mother-of-God."

"Do you pray to the Virgin Mary?"

Emilio ignored this question. "The fish look small, but they're long and skinny, and dig deep holes to live in. They move into them backward"—he illustrated by sticking his own rear end out and shaking it back and forth a bit—"and when they're scared they zip back into those holes so fast it's hard to catch them."

By now they'd come to a place where an isolated group of half-submerged rocks lay scattered on the beach, as if the child of some ancient giant had forgotten to pick up his building blocks, giving the sea several millennia to wear away their edges and smooth them into different shapes. Emilio leapt from one rock to another with sure-footed agility until he reached the particular tide pool he was seeking. He crouched down at the edge of the shallow water and gestured for Raul to do the same. "But get behind me," he ordered in a low voice, "your big shadow will scare them. And be still. Like you're frozen."

The look of intense concentration on the boy's face reminded Raul of a soldier waiting for the order to fire, and that turned his thoughts to what Emilio had said about the militia members who patrolled the beach and inflicted "disciplinary" violence on whomever they felt like, without any fear of reprisal. Had Emilio seen that happen with his own eyes? Or was he repeating rumors?

"Do you live near here, Emilio?" Raul asked in a whisper.

The boy did not even look up. He just gave Raul another one of his shrugs. Raul did not pursue the subject any further.

Then, sure enough, several rounded gray heads pushed slowly out from the sand at the bottom of the tide pool. If Raul hadn't been looking so closely he never would have caught sight of them; they were no more than a few centimeters wide and almost translucent, but their disproportionately large eyes and wide droopy mouths did give one the impression of sad people resigned to their dismal fate.

Emilio snapped his fingers over the water, and the fish disappeared so rapidly it seemed as if they'd never been there. He looked over his shoulder at Raul. "What did I tell you?" he asked gleefully.

Raul stood up and reached into his pocket for some change. "Another amazing sight, well worth the price," Raul replied as he fished out a few coins, "but before I pay you, I want to know — did you really see me drop that coin this morning?"

Emilio gave him another shrug, which seemed to offer a wide range of possible interpretations, from a simple, "who cares?" to, "I don't want to answer," or even, "if you're that stupid, what's the point of trying to explain?" He turned away and looked back down at the water.

Raul kept his tone gentle but firm. "I need to know the answer to that question," he said. "It's important that you be honest with me. I'm a paying customer, remember."

Emilio stood up, but he kept his eyes on the water as he answered. "I didn't know that man, the one with you at the café. So I had to figure out a reason to come up and talk to you without it looking like I knew you, in case, well, just in case. When you didn't say hello or anything I figured you'd caught on and were giving me the sign that I shouldn't say anything important in front of him. It was rotten of you to keep my peso. All you had to do was say you didn't drop it, and I still could have asked you to come to the beach again."

Raul was too astounded by this story to apologize. *What a sophisticated little schemer.* Aloud he asked, "But how did you find me? And don't just shrug this time."

Emilio did shrug, but he also looked up a Raul and answered the question. "It wasn't hard. One of the coins you gave me last time wasn't a peso. It had funny writing on it. I asked one of the cab drivers in the square if he knew what it was, because cabbies must get every kind of strange money, right? He said it was Russian, that there were a lot of Russians coming to Cuba. I know you're not Russian — they have those pale white faces and when they talk it's like coughing and shouting at the same time — but I thought if you have their money, you must spend some time with them. So I asked him where the Russians lived and the cabbie told me a lot of them live in the big houses in Miramar. I would go sometimes, you know, checking things out, and one morning I got lucky and saw you come out of a house — a nice one — on a street where a lot of the Russians stay. And I wanted to talk to you yesterday so I got there early, saw you leave, and I followed you."

"I don't know whether to be impressed or intimidated," Raul said as he handed Emilio a handful of pesos. "You're a very clever young man. What grade are you in?"

"School is stupid," the boy responded as he took out his handkerchief and wrapped it around his latest earnings before tucking it back into his pocket.

"Oh, and is that what your parents think?"

"My father doesn't know how stupid it is." He started to walk around Raul, as if no longer interested in the conversation, but Raul squatted so that he could look the child in the eye, and placed his hand on Emilio's too-thin upper arm to keep him still.

"I'm sure your father doesn't think school is stupid," he said.

Emilio looked impatient. "He doesn't know about how it is now."

"Oh, I see," Raul responded sympathetically. "It was different when he was a kid, right?"

"Everything was different, before—" Emilio checked himself.

"Before what?"

"Just before, okay? I don't ask you a bunch of questions."

"That's true enough." *Let it go,* Raul thought, *what business is it of yours if one Cuban kid has a tough life? Don't you have enough problems of your own?* But he found himself asking anyway.

"Why do you think school is stupid, Emilio?"

Emilio's face darkened, and for the first time Raul saw etched across it the ephemeral scars of a youngster whose childhood has been snatched away by tragedy. It was a look Raul knew all too well. He waited, expecting another evasive answer, but Emilio started talking very fast, body rigid, eyes staring straight ahead.

"You know the last day I went to school, the teacher comes in, the new one, not the old nun that we used to have, and she asks everyone, 'who believes in God?' So we all say 'me,' because, you know, what else are you going to say? So then she says, 'everyone pray to God to give you some ice cream, right now, here in this classroom.' So we all pray for ice cream. It's stupid, but we do it anyway, and then she says, 'open your eyes. Did God give ice cream?' 'No,' we all say. Stupid, right?

"Then she says, 'Now ask Fidel for ice cream.' And we're looking around, wondering if Fidel is going to walk in the door. But she tells us again, 'ask Fidel for ice cream. Say, please give us some ice cream, Fidel!' So we all say it together, just the way she wants us to, and right then three other teachers come in with trays of ice cream. Trays of it!

You know, the kind in the paper cups? And they start handing them out. So we start eating as fast as we can, because if it's a trick, you know, better to eat it quick. Then the teacher says, 'Remember, Fidel can give you what God cannot.'"

Fidel is learning fast, Raul thought to himself, remembering a similar event from his own early days in the Soviet Union. To Emilio he said, "And what did your father think of this?"

Emilio glanced up at him. "He doesn't know. He's in prison." And with that he broke free and bolted, his small heels kicking up puffs of white sand as he raced down the beach.

CHAPTER TEN

T he morning of my second day in Cuba I ordered a room service breakfast for two, waited ten minutes, and then turned on the shower. I rumpled both pillows and tossed the covers around to make it look like I hadn't spent the night alone. By the time the waiter knocked on my door I was wrapped in a robe, hair up in a towel turban, sitting languidly in a chair by the window, smoking a cigarette, and trying my best to look — well, sated. He didn't say a word, but when his eyes cut to the bathroom door, behind which the shower water was still blasting full force, I knew he was thinking what I'd hoped he would think. I gave him a large tip as he left, ate most of the food, drank both coffees, and shoved the tray into the hallway.

I waited a few minutes before calling down to the front desk. "I'll be doing some sightseeing for the next few days, you know, Santiago and all that. May I leave one case here until I return? Such a nuisance, lugging all that around. Yes, now's fine. No, no need for a cab this time. All of my needs are being *well* taken care of."

When the bellhop knocked I handed him my suitcase, which contained most of my decoy clothes. Then I began my transformation.

I'd let my hair dry naturally after I'd showered, and with the help of the tropical humidity my natural curls had reached a new level of manic unmanageability. I leaned over the bathroom sink, pulled all my hair up into a high ponytail, grabbed my scissors, and chopped off a good five inches. I flushed the clippings down the toilet, making sure there were no tell-tale strands left behind, then fetched the bottle of temporary hair rinse I'd brought with me. Fifteen minutes later I had very frizzy, dark brown hair.

My actress friend had also given me a makeup lesson. I brushed some foundation over my face so that I didn't look quite as pale, and my freckles weren't quite as noticeable. Wincing, I pulled off the false eyelashes (how they'd stayed on that long I don't know, but whatever adhesive that beautician had used pulled several of my real eyelashes off along with it). I then put on one of two seriously unflattering dresses that I'd brought with me (rolled up inside my vixen clothes) and an inexpensive pair of ugly but very comfortable shoes. I tied a dingy scarf around my hair, pulling the front low over my forehead. I grabbed a canvas bag I'd brought with me, threw in my remaining belongings, and left the room.

The drably-dressed, slouch-shouldered woman who walked out of the service entrance moved nothing at all like the red-haired vamp who'd been staying in room 364 with her mystery lover. No one gave me a second glance.

* * * * *

I wanted to get to a part of Havana where tourists wouldn't have any reason to go, so I took the bus and was rewarded by casual indifference from the other passengers, which let me know my altered appearance had succeeded, at least initially, in allowing me to blend in.

The section of the city to which I was headed had no grand homes or historical buildings to attract a visitor's attention. Most of the people who lived there worked for other people in shops, restaurants, or factories. Or else they ran their own small businesses. I wanted to find out what they thought of Castro when they weren't cheering for him during one of his stupendously long speeches, and what they expected to happen under his regime.

I descended the bus stairs as if I knew precisely where I was going, took off my scarf, and headed to the first café I saw. Two old men sat out front, on portable metal chairs pulled up to a scuffed wooden table. They showed as many signs of wear as the table did; the sun had molded their skin into taut folds, brown and crackled, rather like the hide of a crocodile Their teeth and fingernails were permanently stained by tobacco.

One of the men was speaking in rapid-fire Spanish, with the rounded vowels and musical rhythm of Cuba's unique treatment of that language, making it hard for me to understand everything he was saying. The other man listened intently, his fingers poised to bring his cigarette to his mouth, but he kept bobbing his hand back and forth a few centimeters, as if he didn't want to miss the opportunity to make the right comment, at precisely the right time, by having the thing in his mouth when he wanted to speak.

I walked within four feet of their table, and that was all it took for them to stop their conversation. "May we help you, lovely lady?" asked the man who'd been talking. His eyes danced with curiosity — and a decent measure of appreciation, despite my efforts to appear unattractive. His reaction reminded me of my brief time in Italy. There, too, life was never too busy for some socializing, and female newcomers were always interesting. In Cuba all that would soon change, but Castro's more draconian measures of collecting information had yet to be put into place, and the Cuban national character was still warm and gregarious.

"Yes, thank you," I answered, "I'm looking for a pawn shop."

"Oh, sit, sit."

"Have some coffee."

"What would a sweet young lady like you be doing at a pawn shop?"

"Are you in trouble?"

"Do you need money?"

"We can treat her to one coffee, can't we, Carlos?"

"Of course! Sit down and join us."

The man called Carlos stood up (his old bones did not seem happy with that decision) and called into the café, "Mario, Another chair!"

At their insistence I took his seat while the other man introduced himself. "I am Luis, and this is my friend, Carlos." A large man with furry arms walked out of the café, carrying another metal folding chair. He set it down, took a cloth from his bulging back pocket, and whipped it across the seat before placing the chair to my left. Carlos sat back down with a soft, short groan. He probably made that sound so often he no longer heard it.

"You will have a coffee with us, yes? Cuban style? Of

course. Mario, a coffee for the lady," Luis continued. Mario grunted his assent and disappeared behind the torn screen door that served as the entrance to his establishment.

"So tell us your name, pretty lady," Carlos said, "and why you need to go to a pawn shop. Terrible places, you know. Cheats and swindlers, preying on the misery of others."

"Like the Imperialists," Luis countered, and at this they both threw back their heads and laughed.

"Imperialists?" I asked, "You mean, like the *yanquis*?"

"Oh, it's too early in the day for politics," Carlos replied, nodding his thanks to Mario as he put a cup of coffee on the table in front of me, "Tell us your troubles—"

"Maria," I said, glad for the first time in my life that my first name was Mary, and could be easily translated into almost any language. "But I don't want to burden you with my complaints. I know what I have to do, but I need to know where I can do it."

Luis looked thoughtful. "That's not a Cuban accent you have. Where are you from?"

"Me? I'm from P—"

"Puerto Rico," Carlos answered for me.

My eyes widened with genuine surprise. "How did you know that?"

Carlos looked smug. "Your accent is not Cuban, or old country Spanish, either. You don't speak Spanish like an American"—here Luis snickered and muttered something that may have been 'thank heaven'—"but you have a touch of that boldness that some American women have. Not a bad thing, mind you, but noticeable to an old man like me who has the benefit of experience with many beautiful ladies, praise God—"

"Don't listen to him," Luis interrupted, "he doesn't have nearly the experience he'd like you to think he does. Just an active imagination."

"Why do I call you my friend?" Carlos bantered back. "I can get insulted by people I don't know."

"You're changing the subject, old man," Luis responded. "We've yet to hear why the lovely Maria needs the services of a pawn broker."

By now I was laughing. I took a sip of my coffee. It was piping hot, dark, and incredibly sweet. I don't think any other country in the world has a national sweet tooth to rival that of Cuba's.

"Why else would a girl need money?" I said, putting my still-too-hot coffee down carefully. "A man has broken my heart. I want to go back to Puerto Rico, and I don't have the money for a ticket."

"Oh, a tragic love story," sighed Luis. "You'll share it with us?"

I shook my head, looking sorrowful. "No, I would cry, and embarrass myself, and ruin your morning. But if you would please tell me where—"

My voice caught in my throat. The boy I'd seen at the beach the day before was running toward us. When he reached the table he stopped abruptly, looked at me, and then spoke to Luis, shifting his shoulders to face him but not taking his eyes off me.

"Papie, Mommy wants you."

"Emilio, where are your manners?" the grandfather remarked, without any real reproach. "This is our new friend Maria...." He looked at me expectantly. I decided not to complicate matters by volunteering my last name.

"Just Maria is fine."

"Very well. Maria, this is my disrespectful, badly raised grandson, Emilio."

I held my breath, expecting the child to say we'd met before, but he just gave me a devilish smile. "Pleased to meet you."

"The pleasure's mine," I murmured uncomfortably.

"Now, did your mother say why I needed to rush away from this lovely lady?"

"No. But I think it has something to do with—you know."

Concern replaced the gaiety in Luis' expression. "Has she heard—?"

Emilio shook his head, as if to warn his grandfather against embarking on a forbidden subject. "She said she wants you to come home."

"Don't you reprimand me, you impudent pup," Luis said as he rose from his chair.

Carlos dropped a few pesos on the table and stood up, too. "Emilio, Maria needs to go to Hiram's. Show her where it is, will you?"

"But don't go inside yourself, you hear me?" Luis admonished his grandson. "He'll clean you out of your hard-earned pesos in minutes."

I started to rise, but Luis waved me back down. "No, sit and enjoy your coffee. Emilio knows where to take you. But don't let him side-track you, either. He's like a travel-ing salesman, always finding something new to con a peso out of you." He patted the boy's cheek, and that fond gesture took the sting out of his words. Emilio grinned and looked down at the table, but said nothing.

Carlos and Luis headed off, still talking, but with lowered voices. I could see that Carlos had a bad hip; he rocked to the left and swung his right leg out to the side with every step. Both of Luis' legs moved stiffly, and he swooped and bobbed his shoulders while he walked, as if this odd motion could help propel him forward. Together they looked like two ancient marionettes.

Emilio was also watching them, and when they were beyond hearing distance he turned back to me and flung himself into one of the empty chairs, fairly quivering with excitement. "How did you know that I lived near here?" he asked in a stage whisper. "Did you change your hair as a disguise? When did you meet my grandfather? Have you cast a spell on him to make him fall in love with you? Mermaids can do that, I know."

I held up my hand to stop the onslaught while I gulped down the rest of my coffee and took a few seconds to think. When I'd finished I said, "Emilio, I came to find you because I need your help with something very serious. Are you good at keeping secrets?"

"Of course," he answered dismissively, "how could I know everything I know if I couldn't keep secrets?"

"I thought so. I have a very, very important one to share with you." I leaned forward and gestured for him to do the same, cupped my hands around his ear and whispered, "I need you to help me find my tail. Someone has stolen it."

I sat back, gazing sadly at him with my unique version

of a damsel-in-distress look, which has never been very successful, but it was the best I could do.

"When?" he asked, looking aghast.

"I went to check on it this morning, but it wasn't there." *This is a new low, Mary Katherine Anne O'Connor, lying to a child. Surely he won't believe you. How could he? You were five when you stopped believing in leprechauns. Or the tooth fairy.*

But if Emilio was inclined to call my bluff he showed no evidence of it. He bent forward and rested one elbow on the table, brow furrowed, and propped his chin up on his fist, like Rodin's famous statue, "The Thinker," and looked so serious that I had to turn a giggle into a cough. He kept thinking.

"Does it have to be kept in water?" he asked after having pondered the problem.

"It's okay for a few days, before it dries out."

"Is that why you want to go to Hiram's?"

I nodded. "I know that sometimes people go to pawn shops to sell valuable things that they don't know what else to do with, so I thought that whoever stole my tail might try to sell it there."

"I can't see why he'd buy *that*. Doesn't it look like a big stinky fish tail?"

"Oh, no, not when I take it off. On land it looks more like shiny green cloth, all covered with sequins. They're scales, of course, but human eyes can't tell the difference. And it folds up like a big table cloth. Only mermaids know that it's a tail and not table linen."

Emilio looked impressed. His mercurial face changed

expression once again, and he looked at me with concern. "What happens if you don't find it?"

"Oh, well, we don't have to worry about that yet. I'm sure we'll find it."

He jumped off his chair. "Okay, let's go," he said, and set off at such a quick pace I had to take extra long strides to keep up with him.

He slowed just once, in front of a large, rundown house. The paint was peeling on most of the buildings in this part of town; paint never prevailed against the relentless onslaught of sun and humidity, and this was not a neighborhood where the homes were regularly cleaned and freshened up. The paint on this one looked worse than most, more like a mosaic made out of chips of old paint. Clothes that had been washed way too many times dangled from a cord stretched between two upstairs windows. Several windowsills were rotted out, and most of the shutters tilted listlessly.

"Do you know who lives here?" I asked.

"I do," Emilio answered, and took off again.

We arrived at a plain storefront with the word "loans" emblazoned across the window. A few tantalizing items were displayed in the window: a guitar, a portable radio, a gold cross on a chain, and a pair of high-heeled shoes that may have been Chanel, although I am not the person to give a credible opinion on anything fashion-related.

Emilio started to open the door but I lunged, grabbed the handle with one hand, and latched onto his shoulder with the other.

"No, sir. Your grandfather said for you not to go in."

"Come on," he sputtered. "He said not to let Hiram sell me anything. That doesn't mean I can't go in."

"That's not the version I heard. Wait out here."

I pulled him back from the door and gave him a hard stare. He returned it in full measure. At last he dropped his eyes and muttered, "Don't take too long." I released my grip on him and walked inside.

Pawn shops are a remarkable barometer of economic wellbeing. When people go broke they sell things they'd rather not part with, but you can't eat your grandfather's watch. Hiram's establishment was no better and no worse than others I'd seen. It was full of the usual stuff — cameras, musical instruments, jewelry and watches, leather goods, power tools, and a couple of sets of golf clubs: all those unredeemed items that people with broken dreams had used as collateral for loans equal to a small fraction of their real value.

The proprietor was well into middle age, rather short, with graying black hair and very fair skin. I suspected he'd not begun his life in Cuba, but then Americans weren't the only people attracted to life on the island. He was sitting at a chair behind a glass counter, but rose to greet me when I came in.

"I have something I would like to sell," I said, moving over to where he stood.

"I don't buy things. I can give you a loan, if you have the proper collateral," he explained rather kindly, gesturing toward the contents of the case in front of him. There wasn't much there — a few rings with colored stones, a couple of old Spanish coins, a mother-of-pearl rosary. I did notice that the door behind him was covered with iron bars.

"If that's all you can do—but I won't be here long enough to pay off a loan," I said, trying to sound pitiful.

"What do you have?"

I opened my bag, pulled out a small box, and flipped it open. Inside lay a medal from the Spanish–American war. A fierce bronze eagle stretched its wings across the top of a mini American flag, at the bottom of which was a cross-shaped medallion that read, "Cuba, Philippines, Puerto Rico."

"Well, look at that," Hiram said.

"Thank you," I responded, gazing longingly at the medal, like a woman forced to say goodbye to her lover. I may have even sighed.

"But I can't loan money on such a thing."

"But this was my grandfather's." It wasn't, of course. I'd picked it up in a pawn shop in New York before I left.

"Yes, señorita, but so many people come to me now, asking for money for this ring or for that gold chain—the only things of real value they own, not sentimental trinkets like this. They have no intention of paying back their loan, either, and how many of those things do you think I can sell?"

This told me what I'd wanted to know. It wasn't just the rich who were fleeing Cuba. I slowly closed the box and slipped it back into my bag, letting my shoulders sag with disappointment. "I see."

I jumped as the front door opened with a crash. Two soldiers stood at the threshold, one with a machine gun at the ready, as if they'd expected armed resistance upon entry. "Don't move," the one without the gun shouted, "hands in the air!"

I'd been in tricky situations before, but until then I'd never had a large gun pointed in my direction. My hands flew up as my stomach did an interior tumble like nothing I'd felt since the first time I'd ridden the roller coaster at Coney Island. I glanced at Hiram, who'd also cooperated with the order, but he looked astoundingly calm. *Keep steady*, I told myself, *don't give them an excuse to pull that trigger.* I concentrated on my breathing, and focused on what was happening around me.

Both men were dressed in the standard revolutionary uniform of olive fatigues, boots, and cap, and both sported a scrubby beard at the base of the chin—or tried to, anyway. Neither of them looked older than twenty. The one on the right, shorter and skinnier than his counterpart, looked edgy, as if he wasn't sure whatever they had planned was going to come off that well. His eyes kept darting from me to Hiram and back, as if he expected one of us to charge them, and his finger was planted right on the trigger of his gun.

"Hiram Kassam, you are arrested in the name of the people of Cuba for usury, sedition, and encouraging counter-revolutionary activities," barked the taller soldier.

"Go to hell." Hiram's response was understandable but not wise. The soldier who'd spoken crossed the small space between Hiram and the door and grabbed the poor man by the collar. I took a step backward, trying to figure out how brave I was prepared to be if things got any worse, when a small blur rushed past the soldier at the door and raced to where I stood. Emilio wrapped his skinny arms around me and looked up, his face distraught.

"Mommy, you have to come home! Grandpa's fallen again!" he cried, as if he didn't even notice that two armed soldiers were in the room.

"Let them go," Hiram wheezed, his voice constricted by the soldier's grip. "I've never seen them before. She doesn't know anything. Let them go and I'll open the safe."

The soldier didn't release his hold on his captive, but he glanced at me, then jerked his head toward the door. I hesitated, but Emilio was pulling on my arm, pleading. "Come, Mommy, come on!" I couldn't jeopardize his safety, so I let myself be led away.

A small cluster of cautious onlookers had gathered across the street, and Emilio walked calmly by them, still holding onto me. When we were about a block away he led me around a corner and dropped my hand. "Follow me, and run," he said, and took off.

I didn't need any encouragement. We whizzed down that street and then cut through an alley, Emilio leading the way. We turned one corner, and the next, then charged up a narrow set of marble stairs that led to an interior balcony overlooking a small courtyard. There he stopped and leaned over slightly, resting his hands on his knees while he caught his breath.

I leaned back against the wall. "Thank you," I gasped. "But you shouldn't have taken a chance like that."

He grinned at me, justifiably delighted with himself. "I saw them go in. Soldiers like that," —he narrowed his eyes, adopted a fierce, bullying look, and pretended to be holding a machine gun—"they're up to no good. I had to get you out of there. And I did, didn't I?"

"What you did was brave, but very stupid."

He dropped his arms and glowered at me. "Some thanks I get."

"Don't get me wrong, Emilio. I'm very, very grateful. But how do you think I'd feel if you'd been hurt?"

"Better than if you were dead."

I was about to say, "I wasn't in that much danger," but I stopped myself. I'd seen the look in the eyes of the man who'd grabbed Hiram by the throat.

I slid down the wall and sat down. "Talk to me. How did you know there was going to be trouble?"

"I told you," he said as he folded himself into a cross-legged position next to me. "Those *Fidelistas* are up to no good."

"But isn't Fidel the hero of Cuba? Why do you think that his men want to cause trouble?"

He gave me an appraising look that was much too sophisticated for his age. "Who's telling you that Fidel is the hero of Cuba?"

I gave him one of his own shrugs. "Everyone."

"Don't believe everything you hear." With that he sprang up and darted away, shouting over his shoulder as he did so, "I'll see you tomorrow. Try and stay out of trouble, okay?"

CHAPTER ELEVEN

E milio fell in step beside Raul as he was walking back
from dinner. He barely looked down when the boy
appeared, and did not slow his own stride.

"You're alone a lot, aren't you?" Emilio asked, quick-
ening his own pace to keep up with Raul.

"And you know that how?" The only answer he
received was another of Emilio's shrugs. Raul came to an
abrupt stop.

"You can't keep following me around. You'll get into
trouble."

"Why? Are you a spy?"

Raul looked around reflexively, grabbed Emilio's
upper arm, and dragged him over to an empty doorway.
"Don't joke around about that. Of course I'm not, but it
doesn't take much to fall under suspicion, and if you're
following me around all the time, someone's going to
notice and wonder why."

"So what? I'm just a kid."

"Kids have been used as spies. You think these people
don't know that?"

"What people? Are there other people following you?
You must be a spy."

Raul swore and let go of Emilio's arm. "Piss off, kid."

There was that look again—all the bravado gone,

replaced by poignant longing. The boy's large brown eyes seemed to expand with it.

"So you don't like me?"

Raul sighed. "That has nothing to do with it. Of course I like you. That's why I don't want to see you get into trouble. And I'm not talking about a paddling or an extra Hail Mary after confession—I'm talking about serious trouble. For you, for your whole family."

Emilio's eyes narrowed. "What do you know about my family?"

"You told me yourself your father's in prison. What would he do if he knew you were getting into trouble? Your job is to help your family, not run around in the streets. Does your mother know you're out at this hour?"

"She's working."

"This late?"

"She works in a restaurant. So you see, she's not even missing me. And I need your help."

Raul's hand went to his pocket, but Emilio grabbed his wrist. "Not that kind of help. Haven't I earned my money fair and square? Well?"

Raul's face relaxed into a smile. "Yes, you have. Fair and square."

"Okay then," Emilio continued, letting go of Raul's arm and looking remarkably businesslike for a ten-year-old. "I need your help finding something very valuable. But it's a secret."

"I don't think I can help with that."

"But you haven't even heard what it is yet." The disappointment on the boy's face went straight into Raul's heart and nudged his common sense into a corner. *You'll kick yourself for this later,* he thought, squatting down so that he could look into Emilio's eyes as he spoke.

"Okay, Emilio, tell me what you need to find."

The boy stared hard into his eyes, as if trying to peer into Raul's soul to confirm his sincerity. He leaned to whisper directly into Raul's ear.

"A mermaid tail."

Raul grinned. "Oh, I see. Are you on a quest of some kind?"

Emilio looked annoyed, obviously not happy that he wasn't being taken seriously. "She lost it, and asked me to help her find it."

"And you believed her?"

"Why not?"

"Well, you don't seem to be the kind of kid taken in by fairy tales," Raul answered, and as he uttered the words thought, *dragons? A cursed village?* Whatever problems life had brought to Emilio and his family, it was clear that the child sought refuge in a rich fantasy world of his own creation. Why wouldn't he go for a mermaid?

Emilio nodded matter-of-factly. "Yeah, I know it sounds stupid, but my grandmother always told me not to believe or disbelieve stuff like that. Like with the Orishas. She said they might have power, or they might not, but better to respect them, just in case. So I figured it was the same with mermaids."

"And what made you think she was a mermaid? Because she told you so?"

"Oh, no. I saw her swimming, and she stayed underwater for so long, I guessed." His self-confident grin returned. "I was right, too, even if she didn't admit it at first."

Raul stood up. "Do you want to finish plotting our strategy over some ice cream? And then I'll walk you home. You know where I live, so it's only fair that I know where you live, too."

"Sure. And I know the best place to go. Great ice cream *and* not crowded. A good place for a talk. You can follow me, you know, from a distance, so no one thinks we're together until we get there."

Guess I had that coming, Raul thought as he followed Emilio down the street.

CHAPTER TWELVE

E milio showed up at my door the next morning with a small bouquet of wildflowers clutched in his hand. "Hello, Miss Maria. How are you? I picked these for you," he said as he edged into my room and thrust the scraggly bundle at me.

No one had ever given me flowers (which tells you everything you need to know about the history of my love life). As I took the bundle of yellow, purple, and white blossoms — one of which I was fairly certain was a noxious weed — I felt my heart soften, like a stick of butter left out of the refrigerator for too long.

"How did you know where to find me?" I asked as I poured water into the one not-very-clean glass that my innkeeper had provided, and propped the flowers up in it. I'd taken a room in a shabby boarding house. It had a scrawny twin bed, a tiny sink, and a small chest of drawers. There wasn't even a closet. But my room was located on the ground floor, right inside the front entrance, so I could get in and out without calling too much attention to myself, and the landlady was willing to take phone messages for her guests. She didn't have too many rules — except that one had to pay in advance. Nor did she seem too interested in who I was or what I was doing in Havana.

"There aren't too many places to stay around here, I mean, if you don't live here," Emilio explained, "no hotels or anything. So I got the idea about the flowers, and asked at a couple of places where they rent out rooms if they had a lady staying who had curly brown hair, freckles, and a foreign accent, because I was supposed to give her these flowers, and the third place I tried — here you are."

I remembered what Emilio's grandfather had said about him being a diminutive con artist, and the appeal of his floral offering diminished ever so slightly. The boy was now scrutinizing my room, so I took a quick glance around myself to make sure he wouldn't see anything that could expose my real reason for being in Cuba. My small suitcase was under the bed, closed, and I had nothing obviously American in origin lying around.

"So, any luck so far?" he asked.

"What?" I gave a start, not realizing at first that he was of course asking about the alleged loss of my imaginary mermaid tail, and not about my hunt for a great news story.

He looked at me curiously. *Kid doesn't miss a trick*, I thought.

"You know, finding your tail?"

"No. Not so far. Any ideas?"

"Maybe. I mean, there's someone I want you to meet." He looked down with a shyness I was certain he didn't feel. If the floor had been made of dirt he'd have been digging his toe in it for emphasis. "A friend of mine," he explained, "but he's not a kid. He's a grownup. I think he could help us."

"How's that?"

"He's an engineer, and they know how to dig, and how to find good spots for digging. So if someone's buried your tail, maybe he could figure that part out. And, he knows a lot of people. Russians, even. So he might be able to ask around, because, you know, he seems like the kind of person who'd believe in mermaids, and dragons, and stuff like that. Not everybody does, right?"

"You mean you told him I'm a mermaid?"

"Well I had to, didn't I? How else could I get him to help us?" he answered, dropping his shy routine and looking up at me, eyes wide. "You're not mad at me, are you?"

Not as long as this guy's not a complete loon, I thought. "No, I'm not mad. If you trust him, I'm sure I can, too." And as embarrassing as it was getting caught in a stupid game of make-believe with a kid, the previous evening I'd been able to contact two of the leads that Bentley had given me, and I hadn't obtained any intriguing information from either of them. If this guy knew a lot of people, including Russians, he might be a good source.

But I wasn't so desperate that I was going to let Emilio put himself in harm's way again. "Does your mother know what you're up to?" I asked.

"She's working. She lets me go to the beach and stuff when she's working."

"You sure about that?"

"Did *your* mother know about everything *you* did when you were a kid?"

He had me there. I couldn't count the number of times I'd been punished for being somewhere I wasn't supposed to be, or not being where I was supposed to have been.

"No," I said, smiling despite myself, "but I wasn't living in a place where there'd recently been a revolution."

"I know how to stay out of trouble," he said with an air of superiority that was almost comical. "So, do you want to meet this guy or not?"

"When?"

"Now, if you want to."

"What—is he waiting outside?"

He shook his head. "He's at the beach."

"Why?"

"Well, isn't that where you hid your tail? Don't we have to start at the scene of the crime?"

"What a brilliant idea. I knew you were the right person to help me with this." I smiled at him, and he bowed, just like a little gentleman... or Rumpelstiltskin.

* * * * *

When I saw Emilio's friend standing on the beach, he didn't look at all like a lunatic—not from the outside, anyway. From a few yards away his relaxed posture and calm features emitted the elegant, self-contained detachment so admired in Europe. *Insouciance,* the French call it: a casual indifference, sprinkled with a touch of irony. But as I drew closer I could see that while his body was calm his eyes were not; they were sweeping in wide circles like the wand on a radar screen, missing nothing. Here was a man well-practiced in the art of being on his guard without showing it. Interesting.

His looks didn't detract from my overall impression of him. He wore the tan khaki pants, short-sleeved, collared shirt, and leather sandals worn by most of the men on the island, at least those who weren't in fatigues. He didn't have the body of someone used to a lot of manual labor; in fact his shoulders were on the narrow side, but he had a strong chin, and it evened out the overall masculinity of his features like a well-chosen weight on an old-fashioned scale. He had an impressive Roman nose, but there again one didn't focus on its size for too long because of his eyes: spaced perfectly apart, large, dark brown, thick-lashed eyes that lost their wary look as Emilio and I approached.

"Mr. Raul, this is Miss Maria; Miss Maria, this is Mr. Raul," Emilio said with impeccable style. For being what his grandfather had called a "badly raised" youngster he did have lovely manners, at least when he decided to use them.

"Delighted to make your acquaintance," Raul said with a slight bow. He spoke Spanish with a Castilian accent, no Caribbean influence at all.

"You honor me," I responded in my most polite Spanish. "Any friend of Emilio's is a friend of mine. But he didn't mention that you're not from Cuba."

"And neither are you. At least from what Emilio tells me..." He finished his sentence with an open-handed gesture toward the sea.

I couldn't hide my chagrin. "Oh, well, that—you know."

Emilio was looking from one of us to the other, grinning madly, which made me wonder what had been going on in that impish little brain. Did he fancy himself some prepubescent matchmaker?

"Please, Miss Maria, I understand the need for discretion in these matters," Raul said, with the gallantry of a Spanish courtier, "no explanations are necessary."

"Thank you," I replied, sincerely relieved.

"But there is the matter of your lost tail," he continued. And then, I blushed.

I'm not the blushing kind. You shouldn't be a reporter if you embarrass easily. But something about the whole situation—being called a mermaid, the charming child—not to mention Raul's smile—it all caused my circuits to misfire somehow.

"That's right," I said, unable to meet his eyes until my face cooled.

"So, is it time to talk about the case?" Emilio asked.

"Sure," I said, glad to have a reason to look somewhere other than up at Raul, "shall we walk and talk?"

So we strolled down to the shore. Emilio had raced ahead, looking, he said, for clues.

"I don't think I've ever been so perfectly played in my life," I said as soon as Emilio was out of earshot, still looking down at the familiar and comfortable view of my own feet.

"Yes, he has reeled us in like fish, hasn't he? Or should I say like mer-people? He's quite something, that one."

"About the mermaid thing—"

"There's no need to explain. He's already taken me to see dragons and a village of people turned into fish by the curse of a witch. Be careful, though. If we like each other I'm sure he'll be asking for a referral fee. He's a very good businessman."

I shook my head and emitted an ungracious sound that was something between a chuckle and a snort—classic

Katherine—before I asked, "How did he convince you to come and meet me?"

"Oh, even at this tender age he knows the powerful lure of the damsel in distress. A mysterious woman, who has the power to stay underwater for an extraordinary amount of time, needs help finding the one thing that will allow her to escape this island and go back to her own people—how could I refuse?"

"It does sound pretty irresistible when you tell it that way."

"I assure you I'm not doing justice to his version of the tale."

"And did you suspect—?"

"I didn't know what to expect," he said. "I did not anticipate that he was a budding matchmaker, but I can't say that I'm disappointed to meet you, either."

I felt my cheeks get warm again. "So where are you from, if not Cuba?"

"Spain, of course. Can't you tell?"

"Why would I know that?"

"Magic? Or keen powers of observation?"

I looked up at him. "Now you're giving me too much credit. All I noticed was the lack of a Cuban accent."

"And yours is from where? Not Cuba, not Spain. Mexico?"

"Puerto Rico."

"Ah. An American then," he said, and the downward movement of his eyebrows told me that he was not comfortable with that fact.

"Involuntary American is more like it," I replied, "and

please don't tell me that I speak Spanish with an American accent."

He found this very funny. "No, that you don't," he said after a good loud laugh. There was something special about that laugh, as if it were a rarely-used talent.

Raul's laugh had intrigued Emilio as well. He came racing back to us, demanding to know what joke he'd missed.

"It was about King Neptune," I said, and then wondered why that had popped into my head. *Getting carried away with the mermaid thing, are you?*

"So tell me," Emilio demanded.

I paused, unable to think of even one non-adult joke. Throw a few journalists in a bar and they don't come up with knock-knock jokes. Not clean ones, anyhow. To my relief, Raul jumped in.

"It seems King Neptune snores very loudly," he said. "You know, when you hear the waves crashing at night? That's him snoring. So, one night he snores so loudly that he wakes himself up. So he calls the royal physician, who isn't all that pleased by being woken up, either. And Neptune tells him, 'Doctor, I have a problem. I snore so loudly, I wake myself up.' And the doctor says, 'Well, then go sleep in a separate room!'"

Emilio gave Raul a quizzical look. "And you thought that was funny?"

At this, both Raul and I both burst out laughing, causing Emilio to shake his head at us with complete disgust. "Have you solved the case?" he asked in a rather snippy tone when we'd caught our breath.

"Not yet," I answered.

"We might be making some progress, though," Raul added.

"So tell me," Emilio said, his head tilted up in the manner of an excitable dog that's caught a whiff of a new scent.

"It might not have been a person at all," I said, entering into the spirit of the game. "It might have been a big fish, like a grouper, who wanted to try it out for a while to see if he could swim faster wearing my tail."

"But how will you get it back?" Emilio asked.

"Oh, everyone under the sea will know it's a mermaid tail," I said. "He wouldn't dare keep it. He'd get into trouble. It doesn't belong to him."

Emilio's face darkened. "If it's a grouper from around here, he might take it anyway," he muttered bitterly.

"Why do you say that?" I asked.

He looked at me uneasily, like any kid who'd been caught saying something he'd been forbidden to talk about. "No reason," he replied, and I noticed he did not shrug this time. Evidently he didn't use that gesture when he was lying through his young teeth.

I glanced at Raul, who was looking at the boy with grave concern. "Sometimes the rules change, Emilio. That's how life is," he said.

At this, Emilio looked so terribly sad that I almost reached out to hug him—another rare reaction on my part—but his expression changed again before I could act on the impulse.

"I found a magic shell," he said.

I knelt down in the sand in front of him. "You did? Can I see it?"

"Well, you know, a guy has to make a living," he answered evasively, and for the third time that morning Raul exploded into laughter.

* * * * *

Emilio was extremely pleased with himself by the time Raul left to catch the bus back to town. He'd persuaded me to pay him a couple of pesos to listen to the magic shell— which had been a little magical; I'd never held a shell to my ear and heard the ocean before. And Emilio was also gloating over the success of his match-making endeavor.

"You like him, don't you?" Emilio asked as we walked up the path that led from the beach back to the main road.

"He seems like a decent guy." Raul Garcia had asked me for my full name and number before he left. I told myself I'd given him the information because I thought I might be able to get some intriguing information from him about the Russians' presence in Cuba—I'd never mixed business with pleasure, and I wasn't about to start. Although I'd been tempted from time to time to accept an invitation to "come up and have a drink" in a colleague's hotel room, the possibility of becoming the topic of conversation at some popular watering hole the next day always had a profound chilling effect on my desire to exercise certain of my inalienable rights.

Nor did I come across a lot of datable men who weren't in my profession. Nice, single men weren't usually involved in the type of news events I covered, and stereotypical "bad boys" never held any appeal for me. I'd seen too many women fall victim to charismatic

118

charlatans, and I'd never met one who'd given me the impression he'd be worth the trouble he caused—in bed, or anywhere else.

And with respect to married men, well, despite my willingness to let go of many of the rules imposed by the strict Irish Catholic faith in which I'd been raised, I could never have an affair with a married man. Quite apart from the possibility of eternal damnation, the thought of the look on my mother's face if she ever found out was sufficient to quell any bubbling desire along those lines.

Of course it would have suited my purpose better if Raul had given me his number, but no respectable woman with a Spanish heritage would have asked a man for his phone number back in 1960, and I didn't want to raise his suspicions that I might not be who I'd said I was.

"I knew you'd like each other," Emilio said, still gloating. "You're both nice, and he's lonely, and your heart's broken. So why wouldn't you like each other?"

"What makes you think I'm heartbroken?"

He gave me an entirely too-self-satisfied grin. "My grandfather told me. He said love brought you to Cuba, and now that your heart is broken you want to leave."

"Do you live with your grandfather?"

"We do now. Since—for a while."

"And 'we' is?"

"Me and my mother. She works at a restaurant, and at another shop. She works all the time. My grandfather is old and sleeps a lot, so I get around, you know, to the beach and other places." He did not mention his father or any siblings, and I filed that fact away in my head.

"So now it's my turn to ask you something," he continued.

"Shoot."

"You aren't really a mermaid, are you?"

I shook my head. "No, not really."

He looked thoughtful. "I didn't think so, but you never know."

"You notice a lot of things, don't you?"

"Yeah. Like that sandwich shop over there," he said, pointing to a small outdoor kiosk from which wafted the delicious smell of roast pork. "Are you hungry? Do you like Cuban sandwiches? With fries and a Coke?"

"I can't wait to try one. Lunch is on me. It's the least I can do for the young man who got me out of what could have been a very tricky situation."

We ordered our food and settled into some folding chairs that the shop owner had tucked under the shade of a palm tree. So far the heat and humidity had been bearable, but I wasn't used to the tropical midday sun, and knew my fair skin would get fried pretty quickly if I overdid it. Emilio sat next to me, swinging his legs back and forth as he sipped his Coke through a straw. *He's never still,* I thought. He reminded me of myself as a kid— constantly in motion, insatiably curious, and supremely, stupidly self-confident in the face of possible danger.

"So Emilio, why do you think those soldiers arrested Hiram?"

"How should I know?"

"Oh, I thought for sure you'd have a theory, being the observant person that you are."

The woman at the cash register announced that our

sandwiches were ready, so I went to fetch them. When I returned Emilio was on his feet, his nose inches away from the trunk of the tree under which we were sitting.

"What are you looking at?" I asked.

"A big bug." He came back to his chair and I handed him his lunch.

"Thanks," he said, before stuffing two whole fries into his mouth. I took a large bite of my sandwich and tasted freshly baked bread, warm roasted pork, ham, melted cheese, mustard, and pickles. It was delicious.

"Have you been to America?" Emilio asked out of nowhere. My mouth was still full so I just nodded.

"And is everyone there rich?"

"No," I managed to get out before swallowing.

"But they're not super poor, like here in Cuba, are they?"

"I haven't seen that many poor people in Cuba."

"Have you been to the country?"

"Not yet."

"When you go, you'll see. And Fidel will make the rich people poor but he won't make the poor people rich, that's what my grandfather says, and that's why everyone's leaving. He said that's why Hiram was arrested, because he'd been giving money to people for their stuff, so they could leave Cuba."

"They?"

He looked around furtively, as if he realized that he'd said too much, and then with uncanny finesse shifted the topic of conversation to safer ground.

"Have you been to Miami?"

"Once."

"Is it as nice as Havana?"

"No. Havana has a history, and beautiful old buildings. Miami is new. So it's busy, you know, with a lot of people, but it's not pretty."

"Is the beach like this?"

I looked around, taking in the palm trees, the golden sand, the vast expanse of blue sea visible behind the low dunes. "No, it's not as nice as this."

I could tell that my answer did not please him. "Why, is your family planning on going to Miami soon?" I asked.

"No, but a lot of people are going."

"So I've heard."

We ate in silence for a while, and watched a group of seagulls jockey for position a few feet away, working their way closer and closer in order to be able to retrieve any errant crumbs.

"They always look so desperate," I said. "Like they never get anything to eat, and one crumb would save them from starvation."

"And they never take their eyes off the food," Emilio responded. "Watch." He leaned closer to the cluster of gulls and held out a single French fry. Every bird froze in place, eyes glued to the prize. Emilio raised it higher, and a dozen heads moved in unison, never breaking eye contact. He moved it right and then left, and the whole group bobbed back and forth. Up and down, back and forth, he directed their movements like a concertmaster until I started to laugh.

"I don't know if that's funny or just mean," I said when I'd finished chortling.

Emilio reacted by tearing the fry into four pieces and

chucking them into the wind. The birds flew after them, shrieking and pecking at each other in their effort to get at them first. "They're just greedy," Emilio said as we watched the birds battle over the spoils, "like most people."

It struck me again how oddly mature he was. "Emilio, how old are you? Eleven?"

"Ten."

"Don't you have friends your own age?"

"Not anymore."

"What do you mean?"

He looked around to make sure no one was within earshot, and then said, "Because I'm dangerous."

"I know you're smart," I chided him, "but dangerous? Who says so?"

"Fidel."

"Oh, come on."

"It's true." He lowered his voice even further, but spoke in an exaggerated, melodramatic tone, not unlike a narrator in a detective show from the golden days of radio.

"My father is a traitor. So parents are afraid of letting their kids be seen with me or my mother. My father goes to prison and everyone we know treats us like we're invisible."

I had not expected this. "I'm sorry, Emilio. That's not fair. It's only because they're —"

"Afraid, I know. They're all afraid."

"Why is your father in prison?"

"Because he doesn't like Fidel. He did at first, but things changed. I don't know how, exactly, but they did and my dad didn't like it. And then one day the soldiers — like the ones yesterday, only more of them — they showed up at the house and took him away. Just like that, he's gone."

It's one thing to hear a horror story from an adult, but much worse to hear a tale like that from a child. What could I say? "Thank you for sharing that with me," I said at last.

He stood up and wiped his hands on his pant legs. "I know you won't tell anyone. I have to go now. I don't want my grandfather to worry, and he will if I'm gone too long. I'll ask him if you can come over for dinner. Tomorrow, maybe. He likes you." He leaned down and said softly, "You see? I told you Fidel isn't a hero." With that, he walked away, proud and erect, and my heart ached for him.

CHAPTER THIRTEEN

After Emilio left I decided to go interview — or rather, talk to — the last one of the contacts Bentley had given me. He was a priest, assigned to a parish in one of the less affluent neighborhoods of Havana. Like most of the Catholic clergy in Cuba, Father Guido Lopez was Spanish, not Cuban. Bentley had assured me that he was a trustworthy old friend whom he'd met during the war.

I called Father Lopez from a pay phone. Despite Bentley's claims, I was reluctant to reveal to the good *padre* my real reason for being in Cuba. The man could turn me in for being in the country under false pretenses — but I was also running out of time, and I needed a good lead. So I told him I'd been asked to come by and pay him my respects on behalf of a wartime acquaintance.

He didn't seem surprised to hear from me, and agreed to meet with me that very day, which worried me a bit. Bentley must have told him to expect my call, and that I did not appreciate. I liked to handle my leads my own way.

Still, a priest with his ear to the ground could prove helpful. The Catholic Church and Castro had started out on excellent terms. Fidel had even worn a large, quite visible cross on his chest as he rode triumphantly into Havana a week after Batista fled the country. But commu-

125

nism leaves no room for religion, organized or any other kind, so by the summer of 1960 Cuban Catholics were starting to object to Castro's policies, particularly his rapidly developing relationship with the Soviets. Father Lopez might have some insight on what could happen next.

A few minutes after four o'clock I was sitting in a tiny, sweltering office across a messy desk from a man who looked to be in his early fifties. He bore a disconcerting resemblance to Rock Hudson, complete with square jaw, dimpled chin, and deep-set brown eyes ideally placed over a beautiful, yet somehow perfectly masculine, nose.

After exchanging a few pleasantries I asked him how he'd met Robert Bentley.

"Did Robert not tell you? We met during the war," he said.

"Yes, but that's all he told me. Spain stayed neutral, so I was just wondering—"

"I was in North Africa for much of the time, in a small parish in Spanish Morocco. Robert was part of the first wave that came into North Africa in 1942. As you might imagine, up until the war broke out I didn't see many Americans, but I studied English in school and spoke well enough to get through a simple conversation. So I made the effort to strike up an acquaintance with some of the servicemen I encountered, Robert included."

"Bentley is Catholic?"

This question seemed to amuse him. "Episcopalian, I believe, but I suppose we were the closest spiritual substitution he could find."

"No Episcopal chaplain around? That seems odd."

"Some of the men sent to war were comforted by being able to attend services in an actual church. Is that so surprising?"

"Odd for him, I guess. Robert never struck me as the church-going type."

"War often brings people closer to God."

"Or drives them away from Him."

"I take it you've had some experience in that regard?"

No reason to answer that, I thought. "Just an observation. When did you leave North Africa?"

"In 1944. I was sent to China for a short period of time, before going back to Spain. I came to Cuba in 1954."

"One war and two revolutions. I'd say you've been given some pretty tough duty."

He gave me a small smile but responded with grave propriety. "I go where God sends me."

"Do you think that Castro is picking a fight with the Catholic Church?"

"He's made some unfortunate accusations. I don't know where it will lead, though. Most Cubans aren't big 'church-goers,' as you put it, but they are a people of strong faith. If this government attempts to interfere with that, there will be problems."

"I've heard rumors that the problems have already started."

He didn't take the bait. "So how long have you known Robert?"

"Not long," I answered. "I was in New York for a while—I'm from Puerto Rico, so I know a lot of people there—and we both run with what you might call a political crowd. He's at the UN, part of the press core."

"So he told me in his last letter. I wondered how long he'd stay in Illinois. He may have come from small-town America, but he's seen a lot of the world."

I wanted to talk about Cuba, not Robert Bentley, so I once again changed the subject. This time I pointed to a small statue of what could have been a black African version of the Virgin Mary, although she was dressed all in white, with an elaborate lace veil. "That's rather unique. Is it from here?"

"Yes, although it has roots elsewhere." He stood up and took the piece down from the top of his ramshackle bookshelf. He handled it delicately, so I did the same as I examined it.

"Santeria," he explained, "a blending of the ancient Yoruba religion brought by the slaves from Africa, some Catholic camouflage, and a sprinkling of other animist beliefs. Surely in Puerto Rico you know of it?"

"Of course, but it's more popular here, I think. This is the mother goddess, isn't it?"

"Or the Virgin Mary. Among the poorer parts of the Cuban population Catholicism and the ancient slave traditions have well and truly blended. Have you ever been to a ceremony?"

"No, but I've read about them. And one sees the followers, dressed in white."

"It's an incredible performance. Rather like what one would expect from a biblical demonic possession. I keep her here to remind me to respect those traditions lest I become impatient with them."

I handed the image back. "I think all Cubans are impatient now, for one thing or another."

He put the mother goddess back in her place and sat down, but said nothing, so I pushed ahead. "I hear that many Cubans are disappointed in Castro."

He gave me an appraising look. "There's been an anti-Castro presence in Cuba since he took over. That's common knowledge."

I waved this comment aside. "But it's growing, isn't it?"

"And as a Puerto Rican, this concerns you how?"

"I'm a Puerto Rican interested in freedom for my own country. We expected Castro to lead the way, to help us prove to the US that we can be trusted to govern ourselves. But if he turns out to be just another tyrant, that will make things even harder for us. Especially if it's true that he's a closet communist. The *yanquis* won't go for that."

"Oh, I think it's safe to say that he's more than a closet communist." He opened the front drawer of his desk and pulled out an official-looking document. "Several of my parishioners have come to me with copies of this, concerned about the future wellbeing of their children," he said as he handed it to me.

I speak Spanish better than I read it, so it took me longer than it should have to translate the words in my head. When their meaning became clear I looked back up at Father Lopez, unable to cloak my incredulity. "This couldn't be true. It would be insane."

He shrugged. "They said the same thing about Hitler's plan to annihilate the Jews, didn't they?"

* * * * *

Luis and Emilio came by the next morning to issue my official invitation to come to dinner that evening. Luis, all smiles, said they would expect me around eight o'clock. The late hour did not surprise me. By 1960 Cubans had adopted many American cultural habits, but they still ate on a Spanish schedule.

As I waved goodbye I wondered what, if anything, Emilio had told his grandfather or his mother about the close call we'd had at Hiram's shop. Probably nothing, although Luis would surely know that Hiram had been arrested. Word traveled fast in a place where neighbors still gathered on their balconies every evening to discuss the day's events.

I spent the rest of the day wandering around from café to café, drinking a tremendous amount of coffee while I read and reread one of daily papers and eavesdropped. Several times during the course of the day I heard criticism of Castro's policies, but they were almost always followed by fervently expressed positive platitudes, some taken directly from Castro's marathon speeches, as if the critic wanted to make sure to anyone who might be listening that he or she was publically on record as a Fidel fan.

I didn't hear any discussion of the document that Father Lopez had shown me. It was something right out of Orwell's *1984*: a plan for the State to take control of the raising of all children in Cuba. Children would remain with their parents until they were three years old, and then taken away to be raised in government-run dormitories, in order to be educated and indoctrinated in ways consistent with the values of the Revolution. They would be allowed to visit their parents two days a month.

Despite its formal appearance, I could not imagine that the supposed "decree" was officially sanctioned. It was either a forgery designed to discredit Castro, or a scheme proposed by one of the loonier members of his staff. But as Father Lopez had said, what if people believed it to be true? What steps would they take?

* * * * *

When I arrived that evening Emilio was outside, waiting to greet me and escort me up to his family's apartment. He was wearing long pants, a clean white shirt, and his hair had been brushed straight back and glued to his head with the help of some sort of pomade. If it hadn't been for the shape of his face and those extraordinary eyelashes I might not have recognized him.

"Don't you look handsome," I said.

He pointed to his hair. "My mother made me do this," he said, as if she'd made him an accessory to a crime. "It itches."

I pursed my lips to keep from laughing. "Well," I said when I was sure I'd successfully squelched my giggle, "you do look very elegant."

He gave me a dubious look. "We live upstairs."

The large front door opened onto a marble foyer, and I realized at once that the place was a large home that had been divided into individual units, without much in the way of renovation to assist in its metamorphosis. A grand split staircase connected the entry hall to an upper landing that led to the larger apartments. Instead of heading up that way, we went through a small door hidden underneath the right arm of the staircase, walked down a narrow hallway, and climbed up what must have once been the servants' stairs.

As is often the case when a luxurious home is hastily split into separate apartments, a host of cooking smells flooded the air — one open window can only do so much to dispel fumes from rooms that weren't constructed to provide sufficient ventilation for the private exercise of the culinary arts. Garlic, shrimp, onions, and beans were a few of the odors I identified as I made my way up the staircase behind Emilio, along with some other less appealing ones.

"All these stairs must be tough on your grandfather," I said, but Emilio did not respond.

We went through a door at the top of the stairs and entered a narrow hallway. Emilio stopped at the first door on the right, put a finger to his lips, then burst in and announced in a grand voice, "Miss Maria has arrived."

His grandfather was seated on a sagging, overstuffed loveseat that was pushed up against the wall to the left of the front door. He stood up and hobbled over to us. "How nice to see you again," he said, taking my hand and kissing it, old-world style. His age may have limited his mobility, but time had done nothing to diminish his graciousness.

A narrow door to our right swung open and a woman came into the room, wiping her hands on a cloth towel she tucked into the front pocket of her Betty-Crocker-style apron, complete with a high front bib and ruffled trim. She was slim — perhaps a little too much so — and one glance at her revealed the source of Emilio's expressive brown eyes and beautiful long lashes. "I'm Emilio's mother, Miriam Velasquez," she said, holding out her hand.

"Maria O'Connor," I said, taking it. "Thank you so much for the invitation. Emilio is a great kid. You've done a wonderful job with him." Her smile showed the genuine pleasure she took in the compliment I'd given her, but it was immediately counterbalanced by a rather puzzled look.

"O'Connor? Are there many O'Connors in Puerto Rico?"

"War of Independence," I answered as if I had to address this issue all the time. "Lots of newly-arrived Irishman immigrants came down from New York to help Teddy Roosevelt fight the Spanish, my great-grandfather among them. Found the weather and the women delightful, so he stayed." The gist of this statement was historically accurate, although I had no proof that any of my own ancestors had actually stormed through the Caribbean during the Spanish–American War.

"You know the war that won Cuba its independence from Spain did the same for Puerto Rico," Luis informed his grandson in an impromptu history lesson.

"Yes, Papie, I know," Emilio replied. He was fussing with the radio, which sat on a small end table at the far end of the loveseat.

"Although Cuba negotiated much better terms," I added lightly. "You, after all, became an independent country. We've yet to achieve that."

"Independence is no better or worse than what the people make of it," Luis said enigmatically. "So, can I offer you some rum? You must admit that Cuban rum is better than your Puerto Rican stuff."

"I admit no such thing, but I'd be delighted to give your Cuban *stuff* another try."

"Miriam?"

"None for me," she answered, "but you two go ahead, and please excuse me. I have a few more things to do to get dinner ready."

She returned to the small side room that served as their kitchen while Luis tottered over to a narrow sideboard on top of which sat a bottle of inexpensive rum, a few glasses, and two family photos displayed in simple silver frames. One showed a slightly younger Emilio in the white dress suit worn by Catholic boys when they celebrate their First Communion. The other was a wedding portrait. Given the 1950s-style of the bride's dress I assumed it was a picture of Emilio's parents.

"I'm afraid we have no ice, if that's what you're used to," Luis said.

"Why would I want to ruin good rum with water?"

Luis chuckled as his bent, arthritic fingers slowly twisted the cap off the bottle. I moved closer to get a better look at the photographs.

"So Miriam is married to one of your sons?" I asked him, indicating the wedding picture.

"Armando, my only son. My only child. I never thought he'd catch such a prize, but I suppose he has his good qualities, and luckily for us Miriam was not blind to them."

I didn't inquire any further about Armando's current circumstances. Getting the answer you want often depends on how and when you ask the question.

While Luis carefully poured out two glasses of rum I

took in the details of the room. It was not large, maybe sixteen feet square, and not nearly big enough for the few pieces of furniture it contained. In addition to the loveseat, end table and sideboard, there was a large rectangular dining table surrounded by six chairs. The set was made of some sort of dark wood. It looked antique, but each piece gleamed with fresh polish. The back supports of the chairs were carved into dramatic spirals, across which spans of worn leather still boasted hand-tooled floral designs. Very Spanish, and evidence that the family might not have always lived in such modest circumstances.

Two doors led out of the main room, one into the tiny kitchen, the other into what I presumed was a bedroom. The door of the latter was propped open by a square electric floor fan that brought an anemic stream of air into the windowless room where we stood. *Either Luis or Emilio sleeps on the couch,* I thought, noticing a blanket neatly folded across the back of the loveseat, *and there's probably a shared bathroom somewhere down the hall.*

"Here you are," Luis said, handing me a small glass of rum. "To your health."

During this whole time Emilio had been fidgeting with the radio. He found a station to his liking, and then sprang over to hold out my chair for me.

"We're having chicken," he announced as I took my seat.

"A poor capon even scrawnier than you," his grand-father replied as he lowered his protesting limbs into the chair across the table from me, "but my daughter-in-law is a wonderful cook. A valuable talent."

I touched a corner of the place mat. It was made of

linen and trimmed with delicate lace, although just like Emilio's clothes it was worn thin. *Had Miriam come from a wealthy family?* I wondered, knowing that a bride's trousseau often included table linens. She had the poise and subtle confidence of a person who'd grown up well-schooled and privileged. *How did she and her son end up here?*

Emilio had planted himself in the chair to my right, and gazed at us with the expectant air of a reporter at a news conference.

"Go see if your mother needs some help," his grand-father suggested.

"Why? I can hear everything you say from in there, anyway."

"Don't talk back," Luis said sternly. "When I tell you to do something, you do it."

Emilio gave him a look that stayed a hair's breath away from an eye roll, yet somehow managed to convey a similar meaning. He stood up and went into the kitchen with all the enthusiasm of a prisoner going back to his cell.

When the door closed Luis turned back to me. "He's right, you know, this place is so tiny you can't break wind without disturbing the neighbors," he said. "It would have been fine for me, but with the two of them as well... you see how it is."

"Have you lived here long?"

"About eight months now. We used to live in a nice house, closer to the center of town, but then Armando ran into some... financial trouble. So we're here until he can sort things out."

"I see," I responded, all sympathy. "I'm no stranger to that kind of problem."

"So you've said. But I gather that things did not go well at Hiram's."

"No."

"Emilio told us he saved you from getting into trouble with some militia men. Is this true? Not that he lies, mind you, but he has a vivid imagination, a way of embellishing things."

"What did he tell you?"

"That two *barbudos* came into the shop to rob it while you were there, and he was able to convince them to let you go."

Emilio's head popped out from behind the kitchen door. "I did!"

"Go chop some onions or something," Luis told him. I heard Miriam laugh. It was an appealing sound, very unlike my own undignified guffaw. Emilio grinned and disappeared into the kitchen again.

"That's true," I said, "he did. He came in and pretended that I was his mother and that I had to come home because you'd fallen. Then the soldiers let us go. But I don't think Hiram was as fortunate."

Luis grunted. "Well, my grandson has courage, but not nearly enough sense."

"Do you have any idea why Hiram was arrested?"

Luis took another sip of rum before he answered. "It could be that he was engaging in 'counter-revolutionary' activities. Or they could have been using their guns and uniforms to disguise an outright robbery."

"Does Castro not do anything about that sort of thing?"

Before Luis could answer Emilio came back into the room to offer us some nuts and fried plantains. He'd just set them on the table when we heard a gentle knock on the door.

Miriam came out of the kitchen and looked warily at Luis. "They aren't that polite," he replied in answer to her silent question. I saw her take a deep breath before she opened the door.

A petite woman of mixed race stood in the hallway. "I must talk to you," she said to Miriam. Her voice was calm but her arms were crossed across her chest, and her legs were stiff, muscles taut, as if to prevent them from trembling.

"Please, come in." Miriam stepped back to allow the woman inside, but she didn't move.

"No, not here," she said, looking directly at me.

Miriam turned to look at me as well, and I saw the fear in her eyes. I glanced at Luis. His furrowed brow echoed Miriam's apprehension. Emilio sat back, his eyes going from his mother to his grandfather, sizing up their reactions like a Geiger counter measuring the room's radiation level.

Miriam started to take off her apron. "I won't be long."

I rose from the table. "Nonsense. It's obvious that I've come at a bad time. I promise you I'm not offended. Good night, Emilio. Good night, Luis. Thank you for the invitation."

I thought Luis might make some objection, but he just nodded, too preoccupied to remember his manners. Emilio came over and gave me a hug around my waist. "Can we go to the beach tomorrow?" he asked, looking up at me, his face a study in contrived nonchalance. He was certainly the best actor in the room.

"Maybe," I answered. The visitor looked at the floor as I brushed by her on the threshold. I walked quickly down the narrow stairs and left the building.

Across the street and to my right I saw a darkened archway and headed right to it. I waited in the shadows to see what happened next. I was sure the sudden visit had something to do with Emilio's father.

In less than five minutes Miriam and the visitor emerged. They hooked arms, the way Cuban women do, and began to stroll up the street, chatting in voices too low for me to hear clearly. There were still a few people out and about, so I was able to trail them without looking too conspicuous. But they never once looked behind them; they were either not concerned about being followed, or anxious to look as if they had nothing to hide.

After walking what I judged to be about a mile they entered a small plaza fringed by a narrow one-way street and several modest buildings, one of which was a hotel. A cab sat parked in front of it. Miriam and the other woman hugged, then Miriam got into the cab. Her friend waved gaily as it pulled away. *Look,* she seemed to be saying, *there's nothing suspicious going on here. I'm just seeing my friend off.*

I glanced around but there were no other cabs in the square. No good trying to follow Miriam any further, at least not tonight. Her friend waited until the cab was gone before walking away. I followed, and we soon arrived

back at the building where Emilio and his family lived —
but she'd come back to it via an entirely different route.

She walked past the front door, and I did the same. She
turned down a narrow alley on the far side of the building
that connected the street we were on with the one parallel
to it. I arrived just in time to see a side door close as I
walked by. Must have been the old service entrance.

I didn't stop. I'd noticed something that perhaps
Miriam's friend had not. When we'd walked past the front
of the building, there was someone else, a man, standing in
the same shadowy archway where I'd begun my surveillance, and he was staring right at the front entrance,
through which we'd exited, not more than half an hour
ago.

* * * * *

I wasn't too surprised to see Emilio early the next morning.
He was sitting in the hallway right outside my door,
building a tiny structure with some twigs. I almost tripped
over him as I headed out in search of breakfast.

"Does the landlady know you're here?" I asked him as
I recovered my balance.

"I didn't want to wake you up," he said, as if this
answered the question. "I brought you some chicken.
From last night." He pulled a small packet of wax paper
out of the canvas bag next to him, and jiggled it at me like
he was tempting a puppy with a treat.

I took it from him. "Thank you. Is everything okay?"

"Papie told me to come and tell you that you shouldn't

come back to our house. There's somebody watching us. Really. No games."

"I believe you." The chicken smelled great. "Come on in."

He followed me inside and perched on the edge of the small bed. "How long are you going to stay here?"

"I'm not sure," I said as I unwrapped the chicken. It was the thigh, my favorite piece. I pulled off a piece of the meat and popped it into my mouth.

"Does it cost a lot to get to Puerto Rico?" Emilio asked as I chewed.

"By plane or boat?"

"Isn't a boat cheaper?"

I swallowed and changed the subject, determined to follow up on my initial line of inquiry. "Who's watching your house?"

"Some big goons. They don't know how to spy on people."

"And you do?"

"I found you, didn't I?"

"You should give lessons."

His grin didn't last long. "They're looking for some-one."

"Your father?"

His silence was all the confirmation I needed. *So he's escaped. From where? To go where? And do what?*

"Emilio," I said, "I don't want to make things more difficult for you and your family. But if there's something I can do to help—"

"Like what? Kill Fidel?"

"Please don't talk like that. You'll get yourself in trouble."

He looked sullen, knowing that I was right and resenting me for it, but that wasn't enough to stop him. "But the Americans hate him, too, so they can come in, like they did with Hitler, and—boom—blow him up."

"Not likely."

He scowled. "It would only take one bomb."

"Here, you can finish this." I handed him the chicken and then stepped over to the tiny sink to rinse off my hands. "Let's go find some more food."

"The chicken's good, huh?"

"Very. Please tell your mother I said thank you."

"She's gone, too."

I froze. "They didn't—"

"No, they didn't take her or anything. But they might. And now Papie doesn't want me to go anywhere, either. Like they could find *me* if I didn't want them to."

"But you're here."

"Just to give a message. And the chicken," he said, before ripping into it himself.

"Okay then, we'll go get some breakfast and I'll get you back to your grandfather."

It took a while to find a shop that was open, and the selection of breakfast pastry was pretty meager. Shortages of flour and other staples were already having their impact on the Cuban economy. I bought a half-dozen plain rolls and some milk. Emilio looked so expectant I handed him a roll as soon as we were back outside.

"You'd better not come back with me," he managed to

get out with his mouth full. "They might see you and try to ask *you* some questions."

He was right, of course. And that could get the family into more trouble, not to mention force me to make a quick exit from Cuba. I took one roll out of the bag and handed the rest to him.

"When will I see you again?" I asked.

"Don't worry, I'll find you. Thanks for the rolls," he said, and darted off.

I strolled around, gathering up the day's papers. There was scarcely any real news available in them, but a quick perusal would fill me in on Castro's latest propaganda efforts. Most of the tirades, as usual, were aimed at the United States, the most vitriolic being criticism for the recent expulsion from the US of three Cuban diplomats accused of espionage. Castro also raged against President Eisenhower because word had reached Cuba that the US Congress was considering drastic cutbacks on the importation of Cuban sugar, in retaliation for the seizure of substantial assets owned by Americans. Castro called this an "act of aggression," and threatened to seize all American-owned property if these cutbacks occurred.

I spent a good while reading as I enjoyed two cups of coffee. When I got back to my lodgings I was surprised to see Emilio leaning against the door. His face looked as hard and closed as a Spartan warrior's.

"They've taken Papie," he said.

CHAPTER FOURTEEN

"Come inside." Emilio maintained his stony silence as I let us into my room. I dropped the newspapers I'd been carrying onto the nightstand and sat on the bed. The bedsprings gave me their customary squeaky salute, and I patted the place next to me.

Emilio shook his head and remained standing. "We have to find him," he said.

"How do you know for sure he's actually been arrested?"

"There were a few people standing around in the street —you know, when the *Fidelistas* come around there's always gossiping afterwards. So I asked a lady what happened and she said some soldiers had gone into the house, and came out dragging an old man behind them. He was unconscious, and his head was bleeding, she said. So I went in through a side door, from the alley, the door to our place was open, and a couple of chairs were knocked over." He gave me a challenging look, daring me to come up with an alternate conclusion.

"Emilio, is it possible that your father has escaped from jail?"

Now he sat down next to me. "I don't know. Maybe. Mommy went somewhere last night and isn't back yet, either. Maybe they found her and took her, too."

"No, I don't think so," I said, laying a reassuring arm around his thin shoulders. "I saw her get into a taxi. I don't know where she went, but I think she got away before—well, they might have come looking for her, if your father has escaped, thinking that he'd try to contact her, and when they didn't find her, they took your grandfather."

"Will they torture him?"

"Oh, no." *Let's hope not, anyway.* "They might ask him some questions, or—"

"Or what?"

"Hold him as a hostage, to try and make your father turn himself in." As I said this I realized Emilio would make an even more attractive hostage. *They wouldn't stoop that low. Or would they? The Nazis didn't have any compunction about harming children. What did we really know about Fidel Castro, after all?*

"Do you have somewhere safe to go?" I asked.

He stiffened. "I'm not going anywhere until I find Papie."

"How do you expect to do that?"

He shifted to face me, slipping my arm off his shoulder as he did so. "You can go to the jail, can't you? They can't arrest you. You're not from here. Everyone else would be afraid to go, you know, because they might get arrested, too. But not you."

"Oh, they could arrest me, alright." I said, somewhat ruefully. "But I'll try to find out something. Meanwhile, you better go back to your apartment in case your mother comes looking for you."

"What if the goons come back looking for me instead?"

"Good point. Let's think… do you know where your grandfather's friend, Carlos, lives?"

He looked puzzled but nodded. "Why?"

"Could you go stay with him?"

"I guess so."

"I have an idea." I leaned down and pulled my canvas bag out from under my bed. Opening it, I took out the smallest of my sketch pads and a couple of colored pencils, and handed all this to Emilio.

"Draw a picture of Carlos," I said, standing up and pointing at the sketch pad, "and write his name under it. Then draw a couple more pictures. Stupid things, anything."

He smiled up at me. "Like a mermaid?"

"Sure," I answered, smiling back.

He put one pencil his lips, thought for a second, and then started to draw. At that moment someone knocked on my door, causing us both to jump. I put my finger to my lips, and Emilio nodded, his eyes wide.

"Yes?" I asked loudly.

"Telephone," my landlady answered.

"Coming."

I pulled my key out of my dress pocket, went to the door, and cracked it open, wondering who the hell was calling me when no one was supposed to know where I was. My landlady was walking back down the hall. She looked around at me as I locked my door, and pointed up the staircase. I walked up and saw a telephone sitting on a small table on the landing. The receiver was off the hook. I picked it up and took a deep breath.

"This is Maria."

"Sorry to call so early," said a man's voice, "but I wanted to catch you before you went out. This is Raul."

Some gears in my head whirred, spun, and then clicked into place. "How nice to hear from you," I began, "I was just chatting with the friend who introduced us. He has a small problem I think you might be able to help with."

"Another lost mermaid tail?"

"Nothing so simple. Can we meet somewhere? I don't like telephones. They're so impersonal."

Silence. Then, "I can't get free until tonight. Where is he now?" The caution in his voice let me know that he'd picked up on my unspoken message. *Emilio is in trouble.*

"He's with me," I said, "or at least he was in my room a minute ago. He may have jumped out the window by now, the little monkey."

"Well you can tell me more tonight." Raul gave me the name of a restaurant in Old Havana, and we agreed to meet there at seven o'clock. I hung up and went back to my room. To my relief Emilio was still there, drawing pictures.

"These are pretty good," I said, picking one up. He'd drawn a red-haired mermaid laying on a rock, a sunset at the beach complete with palm trees and seagulls, and was working on the face of an old man. To my surprise, he'd picked up enough of Carlos' features so that it looked a lot like him, in a cartoonish sort of way: square jaw, flat nose, short, curly hair.

"Okay," I said after he'd finished the portrait and written "Carlos" in big block letters underneath the face, "bring these back to your apartment. Put them on the table, kind of spread out. If your mother comes back here she may figure out that you're with Carlos, but to anyone else it should look like a few of your drawings."

"Good plan," he said, gathering his masterpieces. "And Carlos' wife is a good cook, too. If they have anything to eat."

I almost ruffled his hair but caught myself. My brothers had always hated it when adults did that. "I'm sure she'll find a way to feed you. Come back here after you get those into your apartment, and I'll walk with you over to Carlos' place. I'll come visit you tomorrow. We may know something by then. But you have to promise me that you'll stay with Carlos. Don't go anywhere else. Promise?"

"Okay."

"I said promise."

"Okay, I promise." He started toward the door, then stopped and turned to me.

"Thank you, Miss Maria."

"Never mind," I answered, but he dashed back and wrapped his arms around my waist, very tightly. I laid a hand on his head. "It will be okay," I said softly, "don't worry."

I could only hope that my words contained at least a small measure of truth.

CHAPTER FIFTEEN

"And why can't you go and ask about Emilio's grandfather?" Raul asked after I'd explained the situation.

We'd eaten a quick dinner of Cuban chicken and rice and then strolled down to the water's edge, where the sound of the waves lapping against the seawall would mute the substance of our conversation. The bay of Havana stretched before us, a dark navy blue under the last vestiges of light thrown backward across the horizon by a sun that had gone to visit the other side of the world. To our right we had a clear view of La Cabaña, the massive stone and brick fortress built by the Spaniards and now used by Castro as a prison. "I don't know enough about the system," I replied. "I wouldn't know where to begin."

"And you think I do?"

"Don't you?"

"I've only been here a month or so, and I make it my policy to mind my own business."

I hadn't expected this. "Somehow I thought you and Emilio had known each other for a long time."

"Who's the governor of Puerto Rico?" he asked out of nowhere.

"Luis Muñoz Marín, since 1948. Why? Are you testing me?"

He gave me a sheepish look. "Not much of a test, since I had no idea what the right answer would be. Look, Maria, if I go and ask questions about Luis, someone's going to want to know why I care. And if Emilio's father was put in prison by Castro's people, I can't look sympathetic—for all we know he was plotting against the regime. He may have even killed someone."

"But it's not about his father. If Emilio's mother has disappeared, too, Luis is all the boy has left."

"Still no reason for me to start asking questions, and these things can get very complicated very quickly."

"Well, Luis has a beautiful daughter-in-law, and his son is in prison. Suppose you thought if you could find her father, maybe she'd owe you a favor, one that you could cash in on a couch somewhere. Nothing too complicated about that, is there? And it's not an excuse I could use."

His eyes widened in surprise, and then he laughed, that magical sound that brightened every one of his features and relaxed the lines of tension in his neck. "That might work," he said when he'd caught his breath, "a good strategy, given men's simple brains."

"I thought so. And once we find out where he is… well, I don't know. It's a first step, anyway." I looked into those huge, soulful Spanish eyes, and felt a flicker of attraction warm the space between us.

He felt it too, and looked surprised, as if he'd heard a strange noise, but there was no mistaking it. The atoms in the air had rearranged themselves into a subtle wave of erotic energy, the kind that can pull two foreign bodies together—the catalyst for disaster.

I took a step backward and turned to face the water. *Not now,* I told myself. *Not here, not him.*

"You said you came from Puerto Rico with your boyfriend. He left and you stayed. Why?" Raul asked.

I always heard my mother's stern voice in my head when an untruth was about to emerge from my lips. *Lying is the worse sin of all, Mary Kate. It makes all the others possible.* I did try not to prevaricate unless it was *absolutely* necessary. But when I did, I made it good.

"Castro's success has inspired the Puerto Ricans who want us to be an independent country," I said as I turned to face him again. "My ex is a member of the now-outlawed nationalist party, so he was deported. I followed him here. But with him it's politics first, last, and always. Everything else in his life is left to starve."

"I have some experience along those lines, myself," Raul said. His face was close to mine now, too close, and I couldn't back up any more or I'd end up in the bay. I dropped my eyes to the ground to escape the look in his.

"So you understand. You give and wait and give, and get nothing in return. When we came to Cuba I finally saw the light and broke up with him. After that he went somewhere—probably back to New York—to drum up financial support for the cause, and I'm here, trying to figure out how to get home. If they'll let me back in, that is."

"So you're not a nationalist?"

I looked back up at him. "Let's say I agree with his goal, but not his methods." I almost had myself believing in this nonexistent boyfriend by then. Maybe I should have been an actress. Or a politician.

"And what about you?" I asked, anxious to change the subject. "Why did you come to Cuba?"

"I was invited."

"By whom? To do what?"

"By the Castro government, to serve as a translator and help on engineering projects."

"A translator? You speak Russian?"

"Yes. I've lived in the Soviet Union for quite some time."

"Oh. Did your parents leave Spain after Franco won? I've read a lot about the Spanish Civil War. I know that some on the communist side fled to the USSR afterward — when Franco took over."

"It was something like that." He shifted his weight and edged back, as if the conversation were making him physically uncomfortable. "There are quite a few of us here. It's no secret."

"What's no secret?"

"That the Soviet Union brought some technical advisors to Cuba."

"How many?"

"I'm not quite sure. A few dozen, at this point."

"What for?"

"To help recreate the Cuban economy, mostly. Manu-facturing, enhanced farming techniques, road-building, all the things we're good at."

"What kinds of things do you help build?"

"Whatever they tell me to. Big things, mostly."

"Are you working on something now?"

He looked at me curiously. *Ah, you've blown it now*, I

thought to myself. *One question too many. He'll wonder what's up.*

"Well, tomorrow I'm going to work on getting Emilio's grandfather out of jail. That's a pretty big agenda item for one day, isn't it?"

"Yes, it is," I answered.

* * * * *

The San Carlos de la Cabaña fortress had guarded the entrance to the Bay of Havana for over two hundred years. Raul glanced up as he walked through the impressive front gate, which still bore the Spanish coat of arms. He didn't believe in ghosts, but if any place deserved to be haunted, he thought, it was this one. Built by slaves, it had never been called upon to defend Cuba, so it had served mainly as a prison. And a torture chamber, and an execution ground. Castro had continued to use it for all the same purposes. *For all of Che's criticism of Stalin, he and Fidel are certainly following closely in Uncle Joe's footsteps,* Raul thought as he passed into the front courtyard.

The guard at the gate asked to see his identity papers. Raul pulled out his Soviet passport and handed it to him.

"You don't look much like a Russian," the man said, studying Raul's picture closely.

"I moved there when I was very young. You see? Place of birth, Spain."

The guard called over another sentry, who gave Raul a quick frisk. "He's clean."

The first man gave Raul back his passport as the other

went back to his post. "What's your business here?" he asked.

"I'd like to inquire about a prisoner."

"Well, get in line, then," he said jerking his thumb behind him toward a massive archway leading out of the main courtyard.

Raul looked over at it, tucked his passport back into one pocket, and pulled a pack of American cigarettes out of another. Between the cellophane wrapper and the box was a twenty-dollar bill. He took out one cigarette and placed it in his mouth, holding the pack so that the bill was clearly visible to the man in front of him.

"Where did you get those?" he asked.

Raul lit his cigarette. "Someone who ran a shop had to leave Cuba rather suddenly, and a friend of mine helped himself to some of the inventory. Do you smoke?"

The guard shook his head, eyes glued to the pack in Raul's hand. "Not on duty."

"Take the pack. Now, where did you say I needed to go to ask about a prisoner?"

The man took the pack and shoved it into a side pocket of his uniform. "Go through the archway, but turn right. Go down that hall and turn left at the next arch. There'll be a door on your right, flanked by two sentries. It's Alvarez you want to talk to. He keeps all the lists. Tell his guards you're a Russian general or something."

"Thanks."

He found the door easily enough, showed the sentries his passport and told them that he was there on official Soviet/Cuban business, to discuss improvements in the fortification of the prison walls. One sentry excused himself, taking the passport with him, and was back a few seconds later.

"He'll see you."

Raul opened the door and entered a small foyer containing a coat rack and a large, sand-filled flower pot brimming with cigarette butts. He added his to the collection and then knocked on the interior door.

"You may enter."

Alvarez stood and greeted him. The office was extremely tidy, as was its occupant. His fatigues were freshly pressed, and even his beard was neat and trimmed, unlike so many of the other *Fidelistas* who wore their unkempt facial hair as a badge of honor.

Raul introduced himself and took the chair he was offered. "Señor Alvarez," he began, "I must apologize for my subterfuge. I'm here on personal, not official, business."

"I see." Alvarez said, picking up a stray pencil and putting it back in the holder on his desk. "Well, I should be angry, I suppose, but frankly that's something of a relief, as I had no warning that you were coming, and I'm not the person who would attend to that kind of thing, anyway. But it is true that you're here, in Cuba, with the Russians, are you not?"

"Yes."

"Not everyone likes this Soviet influence, you know. I'm not saying I have anything against it, but some people do."

"Hopefully, once we've shared some of our technical expertise, those people will grow to appreciate our contributions to Cuba's revolution."

155

"And what is your area?"

"Engineering."

"That should be useful." Alvarez said as he leaned back in his chair. "So, I imagine you've come to inquire about a prisoner, is that right?"

"Exactly. You see, I know this young woman. Her father was taken in for questioning. He's an old man, not in good health, so naturally, she's concerned."

"And your interest in this is?"

"The woman." Raul gave what he hoped was a lecherous grin. "I thought if I could tell her something encouraging, she would be, shall we say, grateful."

"If her father's a traitor, she's probably also under suspicion."

"I'm sure she has nothing to do with any counter-revolutionary activities. We've spent quite a lot of time together. But now she's worried about her father. And he's not dangerous, or a traitor," Raul said, touching a finger to his own head, "just talkative, and a tad touched in the head. Thinks he's back fighting the Spanish for Cuban independence. Must have said something that someone took the wrong way."

"The name?"

"Luis Velasquez."

"Huh. That sounds familiar." Alvarez sorted through the stack of papers on his desk. "Oh, that's why. Well, I'm afraid you're going to have to find some other way to ingratiate yourself with the young lady. The old man fell, you see, hit his head, and died a few hours after he'd been taken into custody. Perhaps you can be the right person at the right time to console her."

* * * * *

How am I going to tell the boy that his grandfather is dead? What if his mother doesn't come back? Where will he go?

Maybe Emilio could stay with Maria for a while, at least until she went back to Puerto Rico. That would give Raul an excuse to see her again. He didn't know why he was so intrigued by her, but he was. Her facial features were a touch too masculine to be called beautiful, her hair was a disaster, and her figure lacked curves. But she was so full of energy that she sparkled, and he could see real intelligence reflected in those hazel eyes. She was probingly curious, and very quick-witted, yet her behavior toward Emilio revealed a warm heart.

His wife had been very pretty but not very smart, and rather lazy. After a short time they'd bored each other so deeply that it made sense to part ways. But Maria— somehow she made smart sexy.

But she was also an American, although not a willing one, if she was telling the truth. *Must you always suspect everyone?*

Which brought him back to Luis. Had his death really been an accident? Maria told him that Luis had some sort of head wound when the police carried him out of his building. Had that killed him, or did he fall later... or something worse? Alvarez' report was not clear on that subject, which wasn't surprising.

Vagueness could hide a multitude of sins.

CHAPTER SIXTEEN

"Oh, my God. How are we going to tell them?"

"Has his mother made it back yet?"

"I don't know. I left Emilio at a friend of his grandfather's yesterday morning, a man named Carlos. I have no idea what's happened since then. I was waiting to hear from you."

Raul and I were in a small, dismal bar and grill not too far from where I was staying. There were more flies than customers in the place, and the floor hadn't been mopped since Teddy Roosevelt took San Juan Hill. The waiter-cum-bartender was arguing, loudly, with someone in the kitchen, enabling us to talk freely.

"I'm not sure it's wise for me to go with you to break the news. If Emilio comes to me, well—they can question me, but the truth is that I don't know why his father is in prison—or why they took Luis. But his mother is a different matter. You see, there's always a possibility that I'm under surveillance," Raul said, "and I wouldn't want my carelessness to lead the G-2 to her if she is under some sort of suspicion."

"You might be followed? By whom? For what?"

"Oh, there's some gossip that the Soviet advisors have a sort of hidden escort. The US is a mere 90 miles away, you know. Someone could try to defect, I suppose."

"Would you?"

He looked shocked. "I owe everything I have to the Soviet Union, including my life, and I'm not convinced that living in America is so much better than living in Russia."

That's because you've never been to the States, I thought, but I kept this observation to myself. "How do you owe them your life?" I asked instead.

A wave of indecision rolled across his face, and I thought he wasn't going to answer me. He took a long swig of beer before he spoke.

"We lived in the northern part of Spain. The Nazis started bombing there in 1937."

"I know. I've read all about it." And I remembered the pictures I'd seen of small villages burned into rubble, of blackened corpses, and of thousands of women and children crowding onto train platforms, desperate to escape the carnage.

"Well, the Soviets invited the families of the men and women fighting Franco to send their children to Russia, to keep them safe from the war. Other places did too, like Sweden and France." He gave me a sardonic half-smile. "Not the US, of course, because they wouldn't take in the children of communists."

"Typical."

"So after the war, everyone went home. Except us. Stalin wasn't about to let healthy youngsters go back to Franco and be molded into anti-communists."

"What about your parents?"

"They were dead by then."

"Oh. I'm sorry."

"It was a long time ago, and it all worked out for the best. But no, I would not betray my adopted country."

"Of course not. I'm sorry I asked the question. It wasn't meant as a challenge."

He waved a greedy fly off his beer. "So perhaps you can understand that while I'm sympathetic to Emilio's plight, there's not much more I can do to help. My involvement might just complicate matters."

He sounded strained as he said this, almost guilty, but I couldn't blame him for backing away. He hadn't lived though the Spanish Civil War and World War II without learning some survival skills, and minding one's own business is a valuable one, although not one that I've ever had much success in acquiring.

I laid my hand over one of his. "Thank you for everything you've done so far."

To my surprise he pulled his hand away, flipped mine over, and began massaging the fleshy part of my palm with his thumb. I don't think I'd ever felt anything so sensuous, and the signal that other parts of my body were sending to my brain confirmed their agreement with that supposition.

He wasn't looking at me; he was studying my hand. He stopped massaging it and traced his thumb lightly along the deep lines that formed a sort of "M" in the middle of my palm. "A long life line," he said softly, "hopefully it's long enough for us to have the opportunity to see each other again, sometime in the future, when circumstances are more conducive to our being able to get to know each other better."

He looked up at me and gave me a smile that somehow

conveyed a subtle blend of admiration, invitation, and regret. Then, without taking his eyes from mine, he turned my hand over, brought it to his lips, gave my knuckles a soft kiss, and released me.

"Until we meet again," he said as he rose.

In sharp contrast to the rest of my body, my mouth was bone dry, and I couldn't utter a sound. Raul laid some money on the table and left me sitting there, silent, stunned, and breathless.

* * * * *

And then I had to go find Emilio.

The closer I got to Carlos' house the heavier the weight in my chest became, and not just because of the grim message I had to deliver that day. Having to break the news of Luis' death ushered me back to one of the worst moments of my own life: the day the Western Union messenger brought the telegram telling us that Jamie had been lost at sea.

I was only eleven when Jamie had enlisted, but I was furious with him for going. He should have known what it would do to Ma. He should have tried to get a relatively safe posting as an MP somewhere—and he could have, given that he was a policeman in New York. But he'd joined the Navy right after Pearl Harbor, left a week later, and we never saw him again.

My mother never shared the details of her terrors with me, but it wasn't hard to imagine the gruesome scenarios that fueled her anxiety. Right after Jamie enlisted I started having my own nightmares. Sharks swam around me in blood-red seas, while huge pools of burning oil turned the ocean into an inferno. Or I dreamed about being trapped in a metal space that was slowly filling up with frigid water, and I could feel my whole body freezing, inch by inch. And the music accompanying these dreams was always the same: a cacophony of men's voices, all screaming.

In fact, I still have those dreams, sometimes.

Ma, like most women whose men were at war, never saw one of those thin yellow envelopes without focusing on the devastation they might carry within them, and would never open one herself. She always handed telegrams to me to read for her. I didn't mind. I liked being the first person to receive important information, and I wasn't even all that apprehensive when I ripped opened that particular telegram—in fact, the last one that we'd received had nothing at all to do with the war.

People talk about a human heart breaking, and it's supposed to be a metaphor. But when I read that telegram aloud I *saw* my mother's heart shatter. She went white, stopped breathing, and stumbled back to land in a chair that almost tipped over as she collapsed into it. A look of complete confusion came over her face. At that instant, the light went out of her eyes. It never really returned.

Mark's death, nearly a year later, didn't hit her nearly as hard. It wasn't because she didn't love her oldest son. It's just that whatever tiny pieces of her heart that were left after she lost Jamie were too small to break again. Like splitting an atom. It couldn't be done.

To my shame, the sorrow I felt at losing my brother was nothing compared to the anger I felt toward my mother after Jamie died. I wasn't angry because she'd made me the messenger. I was angry because I wanted her to be stronger, for me—for all of us. I wanted her to stay the way she'd always been: brave, resourceful, resilient, and wise. I wanted her to hide her pain so that we could all hide behind her.

My anger at her failure built a wall between us, the bricks mortared together by deep swaths of resentment. For years I gazed over that wall, first defiantly, then wistfully. I wanted her to realize it was there and knock it down. But she never did.

I couldn't bear the thought of seeing Miriam react the way my mother had when she lost Jamie. But I knew I would not be able to live with myself if I left them wallowing in uncertainty when I held the truth in my hand.

Carlos didn't live far from Emilio's place. He owned—or, more likely, rented—a small two-bedroom house on a once-residential block that had become surrounded by blue collar businesses: a gas station, an appliance repair shop, a hardware store. The house was as squat as a beetle, and built out of large cement bricks: practical during a hurricane, but not at all attractive.

I knocked at the door, heard some shuffling inside, and waved at the peephole. "Are you alone?" I heard Carlos ask from behind the door.

"Yes," I said.

The door opened a crack, and I scooted inside. I saw no one except Carlos in the room. "Where's Emilio?" I asked, looking around.

"Here," came a spritely voice from under the couch.

Emilio crawled out, commando-style. "And guess what?" he added as he stood up. "The picture worked. My mother's here."

"That's enough out of you," Carlos scolded. Emilio frowned at him.

"I need to speak with her. With all of you," I said.

"I'm here." Miriam appeared in the archway that separated the small front room from the even smaller dining area. "Did you find Luis?"

"I'm afraid I did. It's not good news."

"Are they going to keep him in prison?" Carlos asked.

"No, that is... I'm sorry, Miriam." I looked at Emilio and saw the fear in his eyes, but I had no way to shield him from the news. "Someone will have to go and identify his body."

Miriam let out a gasp of air and grabbed the wall for support. Carlos cursed. Emilio stared at me for a split second before exploding.

"How do you know? You're wrong! They're lying!" he shouted, fists clenched at his sides as if to keep himself from using them. His mother went to him. At her touch his anger vanished. He turned and hid his face in her skirt, but he did not cry.

"I'm sorry," Miriam said weakly. "They were very close, you see."

"I know. It's alright. He's upset, and he has every right to be." I touched one of Emilio's shoulders and he shrugged my hand away.

Miriam knelt down to look at him, face to face. "I expect better from you," she said, although her tone of voice stayed soothing. "It's not her fault, you know. She's trying to help us."

Emilio nodded, then turned to me. "I'm sorry."

"It's okay."

"How did he die?" Carlos asked from the rickety cane chair into which he'd sunk.

"I don't know. A friend of mine was able to talk to someone relatively senior at the prison. He was told that Luis hit his head and died soon after he arrived, but no one would say whether it was due to a fall before or after they took him into custody."

"So he wasn't tortured," Carlos said. "That's something to be thankful for."

"Tortured? Why?" I asked, finding it easy to look shocked.

"Because of my husband," Miriam answered as she stood up. "He's organizing the resistance to Fidel."

"Miriam, for God's sake," Carlos said sharply, "how do we know she's not an informant?"

Miriam looked at him blankly. "I guess we don't. But for some reason I trust her. Luis liked her, and she's been so kind to Emilio."

Carlos shook his finger at her. "You have to be more careful."

Emilio broke away from her and went over to Carlos. "It's not like I didn't know that already. I want to go where my dad is. I can help him. I know I can."

"Nothing doing," the old man said.

"Emilio, I need you here with me." Miriam walked over to him, leaned down, and put her arms around his shoulders. "Your father told me to tell you that."

Emilio looked up at her. "You've seen him? You've talked to him?"

"Yes, my darling, I have."

"In jail?"

"Of course." *I hope for their sake she's never interrogated,* I thought. *She's a terrible liar.*

"I want to see him," Emilio demanded.

"Prison is no place for children," Carlos responded.

The door opened, making all of us jump. A petite elderly woman let herself in, carrying a small bag of groceries in her gnarled hands. Clearly surprised to see a roomful of people, she put the bag down on a side table and gazed at all of us from behind very large bifocal glasses, the old-fashioned kind that magnified her eyes and made it look as if she were peering out of a fishbowl.

"What's going on, Carlos?" she asked.

"Luis is dead," Carlos said flatly.

She crossed herself. "Oh Mother of God, protect us." She turned her nervous eyes toward me. "Who is this woman?"

"My friend," Emilio answered, "she's helping us."

"Helping how?"

"This is my wife, Delores," Carlos said to me, waving his hand in her direction. "This is Maria."

I held out my hand. She looked at it, then at her husband. "Carlos, should we have strangers in the house at a time like this?"

"I told you, she's my friend," Emilio said, as if he'd been challenged.

"One more rude remark and you'll meet my friend, the

belt," Carlos said. "I'll give you a whipping in honor of your grandfather."

I could tell that Emilio was itching to say something in response, but he managed to keep himself quiet. "I don't think Miriam should go to identify Luis' body," I said. "Perhaps it would be safest for Carlos to go."

I heard a sharp intake of breath from Delores, but Carlos was nodding. "They won't want anything from an old man like me."

His wife glared at him. "Like they didn't want anything from Luis?"

"I don't have a son in prison."

"No, we don't," Delores said bitterly, "because he died helping to bring this monster to power."

"All the more reason for them to trust me," Carlos said, giving his wife a warning look. She turned away, but not before I saw her eyes fill with tears.

"I'll go cook us something to eat," she said, avoiding all eye contact as she picked up her groceries. "I was lucky enough to find some pork at the market."

I knew it was time for me to go; the family needed time alone to share their grief. Before saying goodbye I took a small sketch pad out of my pocket, tore off a sheet, wrote down the telephone number of my boarding house, and gave it to Miriam. "Please call me. Don't say too much on the phone, and don't call from a place that might be monitored, like your house or your job."

"I can't go back to the apartment or either one of my jobs," Miriam said as I gave her the paper. "I can't go anywhere they might look for me."

"Stay here as long as you need to," Carlos said, "no

167

one will bother with an old man like me, who's sacrificed his only son to the Glorious Revolution."

Miriam gave him a faint smile in response. Emilio walked over to me. "I'm really sorry," he said again.

"I know. It's okay. I—I've lost people I loved, too." I didn't know what else to say, so with that, I took my leave.

CHAPTER SEVENTEEN

O rganized resistance to Castro. How strong a movement was it? Who was behind it? Were they armed? What were they prepared to do? And what were their chances?

I knew I was on to something. No journalist had run a story suggesting that the sporadic violence carried out against the Castro regime could be traced to anything other than a few disparate and disorganized groups. The most serious challenge had been led by one Captain Manolo Beatón, who'd fought with Castro against Batista. But when Beatón began to object to Castro's dictatorial tendencies, he found himself convicted of murder. He'd escaped from prison, collected a group of about a hundred men, and led them back into the Sierra Maestra Mountains, where Castro's own tiny band of revolutionaries had begun their fight. Castro deployed a force of 5,000 troops to flush them out, and the leaders were executed soon after their capture.

After that, a few Cuban émigrés had made it back to the island armed with old guns and righteous indignation, but their efforts were quixotic at best, and they'd been caught fairly easily. A couple of inept attempts to bomb an oil refinery and some sugar cane fields were attributed to former Batista cronies who'd managed to escape the firing squads. Indeed Castro blamed every "counter-revolutionary" incident on ruthless Batista supporters, all backed by the CIA.

My best potential source of information was Miriam, but I didn't know when or how I could reconnect with her without jeopardizing her safety — or mine. The only other person I'd talked to who'd been willing to acknowledge his anti-Castro sentiments had been Father Lopez. I decided I needed to talk to him again. Immediately.

This time I showed up without calling ahead. The evening service was well underway so I crept in and sat in a pew in the far back of the church. Father Lopez was celebrating Mass, one lone altar boy at his side. In 1960 many Catholic services were still said in Latin, and I was surprised at how many of the words I knew, given that I had not been to church in a very, very long time.

I counted fourteen people in attendance, all of them very old: not unusual for a mid-week evening mass. The church itself had seen better days. A few sections of the stained-glass window over the altar had been replaced with clear panes, so that several of the saints observing the Virgin Mary's Ascension into heaven looked like incomplete portions of a jigsaw puzzle. Dust-filled cracks riddled the wooden pews, and the religious paintings were so age-stained it was nearly impossible to make out the scenes they depicted. But there was still an aura about the place, either because the fervent faith of the few who were there radiated some kind of spiritual energy, or because despite the agnosticism that had settled into the thinking part of my brain during my early teenage years, a part of me still yearned to feel His presence.

When the Mass ended I had to wait for Father Lopez to greet each member of his small flock before I could get close enough to ask him if he could spare a few minutes. He had a good rapport with them. He greeted each person by name, asked about their health, and their families. When I asked to speak to him privately he gestured to his garment, explained that he needed to change, and told me to wait for him in his office. One ancient matron who was still within earshot gave me a curious glance, but I figured Father Lopez could handle whatever questions my presence provoked.

"Good to see you again," he said once he'd settled in behind his desk. "I assume this visit is not just another courtesy call?"

"No. I'd like to ask you more about what's going on with respect to the growing resistance within Cuba to the Castro regime."

"You seem immensely interested in that particular topic."

It was time to take the plunge. "Bentley told you to expect me, didn't he? So you know I'm here for a reason. Castro has shut down the press in Cuba. The people who feel betrayed by him should be able to tell their story. Hopefully I can do that in a way that will add some fairness to the equation."

"Robert said I could trust you," he said after an uncomfortably lengthy pause, "and that goes a very long way with me." He touched three fingers to the cross that hung around his neck, as if expecting the Almighty to communicate some advice to him through his fingertips. Maybe He did, because the next thing Father Lopez said was, "You'll need to come back tomorrow at noon, with clothes that are good for rough travel. Bring all the American cash you can—it could prove helpful. Can you disappear for a couple of days without causing anyone any undue concern?"

"That will not be a problem."

* * * * *

I went straight back to my room at the boarding house, squeezed myself back into that tight skirt, put on some makeup, wrapped my hair in a colorful scarf, topped it off with my sun hat and sun glasses, and then caught a taxi back to Old Havana.

I stopped a block away from my hotel to study the situation. No one appeared to be watching the place from the outside. After grabbing a newspaper from a nearby kiosk I strolled into the lobby and pulled a classic Sam Spade by pretending to read while keeping an eye on everyone else. No one seemed to be taking too long to light a cigarette, no one dawdled over coffee, and I didn't see anyone lurking for longer than necessary around a doorway. No one else was reading a newspaper, and no one was watching me. At least, no one I could see.

I left the paper on a chair and went up to the front desk. "Good evening, señor. I'll be leaving tonight. I need to pick up the suitcase I left here."

"I trust you enjoyed your stay in Cuba?" the clerk asked, with such false innocence I knew some speculative gossip about my bedroom habits had made the rounds.

Good. No reason for them to think that I was an incognito reporter.

"Lovely," I said, handing him the ticket for my bag.

"We get so few Americans nowadays," he said after he'd rung for a bellman. "We miss them."

"You mean you miss our money," I said, looking up at him through lowered lashes.

"Oh, no," he assured me, "we miss the people, too. So friendly."

"Everyone here has been absolutely charming," I replied as the bellhop handed me my bag. I handed them both a five dollar bill. "And, well, there's a very small chance someone may come by and ask about me and a gentleman friend of mine. It would be very convenient if you knew nothing about my stay."

They both nodded at me, happy to be part of a profitable extra-marital conspiracy. "Of course, Madame," said the desk clerk, "it's no one's business but yours."

I blew him a kiss and left, sashaying for all I was worth.

My timing could not have been better. Within days Castro nationalized all the remaining hotels in Cuba, declaring that the country had no American tourists due to the continuing "aggressions" of the United States, designed to "strangle Cuba economically." The National Tourist Institute would now run every hotel in the country.

And he was just getting started.

* * * * *

There was one other person I needed to see that night.

I ducked into a busy bar and went straight to the ladies' room, where I rubbed off my Femme Fatale face paint and replaced it with a thin coat of freckle-concealing foundation. I switched shoes and changed into the dress that transformed me back into Dowdy Girl, and left my small suitcase and all the Sexy Sadie clothes within it in the stall. If someone was waiting for her to exit the ladies' room, they paid no attention to me as I left.

I walked past the house three times before going up to the door. My hesitation wasn't caused by the machine guns slung over the shoulders of the two young *barbudos* who stood on the porch, or the fact that I was about to put myself into a situation that could severely increase the chances my cover would be blown. And it wasn't a surge of courage that propelled me to the door—more like the pull of an alluring compulsion.

The sentries eyed me with amused curiosity as I approached. "There's a Russian man staying here," I stated flatly, without greeting them.

"There's a whole house full," one said, smirking, "all named Ivan."

"The one I want is named Raul, if he told me the truth," I said, "and he owes me money."

The other guard looked me up and down. "Couldn't owe you much, unless you overcharged," he said, eliciting a chortle from his comrade.

I glared at them. "If there is indeed a Spanish-Russian man here, named Raul, I would appreciate it if you would go get him for me. Otherwise I'll have to ask my brother to come and collect this money. He works with *El Che*, and hates to be bothered. But he'll do anything for his baby sister."

They obviously doubted the veracity of my claim, so I crossed my arms across my chest and pulled my face into a fierce scowl, doing my best to imitate the devastating glower of my fourth grade teacher, a Catholic nun whose condescending countenance could cast terror even into the hearts of her fellow Sisters in Christ.

They must've gone to Catholic school, too. "Oh, what the hell," said the taller, skinnier of the two. He opened the door and shoved his head inside. "Hey, get Raul. He has a visitor."

I heard someone respond. The guard turned back to me. "Wait here."

"Thank you," I said, relaxing my facial muscles just a little.

In a moment Raul opened the door. I saw a flash of elation brighten his eyes. This caused an odd flutter in my chest.

"What are you doing here?"

I wagged a menacing finger close to his face. "You know why I'm here. You owe me money."

Puzzlement, comprehension, and false chagrin moved across his face in rapid succession. "Oh, well, an honest mistake, you know. Perhaps we should discuss this inside?"

I crossed my arms again and tapped my foot in an agitated fashion as I pretended to ponder this invitation. "Very well," I said, "but don't pull any tricks."

Raul looked at the taller guard, who glanced from me back to Raul, then grunted his assent. I slipped inside.

"Come on upstairs," Raul said, gesturing for me to follow him up the marble staircase. I let my hand rest lightly on the railing as I walked up, briefly imagining what it must have been like to be the mistress of such a grand home — and have it abruptly taken away.

Raul's room was large and airy, but the furnishings were spare and mismatched: a double bed, a small chest of drawers, a metal filing cabinet, a specialized drafting table, a floor lamp, and a heavy leather chair that looked like it had been snatched out of someone's grandmother's parlor. Probably was.

"Why the guards?" I asked as I looked around.

"That's a recent thing. Something to do with anti-Soviet protests. What did you say to them? Women aren't usually allowed in here without some sort of advance permission."

"I told them that you owed me money."

"And that worked?"

"Well, I might have mentioned something about a family member who works closely with Che Guevara."

He laughed, that wonderful warm laugh of his, and a pleasant but unfamiliar sensation swirled through the base of my stomach. I watched as he went to sit on the bed, thought better of it, walked over to the chair, swiped some dust off the seat with his hand, wiped that hand on his trouser leg, and then turned the chair around to face me.

"Please, sit down." He held on to the back of that chair very tightly, and his dark eyes radiated warmth — tinged with an alluring spark of hunger. I did not take the proffered seat.

"I can't stay."

He walked around the chair and stepped closer. "How did you find me?"

"Emilio, of course. When he introduced us, that morning on the beach, he'd already bragged to me all about how he'd found out where you lived."

"I should have guessed."

"Anyway, I came tonight because I wanted to say... to tell you—"

"Tell me what?"

I looked up at him as his face drew ever closer to mine, and realized that I had nothing to say, after all.

Words would have been useless anyway, I suppose; our bodies were communicating on a very intimate level. And Raul must have known even before I did the real reason I came to find him. We stayed silent, but my hand on his cheek, his fingertips along my collarbone, my fingers caressing his shoulders, his lips exploring my neck —every cell in both of our bodies did the talking for us. There were no emotional barriers, no misunderstandings, no time when one of us mentally broke out of that private conversation. And when we brought it to a close we even managed to breathe quietly—deeply, but quietly, gazing at each other in shared delight.

He helped me slip on my dress before we spoke again.

"I have to leave," I said.

"So soon?" His teasing smile faded as he took in the seriousness of the look on my face.

"I mean leave Havana. Tomorrow. And I don't know when—or if—I'll be back. Would you please find a way to tell Emilio and Miriam for me? I know you said you didn't want to be seen with them, but maybe you can get them a message, somehow—"

"But why now?" I could hear pain in his voice, and felt my own heart lurch. *Serves you right,* I chastised myself, *you shouldn't have let things get this far.*

"I can't explain. You know how it is. You told me almost the same thing earlier today. There are too many other factors involved."

"Are you in trouble?"

"Not yet."

Sometimes silence is an answer, and sometimes it serves as a medium for the delivery of questions. I soaked in all of Raul's and said nothing. He took one of my hands in both of his and pressed a kiss into my palm. He closed my fingers into a fist, gave me a sly smile, and offered my closed fist back to me. "Here. Something to take with you."

And in that gesture I could see the boy he must have been, once upon a time, before the bombings and the Russians and the war. I covered my trembling lips with my clenched fist, and nodded.

I was able to hold back the tears until I was outside, striding briskly down the sidewalk. Luckily a passing storm cloud now hid the moon and stars, and it had started to rain.

CHAPTER EIGHTEEN

To understate the obvious, I was a city girl. To me "rough travel" meant taking the subway to Times Square on New Year's Eve. As a kid, a nature trip consisted of a visit to Jones Beach or the Bronx Zoo. I could handle rats, cockroaches, spiders, poor sanitary conditions, bad food, occasional gunfire, and anything else normally found south of 42nd Street and Broadway, but jungle travel was new for me. And that's where I was headed.

The morning of my departure I went to buy some appropriate clothes. Up until Castro's takeover pants weren't worn by many respectable Cuban women, but the new revolutionary style made it easy to find olive green or brown khaki slacks—although not necessarily in the right size. I finally found a pair that didn't fall off, as well as a lightweight, loose-fitting cotton shirt to protect my citified skin from sun and bugs. I bought some hiking boots that almost fit, sturdy socks, a canteen, a sun visor, some DEET mosquito repellent, a small tube of zinc oxide (figuring that a white stripe across my nose would be less attractive than a third-degree burn) and a used, soft-sided Boy Scout backpack to stuff it all into. I also bought a bottle of rum and some cigarettes, knowing that these two commodities frequently helped when attempting to make friends and influence people. And I figured I was going to need a

179

couple of shots and a smoke somewhere along the way myself.

Back in my room, I took the bulk of my remaining American cash (about $300), divided it into two equal piles of bills, rolled each stack into something the length and width of a stubby cigar, and covered that with a couple of layers of toilet paper. I cut a slit in the bottom of each cup of my special bra, removed the padding, and replaced it with a roll of bills, adding wads of extra tissue paper padding where needed. To my satisfaction, when I'd finished one could hardly tell that I'd made an alteration to my deceitful lingerie.

I tucked some small bills in my pants pocket, then put my two remaining $50 bills in a sock at the bottom of my knapsack, hoping that if I was searched whoever was doing the job would stop when they discovered the hiding place of General Grant. Next I added my other traveling essentials. Following my brother Tim's advice, I never left home without a Swiss Army knife, some kind of flashlight, matches in a waterproof wrapper, a few band-aids, and duct tape. Yes, duct tape. Tim was a man ahead of his time.

I rolled up my Dowdy Girl dress and added it to the mix along with my boots, identity papers, toothbrush, my smallest sketch pad and some pencils, my extra shirt and (of course) a change of underwear. After checking my inventory, I added the remainder of the roll of toilet paper from the shared restroom down the hall (involuntarily donated by my innkeeper, but I'm sure she would've understood). Thus prepared, I left a few dollars and a note of thanks on my bed, and left.

THE CUBAN CONNECTION

I was to meet my escort in the tree-lined park that ran through the center of Paseo del Prado, one of Havana's oldest and most famous streets. Begun as a simple canopied promenade during colonial times, by the early 1920s the Paseo del Prado Park had been transformed into a neoclassical oasis, with marble benches, ornate street lamps, fountains, and several enormous bronze lions, all much beloved by the citizens of the city.

As instructed, I bought an orange from a street vendor, found a vacant bench along the edge of the park, and sat down. Within seconds a young man approached me. He looked to be in his late twenties.

"Is that all you're having for lunch?" he asked.

"Unless I get a better offer," I answered, delivering my scripted line as naturally as possible.

"Do you like nachos?"

"Sure."

He offered me his hand and I stood up, whereupon he kissed my cheek like an old acquaintance, whispering, "Well done, Maria. I'm Nacho. Come with me, and try to make it look like we know each other."

I offered him a piece of my orange. He took it with a smile. Unlike many light-skinned Cubans who'd retained the western European features of their Spanish forefathers, Nacho looked as if he owed a good deal of his ancestry to the original natives of South America, with prominent cheekbones, almond eyes, and a nose that ended in the shape of an arrowhead. A large percentage of the young men on the street wore the same outfit he did — khaki pants and a white cotton shirt, although he did not attempt a beard — I doubt he could've grown one.

The one conspicuous item was my backpack. They'd yet to catch on as a fashion accessory for women. Nacho took it from me and slung it over one of his shoulders as we started to walk.

"Men in Cuba don't let women carry their own burdens," he said.

"I'll keep that in mind. Do you always go by Nacho?"

"Most of the time. It's short for Ignatius."

"Where are we going?"

"Over to where I left my jeep. I hope you're okay eating beans and rice. We won't have a lot of variety over the next few days."

"I eat anything."

Soon we were walking down a side street. We came to a small plaza where dozens of cars were parked, all American and none of them in very good shape. He stopped beside a jeep that was obviously a reconditioned US Army vehicle. Nacho opened the door for me, dropped my bag in the back, and climbed into the driver's seat. The engine groaned twice before turning over, like a grumpy old man prematurely awakened from his afternoon nap, but it hummed pretty smoothly once it warmed up.

"So what have you been told so far?" Nacho asked me as we headed out of the city center.

"Practically nothing."

"You don't have anything that says 'press' on you, do you? Someone may want to see your documents, and I don't want to have to explain anything."

"No press ID, just a passport."

"Puerto Rican, right?"

"American. All Puerto Ricans are US citizens."

"Oh, right. But how do you prove that you're Puerto Rican?"

"I have a resident card." That had been a remarkably easy document to acquire before my departure. They were very easy to forge. After all, why would someone want to say they lived in Puerto Rico if they don't?

"Well, for the next couple of days, you're a bird-watcher," Nacho said.

"How's that?"

"Look in the back."

I twisted around and saw a book resting on the back seat. Two hummingbirds graced the bright green cover, one with a two-tone green head, the other showing off a brilliant red throat. I read the title aloud as I pulled the book onto my lap. "'Field Guide to Birds of the West Indies, second edition, by James Bond.' James Bond. Why does that name sound familiar?"

"Well if you're into birds of the Caribbean, this is like the Bible. That's your cover. We probably won't run into any patrols, but if we do, you're an enthusiastic birder, and you've hired me to take you around the island to spot some of Cuba's rare tropical birds. Nature tourism is my business, and it gives us a good excuse to roam around. I have a couple of places lined up I use on a 'drop in' basis to put me and my clients up, so we shouldn't have to sleep outdoors, although I brought a couple of sleeping bags just in case. You need to pick up a few essential facts from that book to make your cover more credible."

"What sort of things should I know?"

"The basic stuff. Like the main differences between a hawk and a duck, for example."

"One tastes good and the other doesn't?"

"Is flippancy the technique you normally use when trying to earn someone's trust?"

I can count on one hand the number of times someone other than my mother hit me with a verbal reprimand so completely on target that it felt like a slap in the face. This was one of them.

"I deserved that," I said as the stunned feeling wore off, "but I am here to try and give the people who don't support Castro an international voice, and I do want you to trust me. I'm very sorry."

He hit a pothole in a way that almost sent me into the dashboard, and I'm pretty sure he did it on purpose, but after I steadied myself he nodded.

"Okay, so what's the difference between a hawk and a duck?" I asked humbly as I opened Mr. Bond's master-piece.

"One is a raptor, the other is a waterfowl. It's all in there. A lot of it is common sense. A pigeon wouldn't be in the same family as a hummingbird, right?"

You haven't met my family, was the first thing that popped into my head. "Right."

"So look through the book, get a sense of the main species, and pick out a couple of Cuban birds and memorize all their details, so that you can talk about them with such fervor that you'll be able to bore to complete numbness any patrol that stops us."

"Gotcha. So is there a grand prize bird? One we birders go wild over?"

"The tocolo. See, there? I've marked the page."

"'*Priotelus temnurus,*'" I read aloud, "'Cuban trogon.

Blue crown and nape, blackish face, white chin, throat, and breast, bright red belly, upper parts iridescent bronze-green with green-blue upper tail, distinctive scalloped retrices.' What are retrices?"

"The longest tail feathers, the ones that stabilize a bird in flight."

I studied the picture. I couldn't imagine seeing a bird that colorful in real life. The tocolo looked like something out of a comic book—a swallow zapped by gamma rays.

"How long have you been doing this?" I asked.

"Since I was a kid. My dad taught me. For me and him it was an adventure. An adventure about discovering nature's beauty, and learning how to respect it."

"Did your dad start the business?"

"No. He died in prison when I was still a kid. We never found out the real story. Most people didn't, you know. One day your dad or your brother is there, the next day you hear he's in prison. Or you never hear anything. My younger brother died fighting against Batista, so you can bet I was in the crowd screaming, 'to the wall,' when Che starting executing Batista's assassins at La Cabaña. But now—well, we didn't fight for this. We just traded one tyrant for another."

"So counter-revolution is the only choice?"

"That's Fidel's label. We're freedom fighters. And yes, if he won't hold elections, it's the only way to overthrow a dictator."

"How many of you are there?"

"About a hundred, but more are joining us almost every day. Fidel started with eleven men, remember?"

"Oh, yes."

"So you should read now, before the road gets worse and makes it impossible. Feel free to ask me any questions."

I complied, although I took frequent breaks to study the passing scenery. I'd imagined sugar cane fields encroaching on the very edge of the city, but saw instead a whole lot of nothing. Just long grass, shrubs, and a few small orchards. Here and there a cluster of palm trees. Not at all what I imagined when conjuring up images of a tropical paradise.

"So where are the cane fields?"

He looked amused. "All over the place, but farther inland. You have to burn the whole field before the harvest, and the cutting is done by the poorer people, mostly descended from slaves. The rich don't like 'that kind' living too close, or having to breathe in smoke for weeks on end. So even those who own plantations have a house in the city, or close to the water. Coming from Puerto Rico, I guess you understand that way of thinking."

I nodded, but my train of thought had moved on. "Did you go to university in the States?"

He looked at me for a split second longer than was safe and had to adjust his steering before we hit another pothole. "Yes. Notre Dame. Why?"

"Two things. You have an American way of saying some things. You know, the words are Spanish, but the grammar isn't, in terms of how the sentence is constructed."

"That's true of a lot of Cubans who didn't go to school in the US."

"And there's your faith in democracy."

"Also true of many who didn't go to school in the US."

I shook my head. "Not for most of the revolutionaries in this part of the world. They lean toward socialism."

His reaction to this remark traveled from his eyes, to his mouth, to his shoulders, and then to his grip on the steering wheel. It was like watching a river freeze over.

"Perhaps we need to lead the way then," he said.

"You didn't have to come back to Cuba, did you? With a degree from Notre Dame? Or you could have worked in an office somewhere, earning more respect if not more money. Why did you decide to come back and start this kind of business?"

He didn't answer right away, and when he did his voice had taken on a totally different tenor. "What is it that makes a person attached to the land of their birth? The comfort of being in a place where you and your people are known? Or something even deeper, an instinct as basic as that of the sea turtle, one that enables her to take a measure of the sky, the sea, and the land that is unique, and drives her back to the same beach where she was born to lay her eggs? Cuba is who I am. I never thought about living anywhere else. And sharing her glories with others as a way to make a living, well, it was a risk, but it worked. Until Fidel wrecked everything. And if he does let the Soviets in, they'll destroy what's left."

"Why would you assume that?" I didn't disagree with him, but sometimes to get the most information out of someone you have to play devil's advocate.

He looked surprised. "I thought you were on our side."

"My job is to stay objective. But one thing I can say with complete objectivity is that Castro is clamping down on any kind of criticism, so to the extent not everyone in

187

Cuba is delighted with the way things are going, my goal is to hear their views and communicate them to the outside world."

Nacho scowled. "Okay, have you ever seen any pictures of East Berlin? Or talked to anyone who escaped from Hungary in 1956 when they tried to throw the Russians out? Ever since the war the Russians have sucked whatever they can out of every country they've annexed, and jailed or executed anyone who stood in their way. Cuba is not as backward as some people assume. We have manufacturing capacity, oil refineries, trained labor, nickel —a lot of untapped resources. Very tempting."

"But does Castro have to play ball with the Russians?" I asked.

"This is what you need to know about Fidel Castro. He got along great with the US until it became clear that Americans actually expected Cuba to pay them *something* for the property Fidel and Che were seizing, and to hold the elections he'd promised. But Fidel wants to maintain power himself, whatever the cost, and he doesn't like anyone to disagree with him, even though half the time he has no idea what he's doing.

"The Cuban communist party wasn't involved in overthrowing Batista, but they jumped into the game as soon as Fidel showed up in Havana. Unlike most Cubans, who expected Fidel to lead us to democracy, the communists told him just what he wanted to hear—that the people needed him, that only he could keep 'the masses' in line as Maximum Leader—and since then the communists have steadily taken over. First the military, with Raul

188

Castro and Che making the appointments—the only two people close to Fidel who were communists to begin with.

"So in less than a year Huber Matos, one of the heroes of the Revolution, resigns from his position in the Army because of all the communist infiltration. 'Fidel, you are destroying your own work. You are burying the Revolution,' he pleads on the radio. Fidel promptly puts him in jail for twenty years. That's when some of us knew we'd been betrayed.

"But most Cubans aren't communists, and they don't believe that Fidel is, either. Many of the poor have no idea what it would mean to be living in a communist state. To them Fidel is the Guardian, the Lord of the Manor, who will take care of everyone on his ranch as long as they are loyal to him—and his ranch is Cuba."

"What did you major in at Notre Dame?"

His face relaxed. "Biology."

"I might have guessed history."

"That was my minor."

I nodded and went back to my bird book.

* * * * *

One thing many Americans don't realize about Cuba is that it's big, with a land mass almost the size of Pennsylvania, although its topography is even more varied. The center of Cuba is the most Florida-like: flat and hot most of the year, sweltering in the summer. Even driving in an open jeep the heat and humidity were so intense that the breeze made me feel as if I were being pulled through boiling water. I did see sugar cane there—miles upon miles of it. The plant looks a lot like corn, with layers of thin green leaves that spread outward from a center stalk, and the fields covered every inch of arable soil as far as the eye could see.

The National Highway was the only paved road going through the center of the island, and it was used by every form of transportation: cars, buses, donkey carts, jeeps, and oxen carts. Outside Havana the traffic was fairly light, though, and the gentlemen driving their carts would move over and let us pass with a friendly smile and a wave.

During the first part of our drive I learned a lot about birds of the Caribbean from Mr. Bond. Try as I might, though, the memories of what had happened the previous night kept knocking on the door of the cupboard in my head where I'd expected them to sit quietly until I had more time to reflect. Although sometimes internal reflection is like holding a microscope over a bug. By the time you think you know what you're looking at, you've fried the thing to death.

We'd traveled for almost four hours when we reached the outskirts of Santa Clara, where Che had achieved his biggest victory in the revolt against Batista. The city lay at the edge of the Escambray Mountains. Cuban mountains are not large by American standards, but the change in landscape is quite dramatic. From a distance the ridges rise up from the flat plain like ancient sentries. The tallest range, the Sierra Maestra, lay farther south. It was there that Fidel and his cohorts plotted Batista's downfall. The Escambray were much closer, almost in Castro's backyard.

We took a route that skirted the city and headed south. Nacho soon turned off the paved road onto one that presented new challenges to the jeep's worn suspension system, and I let Mr. Bond retire to the back seat; I needed both hands to hang on as we rattled over ruts and bumps.

"We're lucky it's been dry for a few weeks," Nacho said after I emitted a painful grunt. "Sometimes this road is made of mud. Then it's even slower going, and by now I'd be teaching you how to push."

The terrain changed as we began our ascent into the jungle. The first thing that flashed through my mind was that it looked like the jungle exhibit at the Museum of Natural History in New York, only hotter, wetter, and larger.

At last we came to a clearing where a small thatch hut had been built near a well. Primitive does not begin to describe the place. "Is this one of your guest cottages?" I asked Nacho as he cut the engine.

He grinned at me. "Not up to your standards?"

"I'm not here on a vacation."

A wizened old woman came out of the hut as we approached and greeted Nacho with a huge smile and a kiss on both cheeks. He introduced me as a client, and we were soon sitting at a rough-hewn picnic bench in the shade, eating black beans, rice, and some sort of fried root. A cast iron stomach is another good qualification for international reporting.

After our meal Nacho pulled the jeep around to the back of one of the huts so that it was not visible from the so-called road. He came back with my backpack, his own large knapsack on his back, and a big blue can of Crisco. He presented the Crisco to our hostess. She beamed as if he had handed her a handful of jewels.

"Was that—did you just give her a can of lard as a gift?" I asked him in muted English as I laced up my hiking boots.

"Oh, yes. Lard is an essential ingredient in Cuban cooking, and very difficult to get now that our imports from the US are being disrupted. I'm telling you, if Louis the Sixteenth lost France over a lack of bread, a serious lard shortage might do the same for Castro and Cuba."

"Can the Russians supply lard?"

"Maybe. But it won't be as good as Crisco."

"I'll be sure to put that in my article."

Nacho handed me a small pair of binoculars as we started up a narrow trail not far from where he'd left the jeep. "So we'll be spending the night at another of my guesthouses deeper in. Early twilight is a decent time for bird watching—that's when they come home to their nests —so we shouldn't have to make any excuses if we run into someone. Which we probably won't, because my group hasn't done enough to make Castro take us seriously yet. But that will change soon enough."

As I listened I was also thanking the Lord for whoever had invented DEET. I could hear frustrated mosquitoes buzzing around my head like Kamikaze planes around a battleship.

"Who am I going to talk to?"

"Don't know. Depends on who can get to the designated meeting area. I can't give you names, because Castro could use their families as hostages."

"Would he do that?"

"Go to the prisons. Ask the people who are waiting

outside why their loved ones were arrested. 'Counter-revolutionary activities' is all you'll hear."

We walked in silence for a while after that. Then we heard the unmistakable crack of a rifle shot, a crack over our heads, and I was on the ground.

CHAPTER NINETEEN

Half of Nacho's body covered mine, but he'd pushed me, not fallen on me, so I didn't think he'd been hit. A hiss in my ear confirmed this. "Stay still." His right arm moved, and I saw a small pistol in his hand—he must have been carrying it in the outside pocket of his knapsack.

Now we could hear footsteps, and whoever was doing the walking did not care much about stealth. "You idiot," we heard a voice say, "you didn't hit nothing. If there was something, it's not going to be dinner tonight. A waste of a perfectly good bullet."

"I saw something move, though."

"That would have been us," Nacho said loudly, getting up and helping me to my feet. He tucked the pistol away. "What a nice welcome for my client."

Two very young men appeared before us. They were wearing the rough clothing of peasants—loose cotton shirts, baggy pants, sandals, and cowboy-style hats—and they both looked taken aback.

"Nacho? Oh, I'm s-sorry," stuttered the one with the rifle in his hand. "I—"

Nacho pulled out a cloth and handed it to me to wipe the dust off my face. My pulse was still pounding in my ears. "Never mind," he said, and turned back to me. "Maria, these are two friends of mine, Orlando and Perico.

Or at least I thought they were friends until they tried to kill us."

"But Nacho—"

He held up a hand. "Enough. Let's get back to your place before it gets dark. And Orlando? Take the gun away from that idiot."

"Sure thing," Orlando answered, and Perico meekly handed it over.

They fell in behind us, and I could hear Orlando delivering a stern—if muffled—lecture on the safe use of firearms to his remorseful companion. As the hillside became steeper and the foliage thicker, they also fell silent. The climb required stamina and concentration, leaving no room for conversation.

Just when I began to worry that we'd be carving our way through the undergrowth in complete darkness we saw the flicker of a fire, and Nacho told the boys to run ahead. "Whistle if there's trouble," he whispered. But all we heard was laughter, and after a minute Nacho motioned for us to proceed.

We hit another clearing, with two huts this time, set around a communal cooking fire. Two women were teasing the boys, one a sister, the other their mother, I supposed—and Nacho confirmed this when he made the introductions.

"We'll meet the men you want to talk to in the morning," he said to me after the family had welcomed us. "Now, some rice, and more beans, and bed."

Bed turned out to be a straw mat in the corner of the "girl" hut. Mama snored, but softly, and mingled with the chirping, whirring, and whooshes of the tropical night, the odd medley blended into a sort of lullaby. With my backpack under my head and my knife clenched in my hand, I fell asleep in no time.

* * * * *

We started out again right after dawn and soon hit a path that was fairly wide and pretty clear. It had been a service road to a now-defunct coffee plantation, Nacho explained. Coffee was a precarious crop, but the locals tried to maintain this road after these planters had abandoned their land. Two hours later we emerged from the shade into a small clearing where a small waterfall tumbled out of solid rock into a clear pool, like a magic spring out of a fairy tale.

"This is enchanting," I said.

"Fill your canteen if you want," Nacho advised. "Luckily there's a lot of good drinking water around here. Not much to eat, but a lot of clean water."

I did more than fill my canteen. I soaked every part of my body that I could get in the water without embarrassing myself, including my hair. It couldn't get much wetter than it already was, anyway.

"Ready to go," I said. I was determined to stay chipper.

"No need. We'll wait here."

"Oh. Good." I looked around. "Will they be long?"

"Don't know. Probably not. Unlike Fidel, our commanders don't like to keep guests waiting."

I smiled at this. Castro was notorious for keeping everyone, from family to heads of state, waiting—for hours, sometimes days. There was no such thing as an "appointment" with Fidel, only an expectation.

While we were waiting I took out my sketch pad and started to make some vague drawings of ferns, rocks, and a sorry attempt at a palm tree. Nacho moved over to watch.

"Are you an artist?"

"How can you look at this and think that?"

"Well, a student maybe."

"No. This is how I'm going to take notes. I have an excellent memory, but I'll use some of the items in this picture to help me remember certain details. Slash marks on the palm tree trunk, for example, for numbers. That way if I'm caught, no one's the wiser."

"Not a bad system."

"Let's hope so."

I heard a low, toneless whistle that could have been a bird, but Nacho's reaction let me know that it wasn't. He mimicked it, and seconds later two men joined us in the clearing.

And I realized that I was looking at Emilio's father.

His face was thinner and carried a few more lines, but it was easy enough to connect him with the wedding picture I'd seen. And his eyes, although rounder and more wide-set than his son's, somehow reflected the image of an Emilio who'd grown up and become very, very serious.

"Do we know each other?" he asked as I stared at him.

"No. But I know your son."

He took a rapid step forward. "Emilio? How?"

The man next to him put a warning hand on Armando's shoulder. It was large hand; he was a large man, half a head taller than anyone else there. A curly black beard covered the whole bottom half of his face, except where he'd trimmed it away to reveal a full, sensuous mouth. Just those lips and his wide, dark eyes would've made a whole movie theater full of women swoon if Hollywood ever got a hold of him.

"Maria, this is Blackie," Nacho said, gesturing. "He's the person you need to talk to."

"But I want to know—" Armando interjected.

"Perhaps we should put Armando's mind at ease," Blackie said. "Could you please answer his question, miss?"

"Emilio and Miriam are fine," I said. "I saw them the day before yesterday. They're staying with Carlos, Luis' friend."

"With Carlos? Why?"

"Because—because Luis is dead, Armando. I'm sorry."

I could see the amount of effort it took for him to keep his emotions in check. "And how do you know this about my family?" he asked, without moving a millimeter of his body other than his mouth.

"I met Luis last week, right after I arrived. At a café. He had Emilio with him, and we all hit it off." I left out the mermaid part of the story. "I had no idea that you were connected with this—effort—until someone came to get Miriam the other night, while I was at their apartment."

Armando's eyes widened. "Miriam told me they'd been having dinner with a Puerto Rican woman whom Emilio had befriended—that was you?"

"Yes. And I know it's an incredible coincidence, but no more than that. Your family doesn't know I'm here, they don't know that I'm a reporter, and no one would connect them in any way with any story that will come out about your activities here. Not through me, anyway."

"But my father... how is it that he's dead?"

"The day after you sent for Miriam—at least, I assume that's why she left dinner—the police came looking for you, and took Luis. Someone at the prison said he fell, and now he's dead. That's all the explanation we could get."

Blackie was looking at Armando with such profound sympathy that I found myself swallowing hard. The man radiated empathy. How could he be a soldier?

"Luis knew the risk he was taking," Blackie said to Armando, "and he would have happily given his life to save you, or Emilio, or Miriam. He's at peace."

Armando looked back up at him, and the anger he'd been controlling released itself word by word as he spoke, like a volcano slowly venting steam. "This is too incredible. She must have known I was in prison, and sought out my family. That's how she found us."

He whirled on me. "How do we know you're not a spy for Fidel? That you're not the reason my father is dead?"

"What could Miriam have told me that would have led me here?" I countered, "unless you endangered your family by telling her where you'd be."

"It was Father Lopez," Nacho interrupted. "He sent her to me, but it's been entirely up to us where we take her, and who she talks to. The rest of it is a pure coincidence."

"Or the work of God," Blackie said.

I could have pointed out that Armando's escape from prison was the real catalyst for his father's death, but I

stayed silent. That would not have been a helpful observation, and no matter what I said these men would have to
work out between themselves the extent to which they
were willing to trust me, or Father Lopez — or God, for that
matter.

"Go ahead and talk to her then," Armando said after a
prolonged silence, and I somehow exhaled through my
nose slowly enough to mask the fact that I'd been holding
my breath.

Blackie and I moved away and sat down while
Armando and Nacho took up positions on either side of
the clearing, although no one seemed very concerned that
we might be discovered by one of Castro's patrols. Even
sitting on a rock Blackie was a commanding presence, but
he came across as such a gentle giant that I found it
difficult to reconcile his whole demeanor with his decision
to take up arms.

"Thank you for trusting me. I assure you, I have no
connection with Castro," I began.

"I believe you." He sounded like a prophet when he
said it. Rather unsettling.

"So, why are you here? You, personally," I asked him.
"Oh, and forgive my doodling. It's a kind of picture code."

I showed him my drawing and he smiled. "Sedition
hidden in a palm frond. Clever. Well, to answer your
question, I fought against Batista with the student group
that formed a second battlefront, here in the Escambray:
the Revolutionary Directorate, started by students at the
University of Havana. I was a captain. We were independent from Fidel, although we tried to coordinate with him.
Our leader was Faure Chaumont. And if that king-maker

Herbert Mathews had put Chaumont on the front of the *New York Times* instead of Fidel, we'd have a democracy in Cuba today.

"When we returned to Havana, in January of 1959, the first thing Fidel did was to denounce the members of the Revolutionary Directorate for holding onto our weapons. 'Who needs weapons when we will soon have elections?' he cried out to the people. Of course, that was the first of his many lies. But we were ignorant of his desire to betray us, so we did as we were asked and turned in our guns. Once we were disarmed, our leaders were cut out of the decision-making process. Chaumont was shipped off to the USSR as an ambassador. It was as if we'd never existed.

"I came back to finish my university education in Santa Clara, and was elected head of the University Students' Federation here. I suppose that gave me a public voice. Then Fidel and Che began to steal the land, not just the plantations of the millionaires, but the fields of many small farmers as well.

"That hit this area very hard, as it is a land of *campesinos*, simple people of the hills. These men have nothing. They fought with Fidel, thinking they'd win the right to work their own land. They see work on a collective farm as little different from slave labor, and they don't trust governments of any kind. They want their freedom, and they're ready to fight again to get it. So, some of their leaders contacted me. And because I believe they're right, here I am."

"What do you hope to accomplish?"

"Isn't that obvious? We want to give Cubans what

Fidel promised them. Democracy. Freedom. Not this future of being another Soviet satellite. And as far as guerilla tactics are concerned, many of us are experienced, and we have the best teacher." With this he pulled a crumpled pamphlet out of his back pocket and held it out to me. The title read, "The Art of Guerilla Warfare," and the author was none other than Che Guevara himself.

"Ironic, no?" he commented as I took it from him. "It just came out, in time for us to use everything he wrote against him."

"Do you think that Fidel was always a communist? Or was that Che's doing?"

"It's more complicated than that. I think Fidel started out thinking he would bring democracy to Cuba. But he became hypnotized, addicted to the power—you could see it, on the first day he rode into Havana. It was like the Second Coming of Christ—vast crowds worshipping him, thousands upon thousands of people shouting his name. It must have been what he'd dreamed about when he was in prison, no—beyond what he could have imagined. Who could have imagined that?

"And when you watch that newsreel—you've seen it, yes? The white dove lands on his shoulder as Fidel greets the people who think he's their savior—like he's being anointed by the Holy Ghost. And he's a very powerful personality. He can convince almost anyone of almost anything—and can convince himself of anything at all. Like Hitler. And I mean exactly that. Like Hitler, he's putting guns in the hands of the people who felt cheated by life, who are now drunk with power, and the rest of the population can't quite believe what's happening."

"But how can you hope to succeed, when so many people here support him?"

"More Cubans are waking up to reality every day. Soon there will be no way to make a living unless you work for the government. But even then there aren't enough jobs, and for the people who have work, there's nothing to buy with the money they make. All we need to do is let the people of Cuba know that they have a choice, and they will do the rest.

"That's how you must help us, Maria. Get the word out. Let the Cuban people and the world know that Cuba doesn't have to go down this path. But what we don't have is time. Once Fidel gets his 'people's militia' trained and hands them Soviet weapons—after that, we'll be martyrs. And I'd rather win."

"Castro will claim you're holdovers from Batista," I pointed out, "or run-of-the-mill bandits, or CIA puppets."

"Yes, he will. But you be the judge. I'll be sending several men to talk to you over the next few hours. Each one has a family member who's been tortured or imprisoned by Castro's men, despite the fact that they fought with Castro to overthrow Batista. And as for the CIA—well, better that than the Russians. So far we haven't had any help from America, but we wouldn't refuse it. Perhaps there's someone you can tell that to, as well."

"That's a little out of my line."

"But you have an 'exclusive'"—and he used the English word, letting me know that he wasn't naïve regarding the power of the press and public relations—"so they'll have to listen to you, won't they?"

"I wish it were that easy."

CHAPTER TWENTY

"Mary Kate, what on earth have you done to your hair?"

Trust that to be a mother's first comment when her daughter comes home, no matter what the circumstances. I'd managed to get in a shower before I jumped on the plane, but the temporary brown rinse I'd used on my hair was still making its presence known, not to mention sunburn and a couple of mosquito bites in places where I never thought I'd need to spray DEET.

I touched a hand to my mangled locks. "It's just a rinse, Ma. It'll be gone in a couple of days. Is it okay if I stay for a while?"

"This is still your home. Are ya hungry?"

"Not yet. I need to get to work. I don't suppose there's any chance my old typewriter's still around here somewhere, is there? The portable?"

"It's in the closet," my mother said.

"What closet?"

"Why, in yer room, where else?"

"You actually kept it?"

"Why not? It's yours, isn't it? Look on the top shelf to the right, under the extra blanket. But don't be setting that noisy thing up in the kitchen. Go to the boarder's table. Put a cloth on it first, though. I don't want that contraption scratchin' the wood."

The boarder's table was in the dining room, where for years Ma had served simple breakfasts and dinners to our paying houseguests. When we were young we weren't allowed in there except to help and serve and clean, and even at thirty years old the fact that she'd given me dominion over that realm made me feel like the Queen of the Castle.

There are some stories you struggle over, and some that write themselves. As excited as I was to start this one, it proved pretty difficult to get out. I let people like Nacho and Blackie and even Emilio tell their stories in their own words as much as possible, letting them explain what they'd been through, and why they felt so betrayed by Castro. I talked about the fear that crept into bed with mothers at night, knowing that a sudden knock on the door could tear their family apart.

I couldn't name names, of course, and had to explain that I'd taken no pictures because the family members of those taking up arms against Castro would be in jeopardy if the regime could identify them. I explained how tightly Castro had clamped down on any kind of protest. And I mentioned that he was relying more and more on the Soviet Union, not only for economic support, but also by emulating the ways that it organized its society.

It took me twelve hours, two packs of cigarettes and half a bottle of Jameson's to perfect the story. When it was finished, I called Bentley.

* * * * *

"For God's sake, Katherine, you could've called me before now. I thought you'd been thrown in prison, or been eaten by a wild animal. Or worse." I could practically hear him bristling.

"So Father Lopez told you that I'd gone into the mountains? You two must communicate a lot more often than you first led me to believe."

"I can't believe he let you travel alone like that," he answered, ignoring my comment.

"I wasn't alone. Lopez trusts these men, and I can understand why. I wasn't worried." *Not much, anyway.*

"How long is it going to take you to write the story?"

"It's done. Are you still interested in helping me shop it around?"

"Absolutely."

"We're clear that you're not getting story credit for giving me a couple of leads, right? But if you do sell it to a major paper, or get me an international byline, I'll buy you a drink — and give you twenty percent."

"That's not necessary. Think of all the brownie points I'll get for bringing the editor who's smart enough to buy this piece such a great story. That'll be payment enough."

This did not sound like the Robert Bentley I knew, but I couldn't see the downside. "Okay. Thank you. But if you can't find it a home by tomorrow afternoon, I'll take it to Reuters myself and push. They could use something like this. It's more in-depth than anything they've done in Cuba, and it's a real scoop — proof that some very credible

Cubans are trying to get organized to do something about Castro."

"Well the timing's perfect. The fact that Congress eliminated Cuba's sugar quota has Castro foaming at the mouth. Can I meet you at Wally's in an hour? Buy you another Reuben and pick up the story?"

"Great idea. I'm starved."

* * * * *

It was thirteen long hours before Bentley called me back. I tried to wheedle the details out of him over the phone, but he stayed mum. Said I had to meet him in person. So it was back to Wally's.

"To whom, and for how much?" I demanded with my usual patience as I slid into the booth.

"Have you thought this through?" Bentley asked.

"Thought what through?"

"What happens when this story gets printed."

"Sure. I get paid, and then hopefully I get hired by a newspaper that will send me where I want to go, to write about what I want to write about."

"But that can't be Cuba."

I'd been so excited about the story I'd not stopped to think about the fact that once it hit, I'd never be allowed back in Cuba again. Not while Castro was running the show, anyway.

My face must have communicated my comprehension of his point, because Bentley didn't dwell on it. "These are your choices, Katherine. You can either sell the story with your name on it to the highest bidder and become persona non grata in Cuba; or, you can let it go out *without* a byline through the Copley News Service, and go back to Cuba right away, on salary, as a fully-credentialed reporter for them. No one would trace this story back to you, because no one knows you've been there—not as a reporter—and you'll have the new job you want. And deserve, I might add."

"Hold on—Copley? I don't mean to sound ungrateful, but they've been around, what, five years? It's just some California millionaire's hobby, not a real news service."

"Are you kidding? Copley's family has been in the newspaper business for decades. They own fifteen papers throughout California and the Midwest. Jim Copley has very deep pockets, excellent connections, and he's looking for reporters like you, whose careers he can help build, to make them—and the Copley News Service—household names. And he's very focused on South America."

"So how come you don't work for him?"

"I did, and I hope to again. Copley owns the *Illinois State Journal*, where I was before Reuters. He advised me to get some wire service experience before I tried to go international. That's why I'm at the UN, for a while, anyway."

"You sound like you've talked to him personally."

"I have. And I've talked to him about you. Personally."

"I see. So tell me, by any chance, does Jim Copley happen to be a graduate of Yale?"

He answered my question with an uncharacteristic eye roll, and then handed me an envelope. I ripped it open, pulled out a letter and a check, glanced at the check, and said, "Roberto, the next drink is on me. And the one after that. And, thank you. I must say, the way you Yale boys operate is starting to grow on me."

CHAPTER TWENTY-ONE

My second entry into Havana could not have been more different than the first. I was dressed in my usual uniform: cotton pants, a slim jacket with lots of pockets, and no purse. I hardly ever carried a purse. It slowed me down, and the temptation to carry more stuff than one needs is ever-present when toting a purse.

When I stepped off the plane I was immediately "escorted" to a small office where a member of the G-2 — Cuba's relatively new secret police, conveniently modeled after the Soviet KGB — searched my suitcase with exaggerated detail, all the while delivering a very thorough lecture. I must keep G-2 headquarters notified of where I was staying. I must not leave Havana without permission. I must not try to get any information out of the country without going through official channels. I must not attend any meetings closed to the press, or talk to anyone about what had happened in such meetings.

"And if you violate any of these rules, you'll be arrested and deported, like the reporters for *Look*, and *Life*, and the *Miami Herald*, and *Newsweek*, and the National Broadcasting Company," my official greeter warned, "or you'll be arrested for spying and imprisoned. And," he added, looking me up and down rather dismissively, "don't think you won't come under suspicion because you're a woman."

His English was excellent, so I saw no need to respond in Spanish. "I understand."

From a news perspective I'd arrived at an excellent time. Right after the US refused to buy any more Cuban sugar, Soviet Premier Khrushchev expressed his willingness to provide "rocket support" to Cuba if the US attempted to intervene in Cuba. Eisenhower responded by saying the US "would not tolerate" the establishment of a regime dominated by "international communism" in the Western Hemisphere. Suddenly the Cold War was hotter than it had been since the US had sent soldiers to North Korea, and Cuba was its molten center.

I'd arranged to stay in a small apartment complex not too far from Father Lopez' church, my address duly registered with the G-2. I picked up my key, dropped off my things, went to get something to eat, and by the time I returned my room had been searched. The sheets I hadn't even touched were rumpled, and my suitcase, still closed and locked, was upside down. "Welcome to the neighborhood," I said aloud to myself.

The next day I witnessed one of the rare public protests against Castro. Worshippers at the Havana Cathedral erupted from the noonday Mass shouting, "Cuba, yes! Russia, no!" and "Christ lives!" A few pro-Castro youths shouted back as the crowd burst into the square, but support for the anti-communists grew as they moved down the street. When a large public bus drove by plastered with the typical pro-Castro slogans, the church ladies attacked. It was almost comical watching women in their Sunday best smacking the sides of the bus with their brightly colored purses, shouting invectives at the surprised passengers, but their rage was real. It didn't take long for the patrol cars to show up.

After that, a special Mass was held at a large church in the posh Miramar neighborhood to commemorate the lives lost during the Spanish Civil War. When it was over the attendees poured out of the church, once again crying, "Cuba, yes! Russia, no! Christ lives!" This time they were greeted by plain-clothes members of the G-2, who were ready with fists and sticks, and the demonstration broke up much more quickly.

Three days later, when I called the office to ask if my story about the protests had been picked up and printed by any decent-sized papers, my very surprised editor told me that they'd never received my cable.

It wasn't hard to identify the two young men who rotated as my intermittent G-2 shadows. I wasn't important enough to be monitored every day, and I didn't acknowledge their presence when they were following me, but my room was searched regularly, and that was harder to ignore. They soon stopped bothering to put things back where they belonged, and I started leaving notes for them in Spanish, such as, "While you're under here, could you dust?" Or, "If you find the lipstick I lost, please leave it on the dresser."

Of course were other faces I searched for on the street every time I left my building. It wasn't long before I saw one of them.

I'd gone to La Floridita, Ernest Hemingway's favorite bar and public throne in Havana. Word had made the rounds that he was getting ready to leave Cuba after a six-month stay at his place outside Havana, spent fishing and finishing his latest work. I wasn't a Hemingway acolyte, but I couldn't resist the opportunity to get a glimpse of the legend in person; after all, he'd started his writing career as a reporter. So unless I had a reason to be somewhere else, I took to popping in at La Floridita every day around four o'clock, just in case the Great Man should be there downing a few more daiquiris before heading back to New York or Spain or Key West or Idaho or wherever else he had a home and a fan base.

A week after my return to Havana I got lucky; Hemingway was there holding court. I remember thinking that despite the adoration pouring over him, he didn't look like a happy man. There was a disconnect between the vigor of his speech and the look in his eyes; he was looking too hard for applause. And of course less than a year later he ended his life with a shotgun, so I suppose I was right about that. At any rate I didn't stay long. I didn't want to shake his hand or get an autograph. I just wanted to get a good look at him.

When I left the sidewalk outside the bar was full of people slowing down to glance through the windows, or stopping altogether, murmuring questions about what was going on inside the packed bar. And that's when I saw Raul.

He was standing across the street, hands in his pockets, looking mildly curious as he gazed at the entrance to the bar. When our eyes met his filled with incredulity, and I saw him start forward. I lowered my gaze and shook my head ever so slightly. I didn't think I'd been tailed that day, but I hadn't made any effort to shake one, either. Hoping that the crush inside La Floridita would make any meeting seem accidental, I turned and pushed my way back inside.

He found me planted at the back of a crowd of people trying to listen to whatever Hemingway was saying, as if the old drunk were giving the Sermon on the Mount. Raul and I talked without looking at each other.

"When did you get back?"

"A few days ago."

"What did you do to your hair?"

"This is the way it usually looks. Have you seen Miriam and Emilio?"

"Emilio tells me he's at a friend of the family's. A man named Carlos. That's all I know. When can I see you?"

"I'm not sure." I slipped my business card into his hand. He put it in his pocket. I shouldered my way out of the crowd and back out onto the street and hurried away.

I didn't want to see the look on his face when he read it.

* * * * *

The next day I did something I hadn't done in years. I went to confession.

There was a point in the history of Catholicism when it was incumbent upon practitioners to formally confess their sins prior to receiving Holy Communion. To facilitate this, many churches posted regularly scheduled hours when a priest would be "on duty" during the week to hear parishioners' confessions prior to the celebration of the Holy

Eucharist the following Sunday. That's how I knew exactly when and where I could have a private conversation with Father Guido Lopez.

"Forgive me Father, for I'm not here to confess my sins," I began as I took my place in the confessional.

"Well, my daughter, then why are you here?"

"To talk to you about what's happening in Cuba. I'm Maria — Katherine — O'Connor. Robert Bentley's friend."

"You've chosen an interesting meeting place," he said.

"I made sure I wasn't followed, but I don't think I can drop by every Wednesday. That might make life difficult for both of us."

"Undoubtedly."

"Are you still in touch with any of our old friends? Could you arrange for me to talk to someone?"

"And why should I do that? In the few weeks since your article appeared Castro has publically denied that there's any armed opposition against him, but he none-theless sent troops into the Escambray to crush the non-existent rebellion."

I'd heard nothing about this, and I was surprised — not only because of the swiftness of Castro's reaction to what I'd written, but also because of the condemnatory tone in which Father Lopez delivered this news.

"What — are you blaming me? Those men wanted their story told."

"They wanted to get help. Now, I believe I have some genuinely penitent people waiting to talk to me, Miss O'Connor. Good day."

Before I left the church I wrapped a dollar bill around one of my business cards and dropped it into the donation box. If my article had brought Castro's hammer down on the men I'd interviewed, I wasn't sure what I could do to make amends — but I was pretty sure Father Lopez could think of something.

CHAPTER TWENTY-TWO

"**W**e have an assignment for you," the Colonel said to Raul.

"I'm honored." What else could he say? The man was delivering an order, not an invitation.

"You'll be part of a very small team doing preliminary site scans to identify places where it would be practical to install sophisticated weapons systems. We may need such weapons in the event that the Soviets decide to assist Cuba in defending itself against an American attack," the Colonel explained.

"May I ask why I was chosen for this honor?"

"That should be obvious. You speak Spanish, you're an engineer, and you've proven yourself trustworthy. The real purpose of your exploration must be treated with the utmost secrecy. The Cubans working with you will be told that we're helping them to find sites to build new factories, and to discern the most cost-effective route for another cross-island roadway."

Che was right. I am Raul, the helpful ferret. What if Che found out through some other leak that the Soviets were investigating missile sites? Would he make good on his threat?

Raul knew he had to make a choice: cooperate with Che, or trust the Soviets to protect him. But even as he made his decision, he knew it wouldn't be that simple. Life never was.

"Colonel, concerning our candidness with the Castro regime..."

His comment hung in the air like a fat fly, waiting for the Colonel to notice it. He gave it an impatient verbal swat. "Yes?"

"I was approached by a member of the Cuban government. He requested that I communicate to him any information I might obtain about what we—that is, the Soviet Union—might be planning that could affect Cuba. Information that our leadership might not want to share with the Castro regime, at least not initially."

The Colonel regarded Raul impassively. "And did you report this contact right away?"

"No, sir. It was just a few days ago." Raul had to hope that a small lie wouldn't hurt him too badly at this point. "And I didn't—I wasn't sure who to tell. He made some threats, and if I'd gone to the wrong person, and word got back to him—"

"Who was this 'member of the Cuban government'?"

"Che Guevara."

"I'd say your concerns were understandable," the Colonel said after a small eternity, "but I'll have to discuss this with—others."

"Yes, sir. Of course. But he did threaten—"

"In the meantime, begin work as planned. You'll meet the rest of your team tomorrow. I'll let you know in a day or two what to do about Guevara's request."

* * * * *

"I know how to use a telephone," Emilio said, shaking off Raul's attempt to help him dial the number after they'd crammed themselves into a phone booth.

"So go ahead."

Emilio dialed the digits with meticulous care, making sure the dial spun all the way around to zero before dialing the next number.

"It's ringing," he said.

"I can hear that," Raul replied. The pace of his pulse quickened with each ring.

It rang four times before she answered. "Miss Maria, it's me," Emilio practically shouted, "but don't say my name. You know who this is, right? I'm calling because I have a message for you. An old friend wants to meet you at the place where you met for the first time. Tonight. At nine o'clock. What should I tell him? Okay."

Emilio hung up and optimistically checked the coin return to see if the phone had malfunctioned and kicked out a peso. "No luck," he said with a sigh.

"She said no?" Raul responded, aghast.

"I was talking about the coin return. She said yes, what else? Let's go. It's too hot in here."

* * * * *

Raul pulled Maria's card out of his pocket and looked at it for the hundredth time. Except it didn't say Maria. It said Katherine O'Connor, Copley News Service, with a California address. What did it mean?

219

The night that she'd come to him he felt as if they'd shared some ultimate truth—and he wasn't so romantic or so naive to think it was the sexual act that had created the remarkable harmony between them. It was as if they'd both let go of all the ways one person tries to protect himself from another.

He looked back down at her card. Or maybe he was just kidding himself. Maybe there had been no truth there at all.

And now he was a pawn in the Great Game between the Soviets and the Americans. He could be discarded or crushed at any moment. Or he could plod on, get through this, and be safe. Again. And then what?

He sat on the beach and waited.

* * * * *

Long before he could make out the features of her face he could tell that it was Maria by the way she moved. She stepped harder with her right foot than her left—did she even know that about herself?

"A beautiful night for a mermaid to return to the water, don't you think?" he said when she was within earshot, and instantly regretted it. *She'll think I'm being sarcastic.*

But she smiled, and there it was again, that connection between them. The completion of a circuit.

He took her hand. "Let's go to where we can have some privacy."

"There's no one else here," she said, without taking her eyes off him.

"But there soon could be. The patrol. I don't think they'd give me too hard a time, but better not to issue an invitation."

He'd found a spot close by, underneath the arching branches and enormous leaves of a large tropical bush. Elephant ears, had he heard someone call them? The branches formed a protective cave of greenery, and he pulled her down into it. They sat next to each other on the smooth sand, both cross-legged. She looked so pensive, leaning back on her hands—thinking about a problem that was both here and somewhere else at the same time.

He studied the three freckles on the side of her nose. "It's an isosceles triangle," he said.

"A what? What are you talking about?"

"A triangle, where the three angles are the same size, and the three legs are the same length. Here. I can trace one perfect isosceles triangle between these three freckles."

She reached up and took his hand away from her nose, but she didn't let go of him.

"I like your hair red," he said.

"This is the real me. Not like the me you met before."

"I think I met the real you. Maybe you told me some things that weren't true, or maybe you neglected to tell me some things you should've told me, but I know the real you."

"No," she whispered, "no, you don't."

He brought his free hand to her chest and placed it above her left breast. "I know your heart."

She gave him a look like that of a hopeful child who's been told to expect a present, yet doesn't quite trust the giver to make good on his promise. But she didn't leave her vulnerability on display for long.

"We need to be honest with each other," she said, in a tone of voice that reminded him of a school teacher handing out an assignment, "there's a lot at stake, and we don't—"

"If I'm honest with you, will you be honest with me?"

"Yes." She didn't hesitate at all. That was good.

"Well, then, I will tell you who I am. Who I really am. Do you have time now to listen to my story, Maria?"

She nodded. So he began.

* * * * *

He started with a story about a journey.

He'd been drifting—not in and out of sleep, exactly, more like wafting through a memory of what sleep was supposed to be—when he'd heard someone shouting.

"My butt's turning to ice! Pull me out!"

Raul blinked and looked around, trying to focus on the noise. It was one of the kids from Barcelona—Diego. He was hanging out of the boxcar's one small window: head, shoulders, arms, and legs more or less inside the car, with his rear end pushed through to the outside. Two other boys, Manuel and Juan, were standing underneath him, just beyond reach of his legs, doubled over with laughter. Some of the other children were laughing as well; a few of the younger ones whimpered, unnerved by the older boy's panic.

They'd been on the train for twenty-five days: thirty children ranging in age from seven to fourteen. For the first three weeks the train had stopped once a day. A couple of adults would slide open the heavy door, distribute bread and canned beans, and give the children a chance to find a sheltered spot to squat near the tracks. No one wanted to be the first one to soil the sparse amount of straw spread around the floor that they used as bedding.

But since they'd begun to cross the wide Siberian plain there'd been no stops, no grownups, and no more food.

Raul gently removed his arm from under his sister's head and lifted himself up onto one elbow. He couldn't help but smile—Diego's plight was funny—but he was obviously suffering. The other boys shouldn't have let him stay up there like that.

"C'mon. Pull him back in," he ordered with the authority his age bestowed upon him as the eldest of the group.

"If his ass weren't so big, he wouldn't have gotten stuck," Juan replied.

"Next time I'll shit in your face," Diego shouted down at him. "Pull me out!"

Still grinning, Juan propped his back up against the wall and allowed Diego to grasp his upraised arm. Juan pulled as Diego pushed against the wall with his feet.

"It's not working," Diego gasped, "pull harder!"

"Hang on, lardass," Manuel answered, and joined Juan under the window. They each pulled hard on one of Diego's arms, and with a sudden pop he fell out of the window back into the car, landing flat on his face, pants down to his knees, his bright red buttocks fully exposed.

A gust of frigid air followed him, converting the children's laughter into shrieks of agony. "Close the window, you idiots." Raul yelled.

223

"Get up and close it yourself," Manuel shot back, but he leapt up and grabbed the lever on the window to shut it as he spoke.

Diego hauled himself off the floor. His nose was bleeding. "I can't feel my butt," he choked out, wiping his nose on his sleeve.

"Try pulling up your pants," Manuel suggested, setting off another round of raucous laughter.

One of the older girls stood up, hands on hips, face alight with righteous anger. "That was so mean. We'll have to cut a hole in the floor to do our business. No more behinds out the window."

"Cut a hole with what?" another boy responded. "Your tongue? It's sharp enough."

Raul decided that he wasn't going to participate in the argument, but he wasn't going to stop it, either. As long as it didn't turn violent a good argument helped pass the time, and was more entertaining than competing to see who could pull the biggest louse out of their hair.

He lay back down next to his sister, who was curled up on the floor like a lost and forgotten ball. Raul wrapped his body around hers, his stomach up against her bony back, and stretched his coat across them both in a futile attempt to stave off some of the cold.

Then his sister let out a long, ragged sigh, raspy and guttural. Raul knew what that sound meant, understood the message it conveyed. He sat up, grabbed one of her shoulders, and rolled her over. Vacant brown eyes stared up at him. He lifted her torso off the floor. Her mouth fell open as her head rolled backward. Nothing. He tried to call out her name, tried to summon her small soul back into her shrunken body, but all that emerged from his throat was a long, keening wail.

The sound silenced the other children with the force of a slap. This was not the first dead body they'd seen on this trip, and they all knew it would not be the last.

Their journey had not begun this way. It had not begun in Leningrad, where they were herded onto the train in an effort to protect them from the imminent Nazi invasion. Their true journey had begun four years earlier, in Spain, when thousands of Spanish children had boarded boats that would take them to Russia, where Stalin, their dear "Uncle Joe" was going to educate them and keep them safe while their parents struggled for freedom from Franco and the fascists.

Or perhaps it's more accurate to say that his journey began even earlier, during the late afternoon of a clear day in April of 1937, when he, his sister, their mother, and hundreds of other women and children were all headed home after a day spent sampling and purchasing the wares of the farmers and peddlers who traveled from all over the countryside to sell their produce, meats, flowers, and trinkets, once a week, on market day.

He'd looked up when he heard the planes approaching. His mother didn't notice them at first, but even at ten years old he was fascinated by all technological marvels, particularly those that could fly. He tugged on his mother's coat and pointed; she looked up, swept his three-year-old sister into her arms and shouted, "Run!"

"But see?" he said, pointing at the insignia that was now plainly visible, "they're German planes. Why would the Germans—"

Then the bombs began to fall, and in every corner of the unprotected village of Guernica the mothers and children, fathers and grandfathers, husbands, wives and grandmothers all ran, and screamed, and ran.

CHAPTER TWENTY-THREE

Sometimes looking at me, but mostly just staring out at the dark expanse of the sea, Raul released the memories of his childhood. He moved back and forth through time, always coming back to the war: his sister's death; being saved from annihilation by having a snowball thrown at his head; and working in a factory where no supervisor cared who was maimed or killed, because they had to build airplanes and tanks to keep on fighting the Germans or they were all as good as dead, anyway. And he talked about hunger, so deep and unrelenting that not only your stomach but your blood and your bones all screamed for food.

He told me about the end of the war, and how when he made it back to a classroom he discovered that he had a talent for mathematics, which unlocked the world of physics, and ultimately physical engineering. When he started dreaming about mathematical equations he stopped dreaming about Spain, and when he started building bridges in his dreams he stopped dreaming about the war.

He told me about coming to Cuba, about how Che Guevara had threatened him, and that he was now caught up in a game between Che and the Soviets that he had no interest in playing, but did not know how to escape.

He must have talked for almost two hours, and when he'd finished he lay on the sand and pulled me down next to him.

"I'm sorry you had to go through all that," I whispered into his ear.

"It was no worse than what happened to many, many others."

"But that doesn't lessen what happened to you, Raul."

He turned his head so that we were almost face to face. "Now you know everything about me. No one else in the world can say that, Maria." He kissed me, and I could taste the truth of his gift on his lips. But the kiss did not last long.

"Your brain is running away from me," he said as he pulled away.

"No, I—"

He put one finger on my lips, and when he was sure I had surrendered to silence he used it to stroke my cheek. "Truth is a burden, I know. Easier to ignore than to face. But please, don't run away. Trust me with who you are."

"I'm not from Puerto Rico. But I am an American. An American reporter, from New York. I came here to try and discover the truth about Castro."

He froze, and the connection between us vanished, leaving a hot pain in my gut that felt a lot like grief.

"Whose truth?"

"Not his version, at any rate," I answered, unable to keep the defensiveness out of my voice. Raul sat up, and I felt oddly ashamed and exposed as I lay there alone on the sand.

"So this card you gave me—Copley Press—that's who you've always worked for?"

I raised myself into a sitting position before replying. "No. I wasn't working for a company when I first came, but they hired me to come back. To come back to Cuba."

"Copley Press hired you? Not the CIA?"

"No, of course not."

He closed his eyes. "Of course not."

"Raul, I don't work for the CIA. I'm just a reporter. And I would never say or do anything to jeopardize your safety." I felt an unwelcome frisson of panic rustle through my chest. *Tell me you understand. Please.*

When at last he opened his eyes I saw such deep sadness there that I had to look away.

"My future is beyond my control at this point, whether you're telling the truth or not," I heard him say. "And I knew there was something you hadn't told me, but I confided in you anyway. I—"

I kissed him. I kissed him and tried to tell him in that one kiss that I was sorry I'd ever deceived him, and that he was right about what there was between us even though I didn't understand it, couldn't explain it, and didn't want it to exist at all.

But I hadn't told him the truth that night. I didn't know what the truth was.

CHAPTER TWENTY-FOUR

I came back to my sorry excuse for an apartment to find it in a more abject state of disarray than usual. My clothes were flung around the room as if they'd been the object of an angry debutante's tantrum. The bed linens lay in piles on the floor. My suitcase sat open on the naked bed, its cheap lining in tatters. Even the mattress was askew.

This was not a routine search. The G-2 had either been looking for something specific, giving me a warning, or both. But I was emotionally overwhelmed and physically exhausted, so I grabbed one sheet and a pillow, left everything else where it lay, and crawled into bed. If they'd found anything suspect they'd let me know soon enough.

The next morning I resolved to tuck my tumultuous feelings for Raul somewhere far away from the active part of my mind. We hadn't made any plans or promises the previous night. I didn't know if he ever wanted to see me again, and even if he did, I was afraid that it might be dangerous for both of us to continue our — whatever it was — especially if Raul was a Person of Special Interest to Che Guevara. Moreover, given the attention I'd just received from the G-2, I might not have much time left in Cuba. *No more distractions*, I told myself as I shoved my slacks back into a drawer. *Concentrate on doing your job.*

Luckily it wasn't hard to find news; every day I had something new to report. Castro continued his nationalization tirade. When Eisenhower told the remaining American-owned oil refineries in Cuba not to refine Soviet oil, Castro seized them all. Soon afterward he claimed the power company, two major mining concerns, the Portland Cement Company, the Illinois Glass Company, Goodyear Tire, Firestone, and thirty-three American-owned sugar mills "for the people."

But because the skilled technicians who ran the plants left Cuba as soon as possible after the businesses were nationalized, most of these acquisitions did not translate into more jobs; quite the contrary. Few of those who remained knew how the machines worked or the proper way to manage production, so the equipment sat idle, while the workers received massive pay cuts for the privilege of working for the State.

When calling in copy I had to keep my language as neutral as possible, but oftentimes by translating pieces from *Revolución* – one of the few newspapers still operating, and by now the official mouthpiece of the State – I could let my readers decipher the truth about what was going on. It wasn't difficult to read between the lines when Castro explained that the officials elected to head the professional societies governing lawyers, doctors, dentists, pharmacists and journalists were being replaced because they were not sufficiently "enthusiastic" about "revolutionary policies."

In early September my editor at Copley sent me a cable. Castro was coming to New York to address the

General Assembly of the United Nations. I was to come home and cover the story.

* * * * *

I flew to New York the day before Castro was scheduled to arrive. When I arrived at Ma's house I found her sitting in the kitchen at the large oak table that had served as our family's dining table, homework desk, work bench, and conference table all throughout my childhood. She was saying the rosary. I saw her lips move as she rolled a delicate bead between her right thumb and forefinger, eyes closed, swaying gently as she murmured the Hail Mary.

"Ma?" I asked gently.

She looked at me with a gaze so devoid of recognition it made me catch my breath. Then she furrowed her brows, looked down, and tilted her head, as if listening to some silent voice. Her expression cleared.

"Mary Kate. You've come home."

I dropped to my knees, put my arms around her once-ample midsection, and laid my head against her chest, something I hadn't done since I was a very young girl. "Yeah, Ma," I said, "I'm home."

I didn't bother to remind her that I'd sent a telegram to Tim asking him to call her and tell her that I was coming home —or to come by and tell her in person if she didn't pick up. I knew better than to send a telegram straight to Ma. She'd never open it.

* * * * *

I decided not to waste time covering Castro's arrival. There would be hundreds of reporters trying to get some decent copy about his "Return to US Soil," and anything he said publically would be duly recorded by all of them. I wanted to get up close and personal—a difficult task given Castro's popularity and the security detail surrounding him, which included his Cuban bodyguards as well as members of the American Secret Service.

But I had a plan.

I knew that Castro would attend the opening session of the General Assembly the next day, so I cajoled (or hounded, depending on your point of view) Robert Bentley into convincing someone he knew at the UN to let me slip in through a service entrance. That accomplished, a five dollar bill helped convince another low-level UN employee to spill the beans about the Cuban delegation's exit plan; they'd be leaving soon after the opening address, but not by the same way they'd come in—Castro and his entourage would go down an interior stairway and exit through a service door that led to the loading dock, where their cars would be waiting. (Nowadays you'd never get information like that from the support staff—at least not for five bucks—but this was before Martin Luther King and the Kennedys were assassinated, so security was not as tight as it would become a few years later.)

I planted myself in the middle of the service stairwell and waited.

Ninety minutes into the opening proceedings I heard the upper floor door open, followed by the footfall of heavy boots; most of the Cuban delegation had come dressed in their army fatigues. When the first two security guards reached me they called a quick halt, and one of the Secret Service agents who was with them demanded to see my pass.

"This area is off limits to the press," he barked when I showed it to him. "Get back where you belong before I have you arrested."

"Certainly. Sorry about that. Just trying to find an uncrowded ladies' room," I said sweetly, as I stepped aside to let the whole group walk by.

I'd seen Castro at a couple of the "speeches to the masses" that he'd given in Cuba—including one recent six-hour marathon he'd delivered in the pouring rain, resulting in a case of pleurisy for him and pneumonia for God knows how many others—but I'd never been this close to him. He didn't even glance at me as he went by, looking withdrawn and strangely subdued, exuding none of his alleged charismatic aura.

I waited until he'd reached the landing below me, and then I shouted, "Dr. Castro, who'd you root for? Havana Reds or Almendares Blues?"

Castro stopped short and turned to look up at me. The rest of the group had no choice but to do the same. "Go on, get out of here," the Secret Service agent closest to Castro ordered, looking ready to facilitate my exit personally.

It may have been the subject matter of my question, or it may have been the fact that he despised his Secret Service babysitters, but Castro held up a hand to silence the agent. At the same time I saw one of the Cuban bodyguards bring a hand to his gun belt.

"How does a girl, not from Cuba, know anything about Cuban baseball?" Castro asked loudly, and I could see some of his fabled energy returning to his face, as if some interior switch had been flipped on.

I gave him an utterly guileless smile and answered in Spanish, "Anyone who truly loves baseball knows all about the great Cuban teams. And as one ardent baseball fan to another, I have a gift for you, if you will do me the honor of accepting it."

I figured that even if he was concerned about an assassination attempt, Castro wasn't going to show any apprehension in front of all these men because of a *girl.* Sure enough, he gestured for me to approach. I started down the stairs, but the young man with his pistol at the ready placed his unencumbered hand on Castro's shoulder.

"Allow me, Fidel," he said. Castro shrugged. I stopped, and the guard walked up to where I stood.

"It's in my jacket pocket," I said in Spanish when he reached me, sticking my right hip forward, hokey-pokey style. "Would you like for me to get it, or would you like to fish it out yourself?"

"You," he snapped, annoyed and a tad embarrassed.

I pulled two baseball cards out of my pocket and handed them to him. He looked at them quizzically before an excited grin broke out on his bearded face.

"Hey Fidel! It's Orestes Miñoso!"

You see, as a nation, Cubans love baseball, and in 1960 Cuban fans still loved their two best teams—the Reds and the Blues—as deeply and divisively as New Yorkers loved their Yankees and Bostonians loved their Red Sox. I thought if I could get Castro to start talking about baseball, his world-famous loquacity might lead our conversation into even more fascinating topics. And I'd had a hunch about where I could find the kind of envy-inducing, Cuban baseball memorabilia that could serve as an ice-breaker.

Because the Cuban teams were integrated much earlier than their American counterparts, some of the best players from the American Negro Leagues used to play in Cuba, initially during the American off-season, and as regulars after the American Negro Leagues disbanded in the early 1950s. This understandably created more interest in Cuban baseball among black American baseball fans than was typically the case with most white fans (at least until some of the Cuban greats began defecting to the US in the mid-sixties). So I'd done some research, discovered a well-reputed store in Harlem, gone there the previous day, and struck gold — all for a mere fifty cents.

"That's right," I explained, still in Spanish, "Minnie Miñoso's rookie card. Don't find many of those. And the other one is Tony Oliva."

Visibly intrigued, Fidel climbed the few stairs separating us and took the cards from the guard. He studied them briefly, then gave me a look of sardonic amusement. "You're a very knowledgeable baseball fan — and a very intrepid reporter," he said wryly.

I smiled back at him. "*Diehard* baseball fan, and brand new reporter for the Copley Press."

His expression didn't change, but I could tell he was evaluating me. After a few seconds he tucked the cards into his shirt pocket. "Come with us," he said as he turned to go back down the stairs.

It took all of my willpower not to let go with a victory shout as I followed him.

The Cuban delegation was staying at the Shelburne, a mid-range hotel not far from the UN. I didn't ride back to the hotel in the same car as Castro—I suppose someone in his security detail objected—but no one was going to challenge his decision to bring me along. What Castro wanted, he got; even though, as was often the case, he forgot about it a short time later.

Scores of people were gathered outside the Shelburne when we arrived. I saw a few with placards reading things like, "Free Cuba!" and, "Where's Our Democracy?" but most of them were cheering Castro with cries of "Viva Fidel!"

Inside the situation was even more chaotic. When Castro walked into the lobby dozens of his rabid fans poured in behind him, shoving the hotel's overburdened security personnel out of the way and confounding the efforts of Castro's own security detail to keep them outside. The reporters who'd been able to secure permission to enter the lobby sprang at him, shouting questions, while a barrage of flashbulbs blazed and popped overhead. The assistant manager grabbed the arm of one of Castro's bodyguards and shouted, "Someone has to tell Castro that you people can't bring live chickens into the rooms."

At that point a senior-looking Cuban official stormed up to Castro and declared, in a voice meant to be heard above the din, "They want a $10,000 security deposit against damages. That is outrageous!"

Castro, looking more animated by the second, agreed, just as loudly. "Ridiculous! We were sent to this hotel by the American government in order to be harassed. We'll move to new accommodations. We can camp out in

Central Park. We're mountain people, after all, used to the fresh air."

And that's how, a few hours later, I found myself on the way back to Harlem, this time at the invitation of Fidel Castro.

* * * * *

First Castro & Company went to the UN where they raised havoc, with Castro making accusations and threatening to camp out in the United Nations rose garden. Then one of his men announced that they'd been offered forty rooms at the Hotel Teresa, "the Waldorf Astoria of Harlem," and off we went.

Someone must have started spreading the word that Castro was on the move before his caravan of vehicles left the UN, because by the time we crossed 116th Street hundreds of jubilant well-wishers filled the roads: blowing car horns, whistling, banging pots, clapping, cheering, and slowing the delegation's progress to a crawl. Hundreds more hung out of windows or clung to fire escapes, waving handkerchiefs and dishcloths and throwing make-shift confetti, shouting with unrestrained joy all the while. Many chanted, *"Cuba, si! Yanqui, non!"* the same way Castro's followers did during his mass rallies in Havana.

It was then that the brilliance of Castro's strategy hit me; by throwing the rich out of Cuba and making life intolerable for its middle class, he'd tacitly told "White America" to go to hell, and these people loved him for it. Now, by staying in Harlem, he could advertise his popu-larity among the poor, and rub America's nose in its race problem by putting it under a spotlight. Because where Castro went, the international press followed — and Harlem was not a place the rest of the world usually got to see.

Castro's move was a public relations grand slam, and although I had no proof at the time, I doubted that the decision to move to the Hotel Teresa had been spontaneous. What I did know was that there weren't many reporters along for the ride, which put me in an excellent position.

How would it feel to be treated this way? I thought to myself as I took it all in. Surely being the object of such massive hero-worship could become addictive, perhaps even turn a relatively humble man into a narcissist — and by all accounts Castro had begun life with an oversized ego.

What is Castro thinking right now, I wondered, as thousands of black Americans screamed his name? *'If the people of Harlem treat me like a god, well then, why should I offer the people of Cuba a democracy, when they could be ruled by a deity instead?'*

It was after midnight by the time we arrived at the Hotel Teresa. Although groups of euphoric well-wishers still surrounded the building, they didn't impede our progress as we made our way into the lobby. The handful of other reporters who'd been given permission to come along looked decidedly uncomfortable. Members of the Negro press were already in the lobby, waiting. Almost everyone cheered as Castro shook the hand of the hotel's owner and posed for some pictures. Pleading fatigue, he asked for food for himself and his "guests."

I ducked out and asked a housekeeper if I could use a

telephone. She stared at me wide-eyed, and it took a second for me to realize she must have been astounded to see a white woman in the hotel, much less asking to use the phone. But she directed me to one, and I was able to call in my story before deadline—and well before any of the white male reporters were able to call in theirs.

When I hung up I turned to find one of the *barbudos* watching me, his face radiating suspicion. As I brushed past him Raul's voice floated into my brain, repeating the last thing he'd said when we parted: "Be careful, Maria. People will be watching you. All the time. Wherever you go. There is always someone watching."

CHAPTER TWENTY-FIVE

W hat happened the next day also made headlines around the world. Around four o'clock a few police vans showed up in front of the Hotel Teresa. Several dozen of New York's finest jumped out and began unloading road barriers. Others cleared onlookers away from the perimeter of the hotel.

I dipped into a brogue and asked an officer who had the ruddy, round face of an Irishman what was behind the extra ruckus, hoping he'd be willing to give another progeny of the Emerald Isle some inside information.

"Castro's having company," he said with a wink. "Stay close." I dashed into the lobby of the hotel and secreted myself in the ladies' room so that I wouldn't be herded out along with the rest of the reporters milling around the place. A short time later I heard sirens heralding a VIP arrival. I came out of hiding to see Fidel Castro greeting none other than Nikita Khrushchev, the Premier of the Soviet Union. Once again I was in the right place at the right time, able to call in my story long before most of the other wire services knew what had happened.

I hadn't been able to finagle a private interview with Castro, but I went home that night gloating with pride. *This will make your reputation. You're reporting from the eye of the storm. Not exactly Pulitzer Prize material, but enough to get someone's attention.*

And I was right about that, but the attention I received wasn't from anyone I'd expected.

* * * * *

The phone rang at seven o'clock the next morning. Ma came and woke me up; God knows how long she'd been awake. Regular sleep seemed to be one of the many activities slipping away from her daily routine.

"Hello?"

"Hi, Katherine. It's Robert. Robert Bentley."

"Why are you calling me this early?"

"You've done a fantastic job covering Castro."

"Thanks. But you could've just given me a slap on the back the next time we saw each other, instead of waking up my mother."

"Was that your mother? I'm sorry. I wanted to check on your schedule for the morning. Someone would like to meet you."

"So now you're running a dating service?"

The ensuing silence told me that he was trying to come up with an appropriate comeback, and failing. "This is business," he said at last. "Someone from the State Department would like to talk to you about what you've learned about Castro."

"Other than confirming that he's a baseball fan, I haven't learned anything that hasn't appeared in print under my byline."

"You never know. Sometimes when you look at

something from a different direction, you discover new information."

"How enigmatic."

"Could you get to the East Side by nine o'clock?"

I was tempted to blow him off, but he had been instrumental in getting me to Cuba, and in getting me a job at Copley (which was somewhat strange, given that he worked for a rival news agency, although he'd implied that he planned on returning to the Copley fold at some point).

"How do I know that this will be worth my while?" I asked.

"You'll have to trust me on that one."

This time the pause was on my end. "Okay, I guess I owe you."

"Thanks."

He gave me the address and I hung up. I turned around to find Ma starting at me intently.

"Good morning," I said.

She didn't answer. She just kept looking at me. I waited a few seconds and then started to go around her. To my surprise she grabbed my arm and shot me a question with something akin to her old fire.

"Why do you do it, Mary Kate?"

It was my turn to stare. "Do what, Ma?"

"Go trottin' all over the world, puttin' yerself in harm's way. What good is it doin' ya? What good is it doin' anyone?"

"Ma, you know I've wanted to be a reporter ever since I was eight years old."

"It seems to me that if you're riskin' yer life, you should be doin' some good for someone in the process."

"Who says I'm risking my life? And I do have a reason. The public has a right to know—"

"Damn the public's rights. Make sure you're doin' what you're doin' for a reason other than to see yer name on the front page of some paper that'll be tossed in the trash the next day."

I was well and truly flabbergasted, not only by my mother's use of (even mild) profanity, but also because she'd never asked me why I wanted to be a reporter, or even what I liked about the job. Now I was receiving a lecture on the subject.

But apparently that was all she wanted to say, for she turned away and walked down the hall toward the kitchen. I saw her pull her rosary out of the pocket of her robe, and decided against continuing the conversation.

* * * * *

The address Bentley had given me led to an office building a couple of blocks north of the Metropolitan Museum of Art. He was waiting in the lobby when I arrived, wearing what I'm sure was a Burberry raincoat, garnished with a cashmere scarf that was placed around his shoulders more as a statement than a way to keep warm. He wore his hat at what Jane Austen would have described as "a rakish angle," and looked for all the world like an Ivy League version of Sam Spade.

I had to suppress a giggle as we shook hands. "Come on up," he said, pressing the call button on the elevator. It was bronze or brass or some sort of expensive metal, gussied up by a geometric Art Deco motif. "Posh place," I said as I got in. "State Department must be doing pretty well under the Republicans."

"This is not a regular departmental office."

"Yeah, I noticed the lack of a sign. Nothing saying, 'State Department lives here.'"

"I think it's a temporary space they leased, to bring in some extra people to handle everything stirred up by the UN General Assembly. There's Indonesia, the Congo, Cuba—all kinds of global action. Must need more hands on deck."

"Well, who exactly am I supposed to meet? I have a busy day planned. This better not be a waste of time."

"I'm pretty sure it won't be," he said as the elevator door opened. He took off his hat and let me exit first, very gentlemanly.

The desk where there should have been a receptionist was vacant. I followed Bentley down a hallway, past six rooms, and noticed that not a single door was open.

He knocked on the door to a corner office and opened it without waiting. A thin, balding, middle-aged man with a professorial air stood up and offered me his hand. "Thank you for coming, Miss O'Connor. I'm Walter Pershing, US State Department, Bureau of Cuban Affairs. Please, come in and sit down."

Bentley and I dropped into the two chairs facing his desk. I didn't waste any time. "Could we get right down to business? I need to get to the UN by noon."

Pershing gave me a grave smile. "Certainly." He picked up a large manila envelope, took out a thin stack of photographs, and laid them out in front of me like a row of mug shots. "Do you remember seeing any of these men at the Hotel Teresa?"

They were all pictures of black men. A couple of them had been taken from a distance and blown up so the face could be seen in detail. I glanced at each of them.

"Why on earth should I answer that question?"

"Because your country needs you, Miss O'Connor."

"Is that so? Then tell me who these men are before I go playing games with their lives."

He drummed his fingers on the desk, looked at Bentley, then back at me. I glanced over at Bentley, whose face wore a smug, told-you-so expression.

"They're members of a group determined to bring communism to our shores."

"Geez, I thought Senator McCarthy had rooted out all the commies hiding amongst us," I said. "And any he missed, Hoover and the boys at the FBI would take care of."

Pershing seemed unimpressed by my sarcasm. "You've been to Cuba. You've seen what Castro has done, what he's doing. He came to the US to reach out to men of similar minds, especially within the black population, to inspire them to engage in the kind of terrorist tactics that he's used so successfully."

"Look, I'm no Castro fan, but I don't see him making much headway in America," I said. "In other Latin American countries, maybe, but not here."

"Castro will soon be in Khrushchev's pocket. We could have nuclear missiles pointed at America in no time."

"I thought there were already a lot of Soviet nukes pointed in our direction. Why sweat over a few more?"

"You have no desire to treat any of this seriously, do you?"

"I take everything the Russians do seriously, Mr. Pershing. I know they took the opportunity to slaughter thousands of Polish and Ukrainian political prisoners while retreating from the Germans in 1941. I know about the rape and pillage of Berlin. I know about the mass starvation that resulted from Stalin's determination to impose collective farming. I've interviewed some of the Hungarians who fled when the Soviets cracked down on their efforts to break out from behind the Iron Curtain. I've even heard Khrushchev threaten the West with nuclear annihilation. But what I *don't* know is why I should add another layer of innuendo to whatever you have against these men, without some kind of proof that I'd be helping my country by cooperating. And patronizing platitudes won't do the trick."

"There are other journalists, Miss O'Connor, who work as reporters in order to make a difference, not just to see their names on the front page of some newspaper that will be tossed in the trash the next day."

I blinked. Hard. His words so closely mirrored what my mother had said to me earlier that morning I wondered for a split second if they'd approached her first. *Don't be an idiot. Ma would never keep that a secret from you. It's pure coincidence.* But it was a coincidence that shook me up. More than a little.

"If you won't help us with this," Pershing was saying, gesturing at the photographs, "would you consider getting

247

back in touch with the resistance leaders you interviewed, and then talk to us, in detail, about how they're doing? We've had difficulty making contact with them. It's obvious they trust you. We need to find out with whom inside their movement we can build a relationship."

"Who the hell is *we*?" I asked him. "That sounds like an odd job for the State Department. More like something the CIA—oh, my God."

It hit me like a ton of bricks. I *had* lied to Raul. I'd been working for the CIA all along.

I turned on Bentley, seething. "You rotten bastard. You offered to pay my way to Cuba so that I could go and risk my neck to serve up some intelligence to the spooks at Langley?"

Bentley raised his hand. "Hold on. That's a very unfair and unjustified accusation. All I did was talk to you about going to Cuba, and then help you get a job with the Copley Press."

"No one here works for the CIA," Pershing said calmly.

"Bullshit." I stood up. "I don't know what other reporters do for the so-called 'State Department,' but don't count me among your agency assets."

I couldn't get out of there fast enough. If I stayed another second I was going to do something a lot worse than just kick Robert Bentley to the ground.

*   *   *   *   *

I had a couple of hours before Castro's speech, but I didn't go straight to the UN. I went back home.

I didn't really believe that Ma had spoken to Pershing or any of his minions before my meeting with him, but I was upset enough to want to ask her about it. *They may have caught her on one of her off days,* I thought. *She may not have remembered the conversation.*

I called out to her as I came in the front door. She didn't answer, but this wasn't unusual. I found her where I expected her to be, sitting at the kitchen table, apron on, rosary in hand, her mid-morning cup of tea in front of her.

At the sound of my voice she turned with a jerky sort of movement and looked up at me. I saw her mouth working, but no sound came out. Then her eyes rolled up into the back of her head, and she fell face first onto the table. And I did something I'd seldom ever done in my entire life.

I screamed.

CHAPTER TWENTY-SIX

"She's suffered a stroke. We don't know how serious its effects will be. She could be mildly incapacitated. Or, she could lose a significant degree of her ability to function. Unfortunately, the fact that she fell into a coma after her collapse makes for a more negative prognosis. I advise you to hope for the best, and prepare for the worst."

"And when will you know which way she's headed?" Tim asked the doctor in a way that sounded more like a threat than a question.

"The first forty-eight hours will be extremely important. The sooner she speaks or responds to her environment in any way, the better her odds become."

I could tell that Tim was about to vent his fear and frustration on our mother's treating physician, so I interrupted before he could get his next words out.

"Is there anything that we can do?"

"It might be helpful for a family member to stay with her. Sometimes people in a comatose state seem to react well to loved ones' voices, for reasons we can't explain."

The doctor excused himself and left us standing outside the door behind which Ma lay. A heart monitor told us that she was still alive, but that was all we knew.

Needless to say, I missed Castro's four-hour diatribe at the UN.

Tim needed to get back to his office and apprise his supervisor of Ma's situation, so I took the first bedside shift. Our sister Maureen showed up that evening around seven thirty, looking like the perfectly put-together suburban housewife she was, from her cashmere coat to her small, glove-clad hands, one of which held a white lace handkerchief (although she didn't look as if she'd done much crying).

I came to relieve Tim at eleven o'clock the next morning. He was sitting next to Ma in one of those notoriously uncomfortable chrome and vinyl hospital chairs, reading aloud to her from a thick, leather-bound book. He dropped it under his chair as I entered.

"Has she done anything? Said anything?" I asked.

Tim shook his head. He was wearing the same shirt he'd had on the previous day, and hadn't shaved.

"What are you reading to her? Should I pick up where you left off?"

For some reason this question embarrassed him. "I—I don't think it matters all that much—just so she hears your voice."

I nodded. Tim stood up to let me have his chair. We stood side by side for a little while, looking down at Ma.

"You go on," I finally said. "I'll be fine." Then I leaned down and told my mother, "Ma, it's Katherine. I'm going to read to you, okay?"

Her eyes flew open. Tim gave a start. Despite the tubes and wires attached to every part of her body, Ma raised herself up on both of her elbows and glowered at me as if she'd just discovered that I'd skipped school.

"Mary Katherine Anne O'Connor," she said, "what are you going to do about that boy?"

"What — what boy, Ma?" I stammered.

"The boy on the beach, with the big brown eyes and the magic shell. What are you going to do about *him*?"

With that, her eyes closed, and she fell back against her pillows.

* * * * *

"Do you have any idea what she's talking about?"

We'd stepped outside to let the duty nurse check Ma's vitals after Tim had reported, in a voice that carried across the entire floor, that our mother had snapped out of her coma and spoken.

I knew to whom Ma must have been referring, but I had no way of explaining that to my brother, or to myself. Even if some CIA agent had traced my connection to Emilio and subsequently contacted my mother, I didn't understand how anyone could have known about the details of our meeting on the day that Emilio had introduced me to Raul. Unless someone had been following Emilio?

Or had Raul befriended Emilio to help the Cuban authorities track down the boy's father?

A wave of nausea followed that last thought. I must have looked as ill as I felt, for Tim put his hands on my shoulders and asked, "Hey, there, girlie, are you all right? Can I get you some water or something?"

"No, I'll be fine. Do you think what she said might be

related to that book you were reading to her? Anything in there that may have put a thought like that in her head?"

"I doubt that. I was reading her the Bible."

"What part?"

"Nothing to do with a boy on the beach with a magic shell, that's for certain. Could she have been meaning Jamie, do you think?"

"I don't know what to think," I said, which was true enough.

The nurse came out and looked at us brightly. "I don't detect any changes, but I'll inform the doctor right away. It's a reason to keep hope alive, though, isn't it?"

It was a reason for something. I just didn't know what.

The doctor came by, examined Ma, and then told us the same thing the duty nurse had said (using three-syllable words). I persuaded Tim to go home and get some sleep. Promising that I would call him if Ma so much as blinked. I plopped into the chair that Tim had pulled close to Ma's bed, and felt my foot connect with something on the floor. Reaching down, I picked up the Bible. It looked brand new. Tim must have bought it to read to Ma.

I set it aside and pulled out the newspaper I'd brought with me. *It doesn't matter what I read to her, as long as she can hear me,* I thought. I droned on for a few minutes, then stopped, bored by the sound of my own voice.

"What are you going to do about that boy?"

What *could* I do about that boy? I couldn't think of anything I could do to help him from New York. I'd have to go back to Cuba.

And what good would that do? I was a registered journalist. If I went to see Carlos the G-2 might trail along.

253

If one of my tails caught site of Miriam my visit could result in her taking a very unpleasant trip to G-2 head-quarters — or worse.

I looked down at my mother. "What can I do to help, Ma?" I asked aloud.

She didn't stir.

My mind flashed back to a time when I was five years old, sick with the flu. Ma had come in with a bowl of potato soup and fed it to me by the spoonful. And as she patiently waited for my parched and feverish lips to open, she sang a sort of Irish fairy tale set to music. I'd fluctuated between wanting to get better and hoping that my fever would last just a bit longer — she'd never focused so much individual attention on me. I must have been very sick, indeed.

I found myself humming the tune, and then a few of the words wafted up from the depths of that childhood memory, so I sang them to my mother:

To and fro we leap,
And chase the frothy bubbles,
While the world is full of troubles.
And is anxious in its sleep.
Come away, oh human child!
To the woods and waters wild.
With a fairy, hand in hand,
For the world's more full of weeping
than you can understand.

And I knew what I had to do about that boy.

* * * * *

"You're doing what?"

"I'm going back to Cuba. I think that's what Ma wants me to do."

"Is that so? How convenient, that you interpret her miraculous speech in a way that gives you permission to do exactly what you'd want to do anyway. But then why should you take her wellbeing into account now, when you've ignored her for as long as you have?"

Tim's comment was my cue to fire back with a retort that would turn his accusation around and leave him on the defensive. He'd volley back, and we would go at it until our anger was spent. It was like a dance, every step predictable.

But that familiar script was not going to work this time.

"Maybe you're right," I said. "But the thing is—and I know this sounds nuts—but I think I know the boy she's talking about. He's in Cuba. And she wants me to go help him somehow."

"So this is some kid you've talked to her about?"

I could have said yes. I should have said yes. But for some reason I didn't. Call it honesty. Call it stupidity. Call it a leap of faith—they all amount to the same thing, don't they?

"No. I've never talked to her about him. Or to him about her. But I know she meant him. I met him on the beach. He showed me a magic shell. Not really magical—but have you ever held a shell to your ear and heard the ocean?"

He didn't respond. I shut up. He needed to digest what I'd said.

"It's the echo of your heartbeat," he muttered.

"Right. But the thing is, well, we were raised believing in guardian angels, weren't we? So what if she's his? What if she — went somewhere else — and heard him crying out for help?"

It was a long shot. I don't know how strong Tim's faith had ever been, but he'd said enough after the war to let me know that his opinion of God and His goodness had greatly diminished as a result of what he'd experienced overseas. But sometimes you win an argument despite yourself, because the person with whom you're arguing wants to be convinced. I saw the desire to be convinced in Tim's face, and I leapt on it.

"What else could it be? You're there, reading the Bible to her. I walk in, she wakes up and — "

"It was the parable of the lost sheep," he said, all the anger gone from his voice. "The parable of the shepherd who goes to look for his one lost sheep. Right when you walked in."

Goosebumps ran up my arms to my neck and down my back, as if a troop of microscopic invaders had been let loose across my flesh. *Someone from the CIA said something to her,* I told myself. *Anything else is just a coincidence.*

But the truth was I wasn't sure if Ma's command was a result of a conversation she'd had with someone connected with Robert Bentley, or because something incomprehensible had happened while she lay in a coma in a hospital room in New York.

Either way, I was going back to Cuba.

* * * * *

"Robert Bentley, please."

I telephoned because I knew that I couldn't trust myself to mind my manners if I spoke to him in person, no matter where we met. Nonetheless, if what I suspected was true, I had to keep my conversation vague.

"Bentley here."

Why hadn't I noticed that before? That's the way someone in the military would answer a radio call. Was I correct in concluding that he'd never stopped serving his country?

"I'll go back," I said, without identifying myself, "but first I need to know why you can't send one of your own people in."

"My own people? What do you mean?"

"Any more bullshit and I'm hanging up."

"Can we meet somewhere to talk about this?"

"No. Just answer the question. Why me? Can't my old friend Nacho to deliver the message for me?" *And then I can concentrate on finding Emilio and Miriam, and get the heck out of there.*

I waited while he chewed through his options. "We've communicated our intentions previously," he said at last. "But for reasons that I can't go into, we weren't able to follow through. By all accounts you made an excellent impression, so we're hoping that by sending you as our messenger we'll enhance our credibility—and we don't want them to give up the fight, not now, when we're finally able to assist them."

"Seems someone in your neighborhood has been dragging his feet for way too long. And now you're asking me to stick my neck out after 'your friends' failed to intervene before the monster grew fangs?"

"There's been a distinct difference of opinion on the matter. Idealists on one side, pragmatists on the other."

"And now the pragmatists have the upper hand?"

"Not in public."

"That pretty much confirms the conclusion I expressed during our last meeting."

"This is not a CIA operation, Katherine."

Some advice that my favorite teacher at Columbia once told me bounced back into my head. *Whatever the Constitution says about the right against self-incrimination, there are two types of guilty people – those who protest too much, and those who say nothing.*

Bentley was guilty on both counts, I decided. But I needed his help, regardless.

"I can't just waltz in and go visiting the people I'd like to talk to," I said. "I'll need some support on the ground. Some very subtle, trustworthy, below-the-radar support, to give me some freedom of movement."

"I'm sure we can work that out."

"And I'll need money. Some bundles of ready cash."

"That won't be a problem, either."

"Good." I'd expected push back on this, but apparently the rumors were true. What the CIA wanted, the US Treasury would provide.

"One more thing. Have you or any of your cohorts ever talked to my mother?"

"Your mother? Why?"

"Please answer the question."

"I'm not trying to be evasive," he said after treating me

to another five-second silence, "but if someone has spoken to her, I know nothing about it."

What a stupid question, I chided myself. I couldn't trust Bentley to give me the real story if his life depended on it, so his response left me no closer to the truth.

My truth was that I had no intention of putting my life on the line to help compensate for the inadequacies of the US intelligence service. But I *was* going to find Emilio and his mother, and do my best to get them out of the Garden of Eden that had become Hell on Earth.

CHAPTER TWENTY-SEVEN

R aul looked out the window as they drove through the flat, marshy land that stretched between the road and the ocean. The Cuban terrain did pose some serious problems. There were large amounts of silt and other unstable material below the topsoil, which would make it difficult to build underground silos. But the Soviets had never met an engineering problem (or an architectural one, for that matter) that they couldn't cure with cement; it wasn't a philosophy Raul shared, but it was the one he'd been trained to execute.

He let out a deep sigh. If Castro followed the Soviet lead, the whole island would be so covered up in cement that Cuba might even sink back into the sea—another Atlantis buried under the ocean as a warning not to interfere too much with what God has created.

If indeed God existed, which Raul doubted. The only forces Raul believed in were the laws of physics and the principles of mathematics. Unlike God or human nature, they were immutable and discoverable. If you knew the right formulas you could not only build a dam, you could build a bomb that could destroy an entire country— something God had not tried to do in a very, very long time.

He'd been traveling with a small group of Cubans and

two other *Hispanic-Sovieticos* for several weeks, mapping out surveys and taking core samples. It was a simple enough process, and given Raul's experience rather like using an open-heart surgeon to teach medical students how to stitch up a cut finger. But Raul had never minded showing someone who was interested in learning how to accomplish something, even something simple. *Like tying a shoe,* he thought, and suddenly remembered the hours he'd spent teaching his sister how to lace up her new boots, during their first few days on board the ship that had taken them away from Spain.

Funny how often he'd thought about her since he'd come to Cuba.

Eventually they arrived in the small town outside Santa Clara where they were to spend the night. Raul went straight to his room to record that day's data into his project notebook before they all met for dinner in the hotel's poor excuse for a dining room.

Someone knocked on the door.

"Just a minute."

Raul put his loose papers into his notebook, shoved it under his mattress, then went to the door and looked through the peephole. A woman stood in the hallway. She was dressed in the Cuban militia uniform of cargo pants and khaki shirt, her sleeves rolled up to above the elbow. She looked more Eastern European than Hispanic: high cheekbones set in an oval face with wide-set, hooded eyes. Her hair was dark brown, shoulder-length, and curly.

He affixed the interior chain to the doorframe before opening it a few inches.

"I'm not expecting any visitors."

"We have a friend in common. I believe he told you to expect me." Her dark brown eyes glittered with coy amusement. "May I come in?"

"Perhaps if I knew who it is you're talking about—"

"Oh, I believe you do know." With this she put one hand on the inside of the doorframe.

Raul felt his stomach tighten as he recognized the particular accent with which she spoke. She was from Argentina. *Che Guevara's contact. Tamara.* He looked at her hand. He could no longer close the door without smashing her fingers.

"May I come in?" she asked again.

Still, Raul hesitated. At last he removed the chain, stuck his head and shoulders out the door, and glanced up and down the hallway.

"Do you think I would have knocked if I weren't sure that I hadn't been noticed?" the woman asked mildly as Raul stepped back and let her into the room.

"I don't know you, and I know almost nothing about Comrade Guevara," Raul replied, trying to keep the edge out of his voice, "plus I'm not well-suited for any kind of espionage. I'm just—"

"An engineer. I know," she said as she made her way over to the room's single chair and sat down. She moved with feline grace, supremely self-confident in the power of her own allure.

"Did you know that Che was on the cover of *Time* magazine?" she asked, glancing around the room.

"What? No. In fact I've never read it. Is it even allowed into Cuba?"

She ignored his question. "'Castro's Brain,' they called him. Flattering, don't you think?"

Raul stayed silent. *Engage as little as possible. Do the work you're told to do and don't complain.* These rules had helped to keep him alive since he'd left Spain, and he wasn't going to deviate from them now.

Her eyes came back to his face. "So what do you think of your Cuban adventure so far?"

To Raul's astonishment she asked this in Russian, not Spanish, but she spoke Russian with a distinctly German accent. "Where are you from?" he asked, switching to Russian himself.

"Oh, here and there. Like you."

"How do I know you're the person Che told me about?"

She reached into her pocket and pulled out some sort of identity card. Raul took it from her and studied it. *Haydée Tamara Bunke Bíder.*

"You're German?"

"Originally. I met Che the first time he came over, in 1959. I was assigned to escort him, as a guide and translator."

Raul handed the card back to her. "So what do you expect from me?"

"I'd like a quick verbal report. Tell me anything you've discovered regarding the Soviets' plans for Cuba."

"I don't have anything to tell. Not yet, anyway." His superior had made it clear that he was not to communicate anything to Che until he received permission to do so, and so far no such permission had been granted. "Keep him hungry," the Colonel had told Raul before he'd left Havana, "I'll let you know when to slake his appetite."

She regarded him skeptically. "No piece of gossip, no odd coincidence, nothing?"

He shook his head. "All I've been doing is running around scouting out sites for potential factories. Pretty boring, actually."

"Can I see your notes?"

Raul shrugged. "Sure." His notes contained nothing but raw data. No one without an engineering background would be able to make sense of them, and he'd not drawn any conclusions yet. He wouldn't prepare his full report until he was back in Havana. So he went to his bed and retrieved his notebook out from under the mattress.

She glanced through it. "You've been busy."

Once again, he said nothing.

She stood up and handed the notebook back to him. "I'll be in touch."

As soon as she closed the door behind her Raul went to his duffel bag and pulled out the bottle of Russian vodka that Tito had given him as a bon voyage present when he'd left Havana. He didn't even bother to try and find a glass.

The Russians wouldn't let Che traipse through East Germany without keeping an eye on him; they'd send someone along from the intelligence service to be at his side, watching his every move and monitoring his communications. Which meant if that woman had been assigned to escort Che when he was in Germany, she was undoubtedly a member of the Stasi. *And I bet she did more than translate for him,* Raul thought, taking another enormous swig.

But that meant, while in Cuba, she should be working

for the Russians, not with Che against them. Was her possible defection something he should pass on to his superiors?

Or would that give Che all the reason he needed to make sure that Raul never made another report, of any kind, to anyone, ever again?

CHAPTER TWENTY-EIGHT

I didn't have any trouble getting back into Cuba, although this time the G-2 seized my suitcase at the airport. I had to hang around the terminal until they returned it—which they did, two hours later, minus the entire interior lining and two very nice ballpoint pens.

Don't ever bother investing in nice luggage, I told myself as I hailed a taxi.

I dropped my meager belongings at my apartment, happy to see that the G-2 hadn't been in while I was gone —or at least the agents had tried to be less obvious about ransacking the place. The delay at the airport had put me way behind schedule. It was Wednesday. I needed to go to confession.

This time Father Lopez was expecting me.

"I've noticed a pattern," I said as soon as I heard the small divider that separates priest from penitent slip open, "You've served the Lord in North Africa, China, and Cuba —all places where US intelligence operations must've been very active. Does the CIA have to get permission from Rome to put a priest on the payroll?"

"I have no idea what you're talking about."

"Right. Never mind. How much of an explanation did our mutual friend give you regarding my return?"

"He said that you wanted to go bird watching again."

"Yup. Gotta spot that *priotelus temnurus* to earn my Scout Badge."

"I have to warn you. The situation is much more precarious."

My heart dropped into the pit of my stomach, bounced back up, and lodged in my throat. I wanted to attribute this reaction to my concern for Emilio's father and his comrades-in-arms, but in all honesty I was also concerned about my own skin. *Now's not the time to get jumpy.*

"I understand."

"Two members of the British Embassy staff are going with you. They're big birders, those Brits."

I wasn't too thrilled about this. "Won't that make travel more difficult?"

"Not at all. Protective camouflage. And there's one other thing."

"Why does that not surprise me?"

"It seems that you're having a tryst with a low-level diplomat from Venezuela."

"What the—?"

"Who is prepared to swear on a stack of Bibles that you've spent every night with him since you've been back in Cuba, in case anyone wonders why you haven't been back to your own apartment. Now, go light a candle under the painting of the Virgin Mary. Under the plate you'll find a love letter from him, a photo, and enough of a description to add some credibility to his claim. Although someone will come by your place and move things around occasionally, to make it look like you've been there."

"I hope this 'someone' is also a skinny redhead."

"Of course she is. She's also an acquaintance of yours

who's using your apartment, with your permission, while you're—otherwise occupied. You'll find a description of her in your packet as well."

"Anything else?"

"Well, as long as you're here, is there anything you'd like to confess?"

* * * * *

Bird watching is an activity best carried out very early in the morning. The little fellas wake up hungry, and leave their nesting place in search of breakfast. This gave me a good reason to be out and about before sunrise.

I took my time getting to the British Embassy, but no one seemed to be tailing me. This might have been because my hair was once again a lovely shade of brown (something between tree bark and tobacco juice) or because my G-2 detail had never seen me get up before sunrise.

As planned, the guards at the embassy let me slip in through the back door. My two companions were waiting for me in the kitchen. One was female, a slight, elderly gray-haired woman with an upper-crust accent and playful blue eyes. She was a bit stooped-shouldered, and despite her thin limbs sported a belly that suggested she'd born more children than was good for her. The second was a tall, middle-aged gentleman who radiated that unique British military stiffness—and wore the perfect mustache to go with it.

The woman spoke first. "I'm Penny Granger. So delighted. This is George Applegate. We're both avid birders. Can't wait to spot a Cuban tocolo."

"Kath—ah, Maria O'Connor," I replied, shaking each of their hands in turn. Maria was the first name on my passport. No reason not to use it—especially now that Katherine O'Connor was in Cuba as a registered journalist.

"Would you like a cup of tea?" Penny asked. "We're still waiting for our driver, Nacho. I believe you've met?"

"Once," I answered, "and yes to the tea." So we sat and sipped tea and chatted about birding while another member of the staff finished preparing a large basket of food. A knock at the door let us know that Nacho had pulled his jeep into the garage. I was to curl up on the back seat, cuddled up in a blanket, and pretend to sleep. That way I could hide without looking as if I were doing so intentionally. *Pretend is right,* I thought, *no sleeping today, even if there weren't so many potholes.*

Penny, who must have been a truly committed bird-watcher, kept up a constant twitter (pun intended) of conversation regarding our feathered quarries from the front seat. I had almost fallen asleep beside George's erect form when an enormous BOOM sounded somewhere behind us.

I sprang up and turned around to see a tall column of smoke rising from somewhere in downtown Havana. Nacho, Penny, and George had not even turned their heads, although Penny did stop prattling.

"What was that?" I demanded.

Nacho turned and glanced at me. "Diversionary tactics," he said with a smug smile.

* * * * *

269

I don't know if the explosion worked to focus the militia's attention on Havana, or if we just got lucky, but we met only one patrol until we were within spitting distance of Santa Clara. The two men who stopped us couldn't wait to let us go once they'd searched the jeep and our luggage for weapons. Penny kept asking them, in that horrible British-accented Spanish of hers, if they'd had any "sightings" lately—of tocolos, kingfishers, owls, and any other bird you could think of. I thought they were going to threaten to arrest her if she didn't shut up. But there are advantages to looking and acting like a dotty old bird—particularly if you really are one. No young man wants to arrest a woman who reminds him, however remotely, of his own grandmother.

"That went well," she said brightly once we were off again.

Nacho looked grim. "I hope the rest of the trip is that easy."

From there we headed south toward Cienfuegos. After a few miles we pulled onto a small dirt road almost hidden by bushy tobacco plants. A few butt-bumping miles later, we arrived in front of a thatched hut that looked to be hanging together through sheer stubbornness.

A man came out to greet us. "Nacho, look at you! Able to keep your business going in times like these. That's what I like to see."

"These are not my regular birdwatchers, Domingo." Nacho replied. "These are the very special friends Blackie told you to expect." He didn't introduce us, but I suppose the fewer people who knew our names, the better. Penny asked for the location of the privy. Nacho pointed toward the hut where our host, Domingo, presumably lived.

"About twenty yards behind the house," he said.

Penny nodded and shuffled off. She came back a few minutes later, walking briskly, her matronly pouch replaced by an almost flat stomach. She held two semi-automatic pistols in one veined and wrinkled hand, a roll of ace bandage, and a small square pillow in the other.

"Glad to be rid of these, I must say," she commented as she handed the guns to Nacho. I stared, dumbstruck. "I'm taking the pillow back with me to pad my bum. Bouncy trip, wasn't it? Do you want to keep the tape?"

"Sure," Nacho answered. "Would you grab that, Maria?"

Penny smiled agreeably, put the roll in my hand and then turned to George. "Ready to go?"

"If Nacho thinks it's time."

"You're clear on where to leave the jeep?" Nacho asked.

"Don't worry, dear, I've been doing this sort of thing for quite some time. It will be there for you," Penny reassured him. I watched, mouth still ajar, as they climbed back into the jeep and took off. Penny gave us a wave and a cheerful smile as they disappeared.

"She was one of the first agents recruited for the SOE in 1940—Special Operations Executive, Britain's wartime covert operations unit," Nacho explained, clearly enjoying my astonishment. "I've known her since I was a kid." He turned back to Domingo.

"How far do we need to go on foot?"

"Until we get past Cumanayagua. Fidel has about ten thousand troops wandering around the place."

"*Ten thousand?* To fight a hundred men?"

Nacho grinned at me as he hitched a pistol to either side of his belt. "There are a lot more than a hundred of us now. I'd say around three thousand, with more arriving every day. Your article gave people hope, by spreading the word that some of us were willing to do what it takes to get rid of Fidel. But we don't have sufficient weapons, and there's not enough coordination between the various resistance groups. We're hoping your friends can help us with both."

They're no friends of mine, I almost said, then caught myself. No point in trying to explain to Nacho the ambivalence I felt about being in Cuba on "State Department" business.

We entered Domingo's hut, where a steaming pot of beans and rice sat waiting for us on a rough-hewn wooden table. "Eat up," he said, "this will be a rough climb. I'll bring some dried beef and crackers to take with us." He left us to serve ourselves, and returned a few minutes later with a canvas-wrapped bundle in his hands.

"Here it is," he said, handing the package to Nacho.

"What's in there?" I asked.

"A gift from your friends at the State Department. The instrument of our salvation," Nacho answered as he unzipped his empty backpack.

"Our death warrant, more likely." Domingo responded.

"Oh, wonderful," I opined with no small degree of sarcasm. "So what is it? A small nuclear device?"

Nacho stood and slung the pack across his shoulders.

"A radio. With this many troops surrounding the Escambray, there's no way to clear a site for a weapons drop more than a few hours in advance. Without a radio, we're done for."

"Hang on—I didn't agree to help smuggle contraband, Nacho. I just agreed to convey to Blackie that the—ah—the 'State Department' is willing to provide more assistance."

"Don't worry about that," he said with a mischievous grin, "we'll get executed just for carrying weapons if we're caught. The radio won't increase our risk one iota."

"How comforting," I muttered. "Shot in the jungle, with beef jerky for a last meal. Exactly the way I'd always hoped to die."

After eating we headed out across the tobacco fields. By the time darkness fell we were making our way up a path so steep and narrow I doubt that any self-respecting mountain goat would've tried to climb it. Tall mahogany trees, pines, and towering cedars blocked out almost all the starlight, but Domingo must have memorized the location of every stone and thorn bush, because we managed to move with remarkable stealth. We had to—the sound of a foot sliding on gravel or even a muffled grunt could serve as an alarm bell to any nearby militia patrols.

At one point Domingo froze in front of me; I looked down to see a large snake slithering across his boot. Reptiles bother me less than some of the politicians I've interviewed over the years, but at that moment it took every ounce of willpower I had to stifle the cry of alarm that leapt into my throat.

We were gaining altitude pretty rapidly; the sweat produced by exertion and tension began to cool and evaporate, taking some of my body heat with it. I started to shiver. Nacho emitted a gentle *wheet,* mimicking the call of some Cuban night bird that was our signal to halt. I turned to look at him. He handed me a knitted wool cap. With a grateful smile I slipped it on, one of my mother's child-hood instructions echoing in my head: *if your feet are cold, Mary Kate, put on a hat.*

Eventually we broke into a narrow clearing dissected by a small stream. By then I'd figured out why water features made good rendezvous spots. They weren't likely to move, couldn't burn down, and gave everyone a chance to refresh themselves, both physically and mentally. Water heals the body, and something optimistic and eternal about the sight of moving water revives the human spirit.

I sagged to the ground, nearly spent. I wasn't used to climbing stairs, much less crawling up a mountainside. Domingo offered me a piece of jerky. I shook my head. I wasn't *that* desperate—not yet, anyway.

We waited almost an hour before we heard the *wheet wheet* we'd been waiting for. Nacho answered, and two shadows drifted out from behind the trees. I could tell by the shape of the silhouettes they belonged to Blackie and Armando.

"Why is she here?" Blackie asked, in a barely audible whisper.

"She comes bearing gifts," Nacho answered, "and promises of help to come."

"From whom?" Blackie asked.

"The CIA," I answered.

"We've heard their promises before," Armando said,

speaking as quietly as Blackie, although his harsh tone made his voice seem louder.

"Yes, but in addition to their personal representative, they've sent a token of goodwill this time," Nacho said. He pulled the bundle out of his backpack and placed it in Blackie's enormous hands. "A radio. You can contact the Havana post, which will in turn send a message to Key West—and you'll have a weapons cache dropped in less than an hour."

Blackie turned to me. "Is this true? You've talked to someone in the US who's in a position to make this kind of commitment?"

Your credibility is your stock in trade. I needed to be honest, but I didn't want to give them any false hope. "Yes, at least I think so. I didn't go looking—a representative came to me, and said that they're willing to help you. Clandestinely, of course. It seemed like a serious offer."

"Where's Tomas?" Nacho asked, peering into the shadows.

"Captured," Blackie answered. The effort it took to conceal his emotion communicated how deeply the loss of Tomas affected him.

"Will he talk?"

"Who knows? A man never knows how strong he is until he's tortured. We hope he'll spill enough to satisfy them, but not enough to do much damage to the movement. We keep the cells small and self-contained for precisely that reason. You can't finger someone you've never seen, whose name you don't know."

Torture. God help these men. I pulled a small screwdriver out of my pocket and started to pry at the sole of one of my boots. "Here's the rest of the contribution," I said as I pulled Mexican gold coins of various denominations out of their hiding place. "They wanted to make sure you could spend it whenever and wherever you wanted to, which is why I didn't bring dollars—rumor has it Castro might soon declare American currency illegal in Cuba."

Despite the fact that I wasn't happy about being a CIA errand girl, I couldn't help but be pleased by their expressions of joyful astonishment. Even Nacho looked amazed.

"You didn't tell me about all that," he said, with real admiration.

"A girl mustn't give away all her secrets," I said as I dug the last coin out of my heel and added it to the small mound on the ground. "And before I leave I'm going to help your family, Armando."

"My family? Why?"

How was I to answer this? *Oh, because my mother, who's in a coma, told me to?* "Because I can," I said with a shrug, "because I thought highly of your father, and I like your wife, and I think Emilio's a great kid. Because you shouldn't have to worry about them while you're trying to take this bastard down."

He may have teared up—it was too dark to tell for sure —but I saw him wipe his eyes with the back of his hand before talking again. "I've seen Miriam once since you were here the last time. I haven't seen my boy for almost a year. They're in a safe house in Santa Clara."

"I'm going to get them out of Cuba, so you don't have to worry about them until this is all over," I said after he'd given me the address. "Soon."

He reached out and grabbed my forearm. "Thank you. I don't know what else to say."

"Say that you're going to win," I said. "Believe it. Don't give up. And try to stay alive. More than anything, Miriam and Emilio will want to come home to you."

CHAPTER TWENTY-NINE

N acho left the guns with Blackie and Armando — now that we weren't protecting the radio, we were safer without them if we had the bad luck to be stopped by a patrol. Our progress back down took almost as much time as the climb up. That's when I learned that you use your shin muscles more when you're going downhill than you do when you're climbing. A lot more. By the time we reached the tobacco fields my shins were screaming for mercy.

An old man with a donkey cart was waiting outside Domingo's hut. He looked to be about a hundred years old, and his animal wasn't much younger.

"Don't tell me," I said to Nacho as we approached, "this is our ride, right?"

"Yes it is. Maria, this is Eduardo, and his donkey, Benito."

"*Buenas noches*," I said to Eduardo, who gave me a near-toothless smile in return. He scrambled up onto the cart and I started to haul myself up after him.

"No, you're riding in the back," Nacho said, grabbing my leg. "Under the hay."

"You must be joking."

"What's the matter? It's more comfortable than riding on the bench. Smells better, too. Two farmers aren't likely to attract any unwanted attention. A young woman with skin like yours riding in a donkey cart is harder to explain."

I inspected the back of the cart, which was full of loose hay. "How long a trip is it?"

"A few hours. Come on. I have to change, then I'll tuck you in."

He came back wearing the loose garb worn by the *campisitos*, complete with cowboy hat. I crawled up into the back of the cart and dug into the hay like a gopher. Nacho arranged some more hay on top of me, until he was satisfied that I was completely hidden.

"Next stop, Santa Clara," he said as he climbed onto the seat next to Eduardo. "Can you breathe okay?"

"Yes." In fact I was pretty comfortable. And before I knew it, I was sound asleep.

Some time later Nacho woke me up by poking me with the handle of Eduardo's donkey crop. "Wake up. We're almost there. And we probably won't get stopped, unless someone hears you snoring. I didn't know a woman could make a noise like that."

I heard Eduardo cackling with amusement. "I only snore when I'm sleeping on my back," I said defensively as I began to wriggle out of hiding.

"No, don't move—just be quiet, for God's sake." Nacho said as he rearranged some of the hay.

I stayed as still as I could, but the more I tried not to move, the more various parts of my body started to itch. Obviously my DEET had worn off somewhere along the way, and the mosquitoes had taken full advantage of my unprotected state. My shins still ached, and other muscles were now also complaining about their forced participation in my nighttime climb. *Don't be a sissy*, I thought. *Poor Tomas would be happy to trade places with you right now. And if you wiggle, you and Nacho may be joining him.* That was all the inspiration I needed to keep myself from scratching.

The next phase of our trip went off without a hitch. Eduardo dropped us at the storage shed where Penny and George had left the jeep. Nacho walked around to the back and changed into his birder-guide clothes, although he kept the cowboy hat on. I changed into a pair of cargo pants, a white cotton shirt, and a pair of comfortable canvas shoes. I put some pesos in my pocket, stuffed my hiking clothes into my duffle bag, and tossed it into the back seat.

"We can't spend much time tracking down Armando's family," Nacho said as he pulled into the street. "And if I remember correctly, the street we're looking for is too narrow for vehicles, so I'll drop you off in the square. Whatever you do, *don't* ask anyone for directions. We don't know who's spying for Fidel, and we don't want to lead any of his minions to one of our safe houses."

When we'd reached a small public square on the outskirts of town Nacho stopped. "I think it's down that way," he said, jerking his head toward one of the streets that led away from the corners of the colonial-style plaza. "I'll meet you back here. You have twenty minutes. And if I'm not wearing my hat, steer clear—that means there's a problem."

I didn't have any trouble finding the place. An elderly woman with the face of an Incan warrior answered my knock.

"Have you any eggs, grandmother? I need a couple to make a birthday cake."

She glared at me, silent and suspicious, although I knew I'd given the correct pass phrase. "May I come in?" I added.

She backed away, pointed toward a rickety couch, and then disappeared. I sat down. A few seconds later I saw Miriam peek cautiously into the room. As she recognized me, her face filled with wonder. She stepped through the doorway to greet me.

"How did you find us?"

"Armando," I said, standing up. "I've seen him. He's fine. And he's given me permission to get the two of you out of Cuba."

She moved closer and gestured for me to retake my seat. "My Armando? Where?"

"I saw him last night. I couldn't tell you where—even if I wanted to—other than we were somewhere in the hills. And he wants me to get you and Emilio out of Cuba as soon as possible."

She sat next to me, shaking her head in amazement. I could see tears filling the corners of her eyes. "This is God's work," she said softly.

I decided not to correct her by explaining it was actually the work of the CIA. Besides, who was I to say that God had absolutely nothing to do with it?

Suddenly a boy-shaped missile headed straight for me. He threw himself into my lap with such force I'm sure the whole couch would've toppled over if it hadn't been pushed up against the wall.

I pried him off and made him stand up. "You've grown. You're taller."

He grinned at me. "Almost half an inch."

Miriam's face was now somber. "Emilio, Maria has come to take you to America," she told her son.

"Both of you," I added.

"No," she answered. "I cannot leave my husband. But Emilio will go with you."

"I'm not leaving either!" Emilio asserted, crossing his arms and punctuating his statement with a look of outraged defiance. "I'm staying here, to protect you, and help Papa."

"You're too young to help, Emilio. And if you stay, Fidel will send you away anyway."

I turned to her. "Miriam, what are you talking about?"

"It's already happening. Two thousand children are being sent to Russia for their 'education.' Soon Fidel will take all the children away from their parents, and raise them in state-run institutions."

My mind flashed back to the document Father Lopez had shown me when I'd first arrived in Cuba. "Are you talking about some sort of program for the government to eliminate parental rights?"

"Yes." All of Miriam's sweetness had vanished. Her voice was bitter, her expression cold as stone. "They'll take the children away from their parents when they're three years old, and brainwash them in collective housing, raising them to be good little communists. There's an official document describing all this. A copy was stolen from the government and circulated. It's everywhere."

"Oh, Miriam. Not even Castro could get away with that."

"They took the children in Spain, didn't they? Everyone in Cuba has heard a story about someone whose child disappeared during the Spanish Civil War, whether taken by Franco as a hostage to force a parent to surrender, or because their communist parents sent them to the Soviet Union for their so-called 'protection.' *Those* children never returned home. So why couldn't Fidel start brainwashing toddlers —"

"They'll never brainwash me!"

Miriam looked at her son. "I know. And so you'll be dead when you're fifteen, the age when young men are drafted. Like the god Saturn, Fidel will eat his own children."

She reached out and put a hand on Emilio's shoulder, conveying a hint of her normal gentleness. "Go with Maria. It's what your father wants. We'll come for you as soon as Fidel has been stuffed into the same prison where he's killed so many others."

His chin went up. "No. I'm not going, and you can't make me."

Without warning, Miriam stood up and slapped him, hard, right across his face. I jumped. Emilio, one hand on his reddening cheek, stared up at her as if she'd never ever hit him before. But she didn't look repentant. If anything she looked even angrier.

"Do you want to stay in this tiny room for months, afraid to move, afraid to breathe? Don't you know your father cannot do what he has to do if he has to worry about you?"

Emilio said nothing.

Miriam left the room. She came back holding a very small leather satchel. Emilio remained motionless, hand still on his face, gazing at his feet.

She handed the satchel to me. "Open it." I did so, and pulled out the contents as she sat down next to me.

"I've heard they won't let you bring a picture out of the country if it's framed, in case there's something stashed behind it, or because the frame itself might be valuable. So this is all I can give you. That's a photograph of all of us at Emilio's First Communion. That's our wedding picture, and this is—this is Luis holding Emilio when he was a baby. And you also have Emilio's baptismal certificate. I wasn't able to get to the strong box at the bank where we keep his birth certificate, so this will have to do if he needs any sort of identification."

At the bottom was a small velvet bag. "That's a watch," she said as I lifted it out. "It was—it belonged to my father. He wanted Emilio to have it when he graduated from university, but I think now's a good time."

Emilio's eyes filled with tears as Miriam took the velvet bag from me and laid it in his hand. "Take care of it, my son," she said. "I know you don't remember him, but he loved you very much."

I glanced at Emilio's baptismal certificate as I put it away. *Emilio Jaime Velasquez*, I read.

Jaime. Spanish for James.

Oh, Ma. Wherever you are, please help me get this little Jamie out safely.

I told Miriam that Emilio didn't need to take much with him. "Better to look as if we're just going on a short trip. I'll be able to buy him everything he needs once we're in New York."

"New York? Why New York?" Miriam asked, her voice faltering. "That's—it's so far away."

"That's where I live. We'll be staying with my mother. Unless you have somewhere else in mind for him? I'm happy to take him wherever you say."

"No, I guess not. One always thinks of Miami, but the Cubans who escaped when Fidel took over, at least the rich ones, they all worked with Batista. Those fleeing now are lucky if they get out with the clothes on their back. There's no one. Oh my God—I can't believe I'm sending my child off with a stranger—"

I took both of her hands in mine. "Armando wants you both out of danger. If you won't come with us, please know that you can trust me with your son."

She closed her eyes. "He's so young, even if he doesn't think so."

"I know. But he's very smart. He'll be okay."

Then they said their goodbyes: Emilio stern and stoic, Miriam trying hard to contain her own emotions. Outside, I took Emilio's hand and walked back in the direction of the square. "I have a friend who's going to take us back to Havana. In a jeep. Have you ever ridden in a jeep?"

I looked up and stopped short. Nacho stood beside his jeep, smoking a cigarette. His hat was on the ground next to his feet. I backed up a few steps.

"What is it?" Emilio whispered. "Isn't that your friend?"

"No. He must've left," I replied quietly, trying desperately to stay calm. "He said that if he wasn't around, that we should take the bus. Any chance you know where to find the bus station?"

"Are you kidding?" Emilio said with a touch of his old bravado. "We came by bus. It's not far. And you know me —I never get lost."

Thank God for that, I told myself as we reversed direction, and I followed him away from the square.

* * * * *

My heart was in my throat the whole way to the bus station. If I hadn't taken responsibility for Emilio, I would have at least tried to approach Nacho. But if he was in trouble, I might be—and if I was going to keep Emilio safe, that meant I had to Get Out Of Dodge. Fast.

I was horrified to see the station crawling with members of the militia. After surveying the situation, I realized that most of them were focusing on the people arriving. *Worried about more people coming to join the rebels,* I thought. I bought Emilio a comic book at the news stand and told him to sit quietly while I went to buy our tickets to Havana.

After that I buried my face in the latest edition of *La Revolution* and told Emilio to read his comic book twice if he had to, as long as he didn't move. When they called our bus he grabbed his little satchel and bolted ahead. I just smiled and called to him, "Save me a seat, you little monkey."

He was on board by the time I made it to the bus. One member of the militia stood at the door, looking bored, glancing over each passenger as they boarded. I smiled pleasantly at him as I waited for the aged gentleman ahead of me to navigate the four steps from the ground into the bus.

I felt a hand on my left shoulder. Another *barbudo* stood there, eyeing me with open hostility. "The sergeant wants to talk to you," he said.

"But I—"

The man on my right grabbed my arm. "He said Sergeant Valdez wants to talk to you. So you'll come talk to him."

I looked up. I saw Emilio's face pressed against one of the bus windows. He watched, terrified, as the two men led me away.

CHAPTER THIRTY

They took me to the back of the bus terminal where another member of the militia was waiting. He was at least ten years older than his junior officers, and had one of those faces that probably looked evil when he was still in his crib. Looking me up and down he said, "I do know her. She's the girl reporter from the Hotel Teresa."

"No, señor, I'm sorry, but you're mistaken. I've never been to a hotel by that name." I responded.

"Turn around," he commanded.

The two young *barbudos* spun me around. "Oh, it's her, alright," the sergeant said. I could picture the sneer on his face. "She had red hair in New York, but I'd know that skinny ass anywhere."

I turned to face him, shaking off my two amused guards as I did so. "But, sir, I'm not the person you think I am. I'm from Puerto Rico. I'm visiting an old family friend here—"

He grabbed my chin before I could elaborate. "It's illegal for American reporters to leave Havana, you know."

I shook my head violently. He loosened his grip a little and asked, "And the boy you were with?"

"Her nephew," I mumbled.

"Is that so? Well, let's go talk about this in greater detail."

He let go of my chin, but the other two grabbed me again, one on each side. They half-pulled, half-carried me out into the street. We made our way to a long, low-slung building that looked like a Mexican jail in an old Hollywood western, complete with cracked stucco, a decrepit tile roof, and a mongrel dog busily licking water from a broken drain pipe. The poor mutt looked up at me as we passed by, and I saw more sympathy in his eyes than I'd seen on the face of any *barbudo* since I'd been in Cuba.

They tossed me into an isolated holding cell. I picked myself up and looked around. The cell was about eight feet wide and six feet deep, with a hard packed dirt floor. There was no furniture, not even a latrine. The one window was way above my reach, and blocked by the iron bars one would expect in such a place.

I tried to come up with a plan of action, but my brain seemed frozen by the knowledge that my life was in serious jeopardy. No one knew where I was or what was happening, so no one was in a position to help me. This man could have me killed, or kill me himself, and the truth about my demise need never be made public.

I should have told him yes, I had been at the Teresa, but that I wasn't in Cuba working as a reporter, I told myself. *As if he'd believe that.* He knew that I was either a reporter with no right to be where he'd found me, or a spy. *And the truth is that you're a bit of both, aren't you?*

I called out for help, for about thirty minutes non-stop, but no one responded to my cries. Blackie's words came rushing back to me: "No man knows how strong he is until he's tortured." I crouched down in a corner and covered my face with my hands, too numb with terror to cry.

It was more than two hours before the guards came back. "I'm not who he thinks I am," I pleaded as one of them opened the cell door.

The other came in to secure my hands behind my back with a pair of handcuffs. "Shut up," he commanded as he snapped the cuffs into place. They led me out of the cell, down a hallway, to another hall where it looked as if a few of the larger cells had been converted to offices; they had wooden doors instead of bars across the front. We entered one, and there was Sergeant Valdez, standing in front of his desk, holding something in his hands that was wrapped in a dirty cloth. He dismissed the two men with a wave.

"So you're not the reporter," he said after they'd left, "but we found your prince, Cinderella. Are you missing a shoe?" With that he threw what he'd been holding right at my chest. It hit hard, just below my collarbone, then fell to the floor. I looked down.

It was my boot, the one with the false bottom.

"If you're not who I thought you were, who the fuck are you?" he demanded.

"But I am—I mean, I'm Katherine O'Connor, the reporter. But I'm in Santa Clara visiting an old family friend. I came unofficially because I couldn't stand the thought of being so close and not being able to see her— she was like a second mother to me when I was younger—"

He moved closer to me. "Hearing a woman lie makes my dick grow bigger. Like the nose on Pinocchio. Keep lying, and you'll find out what a big wooden dick can do to a lying cunt like you."

I started talking again, barely aware of what was

coming out of my mouth. "I swear—call Fabio Oceguera, at the Venezuelan Embassy. He and I—we know each other. He'll tell you that I'm just here visiting."

"Why should I bother to do that, when I'm fully capable of getting the truth out of you myself?"

I felt my knees buckle and stopped myself from falling by leaning back against the wall for support. He shouted something and the two *barbudos* came back into the room.

"Take her to the interrogation unit," he said to them.

"But you can't," I shouted. "I'm an American—"

"And shut her the fuck up."

I saw the back of a hand coming at me, felt it connect with my face, sensed my neck whipping back, and then everything went black.

* * * * *

When I woke up I was lying on my stomach. I pushed myself up slowly. My watch was missing, but thankfully so were the handcuffs. I guess they couldn't afford to waste a pair on someone securely behind bars. So many prisoners, so little time.

The back of my skull throbbed a lot more than my jaw, although that didn't feel too good, either. I sat up and gingerly investigated my wounds. Swelling, but no blood, thank heaven. *The bastard must have knocked my head into the wall when he hit me.*

This cell was a little bigger than the first one, but it had no window, and the floor was wooden, which meant I might be on an upper floor—or in an entirely different building. The door to my cell was also made of a thick slab of wood, with a tiny, bar-covered window no bigger than my face, and a small flap at the bottom. *Just like the Count of Monte Cristo,* I thought, not really amused.

I stood up, still shaky, shuffled over to the door, and peeked out. Some light flowed into the hallway from a small row of windows set close to the high ceiling. Still moving slowly, I turned and looked around my cell. I saw a bucket in the corner and staggered over to it, hoping against hope that it was full of fresh water.

It wasn't.

I checked all my pockets. Nothing, not so much as a match. Then I remembered the gold coin I'd hidden in my bra, in case I needed to bribe an official in order to get Miriam and Emilio out of the country. I felt for it. *Still there.* Would it work as a bribe in this hellhole? If Valdez had been at the Teresa, he was in Castro's good graces. Would a gold coin be enough to buy his cooperation? No, he seemed too maniacal to be susceptible to a bribe. It would have to be someone lower on the totem pole, like a guard.

I didn't know how long I'd been unconscious, but my stomach soon announced its disapproval of my dining schedule, which left me wishing I'd eaten the wretched beef jerky when I'd had the chance. I doubted that dinner would be served promptly at eight.

I was right about that, too. The light faded from the windows. Darkness fell, and no one came.

* * * * *

The sound of the key in the lock woke me. I was on my

feet by the time the guard was in my cell, relieved to see that he was not one of the men from the day before. I shouldn't have been.

"Did you enjoy your beauty sleep?" he asked.

"I could use some water."

"You Americans are so demanding. If you're thirsty, suck my cock."

In another situation I'm sure I would have given him a pithy retort, but I just stared back, weak from hunger and dehydration, in pain, and terrified. I stayed silent while he put me back in handcuffs and led me out of the cell.

We went down a flight of stairs and entered a court-yard. I was momentarily blinded by the bright daylight, but when my vision cleared I saw Nacho sitting in a chair. No, not sitting; his legs and arms were tied to it, making movement impossible. He caught my eye and gave the slightest shake of his head before he looked down. What was he trying to tell me?

My escort flung me into a second chair not too far from Nacho. I heard another door open, and there was Valdez. "So I take it you two know each other?" he asked as if we were guests at a dinner party.

Nacho shrugged — or tried to, given that he couldn't move his shoulders. "She's a client. I took her bird watching, then dropped her off here to meet some relatives or something."

"Ah, yes, bird watching. What a charming hobby." That's when I noticed the binoculars around Valdez' neck.

"These are yours, yes?" Without waiting for an answer Valdez lifted them off and put them around Nacho's neck, backward. He started to twist the binoculars around and around, until the strap was tight against Nacho's throat. "Tell me why you brought this woman to Santa Clara."

"Forgive me if I doubt your credibility," Nacho said in a strained voice. He was having trouble breathing. "But no matter what she or I say, we know we're both as good as dead already."

"Stop it!" I shouted at Valdez. "He doesn't know anything about me!"

Valdez wound the strap tighter. "You don't have to die—just tell us who this woman is."

I saw Nacho's eyes grow wide as he fought for air. "Stop!" I screamed again. "He doesn't know why I'm here. Let him go!"

Nacho's body sagged as he lost consciousness. Valdez dropped the binoculars. They hit the back of the chair with a loud clack.

"He's not dead," the man said smoothly. "Not yet. You can still save him."

But I'd understood what Nacho had been trying to tell me. Don't say anything to jeopardize the others, because we're both good as dead, anyway.

"I—it's just as he said. I was afraid to tell you the truth at first. But I am Katherine O'Connor, and I went bird watching with this guy and a couple of Brits, and afterward he dropped me off here to visit my friend, who asked me to take her nephew back to Havana. That's all there is to it. Honestly."

"So why does your boyfriend at the Venezuelan Embassy say you haven't left his bed in two days?"

"He's—he's trying to protect me."

"How interesting. He destroys your honor by admitting you're a slut, and thinks that's a good way to protect you. To protect you from what?"

"People like you." For this I received another hard slap.

"You had boots with a hidden compartment in them," he said.

"I don't know what you're talking about," I said, as distinctly as I could, given my bruised jaw.

Just then a very young militia member ran into the room, out of breath and bursting with excitement. "Forgive me, Sergeant Valdez. But we've caught them. We caught the leaders."

Valdez looked at him, then back to me. "Put her back for now," he said to the *barbudo* who'd brought me out of my cell. "And give her some water. Maybe something to eat. We don't want her to expire before I have a chance to question her again."

My guard brought me back to my cell and removed my handcuffs. "Wait," I said before he could leave. "I'd like to make a deal."

"What kind of deal?"

My heart was pounding so loudly I was pretty sure he could hear it, too. "I'll pay you to help me get out of here."

He looked interested. "How much?"

"A lot. As soon as I'm free."

"Sorry," he said mockingly, "I don't take IOUs."

"I can pay you something now."

"Is that so?" He closed the cell door. "You must have something with you that I'd like. Let's see it. Off with your pants."

It actually took a second for this to sink in. "No, no.

295

Not that." I reached into my bra and pulled out my gold piece. "Here—a down payment," I said, handing it to him. "The rest—a thousand dollars in gold coins, delivered wherever you want. Or cash. If you help me escape."

He slipped the coin into his pocket. "Agreed. But it'll take me a while to figure out how to do it." He let himself out, locked the door, and then leaned his face near my pitiful excuse for a window. "On second thought, my balls are worth more than a thousand dollars to me, and that's what Valdez will have hanging from his front door if you escape on my watch. So I will have to decline."

I lunged at the door. He stepped back from it and laughed. I heard him continue to laugh as he walked away.

Hours later the panel at the bottom of the door opened and someone shoved a tray inside my cell. I scrambled up, too late to see the face of the person who'd brought it. On the tray was a metal bowl full of some kind of corn gruel and a tin cup full of water. I used the water to help me choke down the porridge. I had to fight to keep it all in my stomach. The stench of the overloaded latrine bucket didn't help, but I managed to keep myself from vomiting.

I'd occasionally hear voices in the hallway, and several times the agonizing moans of someone in pain—but I couldn't see anything through my narrow portal. All night long I fantasized about ways to escape. I could hit the guard over the head with the latrine bucket and take his pistol. *And do what? How far do you think you'd get?* I had no idea how to get around the prison I was in. Had it been a palace once? The city hall? Or had it always been used as a place of torture and punishment?

My second meal came long after dark: mushy beans

and rice with some kind of greens stirred in. I laughed when I saw it. *See what a hundred dollars worth of gold can buy you in Santa Clara?* I thought. But I ate every bite.

Another day passed pretty much the same way. On the morning of the third day a different guard came, took me out of my cell, and held onto me while a service worker replaced my bucket with an empty one. Not clean, but at least, not full. I was tossed back in. The prison chef must have arrived late to work that day, because I didn't get any food at all until early evening.

I'd started pulling splinters of wood off the beams on the floor, with no clear idea of what I'd do with them, but it helped passed the time. I wrote stories in my head. I relived every moment I'd spent with Raul. I tried not to pray. It seemed very hypocritical for me to talk to God only when I wanted something from Him, so I left the praying up to Ma, Miriam, and Father Lopez, hoping against hope that by now at least one of them would realize that something was wrong, and start sending up word that I needed help.

Sometime during the middle of the fourth day another unknown, bearded face came to my door. "Come along," he said as he unlocked it, "we have some entertainment for you." He grabbed me tightly by the arm, but did not put me in handcuffs as he led me away. I tried to keep track of every window, every door, every turn down every hallway. He led me outside, but we weren't in a courtyard. It was more like a very broad alleyway between two old colonial buildings. *So I'm in some kind of compound,* I thought, frantically looking around for the most promising avenue of escape.

Four other prisoners were already there, lined up against one wall, their arms tied behind their backs. Facing them were four soldiers, holding rifles. To my horror I recognized one of the men in front of the firing squad. It was Blackie.

He caught me looking at him and I glanced away. Someone would be watching for any sign of communication between us, and any connection could make things worse for both of us.

Five other prisoners, all young men in peasant garb, were brought out and positioned with me in full view of the firing squad. At last Valdez sauntered out, cigar in hand. "This is your last chance to save yourself," he informed the men standing up against the wall. "Tell us the names of the traitors who've helped you betray the Revolution."

"Down with communism! Long live Christ the King!" Blackie shouted.

"Fire," Valdez ordered. The four executioners obeyed. My eyes closed reflexively at the sound of the gunfire. I opened them to see one man on the ground, bleeding from multiple chest wounds. Another had collapsed and soiled himself, but didn't appear wounded. The other two men, including Blackie, had not moved.

The four gunmen burst out laughing at the sight of the man who'd fainted, but they silenced themselves when Valdez spoke. "Tomorrow all the bullets may be real," he said, with no hint of amusement, "so think well about what you want to tell us today. And as for you," he added, turning to me and the other observers, "unless you want to join these men, you'll do the same."

My guard grabbed me and marched me back into the building.

CHAPTER THIRTY-ONE

I t was three days before anyone else came to my cell, other than to shove food through the door. To my dismay, my next visitors were the same two militia members who'd stopped me at the bus station.

"A special treat today, señorita," one of them said sarcastically as he pulled me up off the ground. "You get to take a bath, so you're all clean for a private interrogation."

There was no doubt about what he meant. I could struggle now, or go along and hope that I'd find a way to escape on the way. It was that or the firing squad.

We went down the same corridor that led to the interior courtyard, but instead of going outside we turned right and went into a small room with a tile floor. A bar of soap, a small towel, and a simple cotton dress were piled onto a backless bench in the center of the room. I saw a drain in the floor,, one end of which was attached to a spigot in the wall. At the end of the bench was a small barrel of what appeared to be clean water.

I could guess what the barrel and hose were normally used for, and it didn't have anything to do with bathing. But the two *barbudos* seemed serious about letting me clean myself, and even stepped outside — leaving the door ajar — while I undressed. I emerged wearing the clean dress, my wet locks having reverted to something closer to their normal color with the help of some soap and water.

"Look at that, she's a chameleon. Changes color and everything," one of my captors said with a chortle.

"Too bad about the face, though. Still purple," the other replied. "But then, he's not going to be looking at her face, is he?"

I did not react to this. I was too busy thinking about how to get away.

To my relief they did not cuff me or tie my hands behind my back, although they were both carrying rifles. They led me down another corridor and then through a huge door that opened onto a narrow alleyway. At the far end I could see a car, parked on what looked like an actual street.

The guy on my left stopped walking. "Hold up," he said, and let go of me to light a cigarette.

That was a mistake.

I shook off the other guard and bolted, ran a few steps, then pivoted and grabbed the first guard's arm as he lunged for me, using his own momentum to throw him forward onto the ground. His chin hit the cobblestones with a thud. I turned to see the other guard swinging the butt of his rifle at me like a baseball bat. I blocked it with my left forearm—probably not the best move, but the first one I remembered from the lessons Tim had given me. The weapon hit my arm with a loud crack. I lost my footing, but I'd also knocked the rifle out of his hands. I fell back onto my rump—thankfully, not too hard.

He reached down to grab me by the hair, screaming curses. I swung my right fist hard up into his crotch as he bent over me. He went down on his knees, clutching himself with both hands. I scrambled over to the gun, lifted it, and smacked the side of his head with the rifle butt as if his skull were a cue ball. I don't think I killed him, but he did lose consciousness.

I stood and turned around. The other guard had flipped onto his back and was reaching clumsily for his own weapon. I brought the rifle butt down hard on his hand, then again into the middle of his forehead.

I may have killed him, but I didn't stick around long enough to find out.

I dropped the gun and looked around. There were no windows to peek through, no one charging into the alley. I took a deep breath and strolled to the street, trying to ignore how badly my limbs were shaking. There was an empty jeep parked near the first car I'd noticed, but no other militia members in the vicinity.

That's when I started to feel the searing pain in my forearm. I cradled it in my right arm and walked along the sidewalk until I saw a church steeple. I headed that way.

* * * * *

When I entered the sanctuary its single occupant was an ancient nun at prayer in the front pew. I crept up, sat behind her and tapped her on the shoulder. She turned around and gave me a look that shot me right back to third grade. I saw her glance at my arm.

"Father Lopez, Havana, Church of the Holy Savior. Please—" I managed to say before her face grew larger.

Then she flipped upside down. No, I was the one who was upside down. Then she was gone.

When I woke up I was lying face up on a pew. The nun was holding a wet cloth to my forehead. "Is anyone looking for you, my daughter?" she asked.

"Not yet. At least, I hope not. I don't think anyone knows I've escaped," I stammered.

"Do you have any money?"

"No, they took everything."

"I'm sure. They robbed this church. A group of that militia scum came in, searched the place from top to bottom, and took anything they wanted. Harassment of the church is increasing every day. I don't know how much longer it will be before we're all expelled from the country. But that's not your problem. I'll go get a wrap for that arm."

She came back with some sort of liniment and a long bandage. When she touched my arm I flinched, but managed to stifle my scream. She smeared goop all over my forearm, then wrapped it up in a bandage.

"The bone may be fractured, but at least it's not split in two. The ointment will help the swelling. There's a bus leaving for Havana from the central station at eleven. A member of our order will be traveling on it. I'll go now and ask her to take you with her."

I nodded. I wasn't happy about getting back on a bus, but I figured I had one advantage; they wouldn't be looking for a redhead.

"Don't worry about being recognized," she said, as if reading my thoughts. "The disguise I will give you will hide everything—your arm, your hair, even the lower part

303

of your face, as long as you keep your chin tucked down. You'll travel dressed as a novice."

The irony of this was not lost on me. "God Bless you," I said.

CHAPTER THIRTY-TWO

"You must leave the country as soon as possible. It's a miracle you're still alive."

"But I have to find Emilio. He's the real reason I agreed to make the trip."

"And how do you expect to help him if you're dead?"

I was sitting in Father Lopez' office. I'd shed the novice's habit, and was clad the shift I'd escaped in. I did not mention that I'd caused some serious bodily harm to two members of Castro's militia. Telling a priest that I might have killed someone, when I didn't feel any genuine remorse, just didn't feel right. So I implied that I'd fallen and injured my arm during my mad dash to freedom.

Father Lopez set my arm, wrist to elbow, with a thin piece of wood and surgical tape, then wrapped it in a makeshift sling. He also gave me some codeine. (I was too grateful to ask him where he'd received his medical training, or what he was doing handing out narcotics.) The painkiller wasn't terribly effective, but at least it made the ache seem farther away.

"I have to find Emilio," I insisted. "How do I know if he made it back to his mother? I can't just abandon him."

"Listen to me. When Castro came back from New York, he followed the KGB's advice very closely. He's organized these so-called 'Committees for the Defense of the Revolution.' There's a committee member on every block, in every apartment, and every office building. He now has spies everywhere. People are afraid to sit on their front porch and talk with a neighbor or meet with friends after church, for fear they'll be turned in as conspirators. Castro is strangling the country. There's no way for you to stay here and be safe, now that you're under suspicion—even if Valdez doesn't yet know that you really *are* Katherine O'Connor, the reporter."

"Yeah, my alibi worked a little too well. Tell Fabio thanks for sticking his neck out for me, though."

He grimaced, then said, "I can get you on the first flight out of Havana tomorrow morning."

"Won't it look suspicious if I try to get on a plane with no luggage or anything?"

He went to the closet and retrieved a valise. "I'll ask my housekeeper to go and buy a few things. It's probably better for you to get rid of that dress, anyway, since that's part of the description they'll be using. Long sleeves will hide your arm, but that bruise on your jaw—you'll have to do your best with makeup. Where's your passport?"

"At the last minute I thought it might be inconvenient to have it with me, so I asked the guard at the British Embassy to hang on to it for me. He said he'd give it to Penny when she got back."

"Well, that decision may have saved your life. Lourdes can pick that up for you, too, I suppose. Now stay here until I get back. In this office. Do you understand me?"

I gave him a look that communicated my reluctant agreement.

"Good girl. How are you at memorizing phone numbers?"

"Better when I'm not drugged."

"When you get to Miami, call this number." He dropped the case and wrote nine digits down on the top sheet of a notepad on his desk. "Increase each of these numbers by one, and then add a seven at the end. Can you remember that? And call collect."

"Add one, add a seven, call collect. Who'll answer?"

He ripped the page off and handed it to me. "Someone who'll want to know everything that's happened to you."

"But am I going to want to tell them?"

"Yes, I believe so."

I looked down at the piece of paper in my hand. "Blackie and the others — how did they get caught?"

"I don't know. But I know their capture won't stop the resistance. Not now."

"Did they get the weapons they were promised?"

"I don't know that, either." He picked up the valise again and started toward the door.

"Do you think they stand any chance at all of getting a prison sentence instead of being shot?" I asked without turning around.

He came back, and placed a gentle hand on my good arm. "Blackie has been executed, along with several others. Their trial was very short, and the outcome was never in doubt. They were shot less than an hour after the so-called 'verdict' was read. A lot of people went to the streets to protest, mainly about Blackie's death. He was well-loved in Santa Clara."

I winced as a pain that had nothing to do with my physical injuries shot through me. "And Armando?"

"His name was not among those executed or imprisoned. We must be grateful for that."

"What about Nacho?"

"No word about him yet. I'm sorry."

I slouched down in my chair with a sigh that shifted into a groan. *You may as well go home now, because you're a failure. A complete and utter failure,* I told myself as Father Lopez left in search of his housekeeper.

* * * * *

Going through the airport, I felt as if I were watching someone who looked a lot like me acting in an Alfred Hitchcock thriller. *Scene: Havana airport. Suspected spy waits for the plane to Miami, showing no signs of her barely concealed panic. A light sweater hides her bandaged arm. A broad scarf tied underneath her chin hides most of the bruise on her jaw. She smiles at the official who looks over her passport, sure that she'll hear the bad guys shout out her name and seize her before she can get on that plane.*

But I had no trouble at all. Apparently Valdez still didn't suspect that I was who he'd originally thought I was, and Katherine O'Connor wasn't on any sort of "stop" list. The guards were far more interested in harassing the Cuban nationals trying to leave than they were in grilling me.

I think I held my breath all the way to Miami.

I called Tim from a pay telephone in the terminal, using all of the change I'd scrounged from Father Lopez.

"Jesus, Mary, and Joseph! Where the hell have you been? Are you all right?" my brother shouted when he heard my voice.

"Sure. That is, mostly. How's Ma?"

"No change. So how did it go? Did you find him?"

"Yes. But I couldn't get him out."

"Then enough of this nonsense. Come on home."

"I'll come back soon. I still need to talk to a few people in Miami."

"What you need to do is come home."

"Soon, Tim. I promise."

After I hung up I pulled out the number Father Lopez had given me. When I did the math I realized it was a Washington, DC number. As instructed, I asked the operator to put the call through collect. After a few rings a woman's voice answered.

"Hello?"

"Collect call from Katherine O'Connor, from Miami. Will you accept the charges?"

"Just a moment." I could tell she'd put the receiver to her chest, or something of that sort, because her next words were muffled. "Jim, do you know a Katherine O'Connor? She's calling collect from Miami."

Next I heard a man's voice. "Yes, operator. We'll accept the charges. Miss O'Connor, this is Jim Copley."

"Hang on... you're my *boss*, Jim-Copley-of-Copley-News-Service Jim Copley?"

"That's right. Heard you'd dropped off the radar screen. We've been pretty worried. Where are you?"

"In the Miami airport."

"Okay, wait there. I'll send a driver to pick you up, and

arrange a room at Eden Roc. Are you feeling okay? Do you need a doctor?"

I was having trouble absorbing all this. "The Eden what? A doctor?"

"I'll send a doctor for my own peace of mind. You must be exhausted. Get some rest. I'll try and get down to Miami by this evening."

"But I don't see—"

"As you pointed out, I'm the boss. Please do as I ask."

I was too tired to argue, so I made my way to the front of the airport. A short while later a black limousine pulled up, very distinctive among all the light-colored cars and yellow taxis. The driver stepped out with a sign. "O'Connor" was printed on it in big block letters.

"That's me," I called to him, ignoring the curious looks of the passers-by. The driver took my valise and opened the door for me. I crawled into the back seat. A blast of cold air hit me full in the face. "Air conditioning," I said aloud. "God bless America."

* * * * *

When I entered the lobby of the Eden Roc Hotel I thought I might be hallucinating. It looked like the interior of an Art Deco spaceship. Enormous metal pillars propped up a sort of cloud-like faux ceiling. The crystal chandelier hanging over the reception desk was so huge it would have killed the entire population of a small town if it ever fell, and I'd never seen so much marble in one place, other than in the Vatican. The architect who'd designed this monument to excess was responsible for several astonishing new hotels in Miami. His motto was, "Too much is never enough," and he'd executed that philosophy perfectly when he designed the Roc.

I'd barely closed the door to my room when a waiter arrived with a meal: tomato soup, a grilled cheese sandwich, French fries, a pot of coffee, and a fifth of Jameson's whiskey. Whoever had ordered that meal knew way too much about my dietary habits. I started with the whiskey.

Soon afterwards, the bellhop brought up a very polite and elderly doctor. He introduced himself, took my temperature, and checked over my injuries. "That arm may be fractured," he said. "You should get it x-rayed."

"What if it is fractured?" I asked.

"You'll need a cast, not a sling."

"Let's go with the sling for now."

He reset my arm with an impressive plastic splint and gave me a prescription for some sleeping pills and a pain killer of some kind. I decided that the Jameson's was all I needed to fulfill both purposes, and within half an hour I was fast asleep on the top of the bed, having removed nothing but my shoes.

The shrill ring of the telephone woke me. I glanced reflexively at my wrist before I remembered that someone had swiped my Timex while I was a guest at Casa Valdez. The ornate clock on the nightstand read 7:30 p.m. I'd been asleep for over six hours.

"Hello?"

"Miss O'Connor, it's Jim Copley. Are you feeling up for a visit?"

"Right now?"

"Anytime, the sooner the better. We're in suite fifteen."

"Who's 'we'?"

"I brought Robert Bentley along. I thought it might be helpful to have him with us."

"What has he been telling you?"

"Why don't we talk about it over a drink?"

"I'll need some time to clean up."

"Fine. We'll be waiting."

I hung up a little too abruptly. *Why was Robert Bentley here?* He didn't even work for Copley. Or maybe he did by now. And how was my multi-millionaire employer mixed up in all this?

A quick look in the mirror made me realize there was not much in the way of "tidying up" I could do without a major overhaul. I didn't even have any lipstick. So I took a whack at brushing my hair and went in search of suite fifteen.

Bentley ushered me in. The place was enormous. I'd entered the combination living and dining room; the bedroom was hidden behind two lavishly decorated metal doors. The whole suite was furnished in that ultra-modern, ultra-uncomfortable style that was considered the height of chic in the fifties and early sixties: all white leather, chrome, glass, and plastic. Huge windows displayed a postcard-worthy view of the Atlantic.

The gentleman I recognized as Mr. Copley was on the telephone. He was a thin man, with a rather professorial air about him, down to his bow tie and horn-rimmed glasses. He gave me a thin-lipped but enthusiastic smile and gestured for me to sit down. I perched on the edge of the white couch in the center of the room.

"What will you have?" Bentley inquired, hovering.

"An explanation."

He responded with the most boyish grin I'd ever seen on that even-featured face. "How about something to help soften the blow? Mr. Copley has some fantastic single malt here."

"Fine. With one ice cube. Please."

Bentley looked me over while he poured my drink from a stunning crystal flask. "Pretty roughed up, were you?"

"You don't seem surprised. Are you back on the Copley payroll?"

"That's right."

At last Mr. Copley hung up and came over to greet me. He shook my hand and then took the glass of scotch Bentley offered him. "I'd like to offer a toast, to an extra-ordinarily brave woman, and one of the best reporters I've ever hired."

"Hear, hear," Bentley said, raising his glass as he took a seat.

I put my own glass down, untouched. "I appreciate the compliment, Mr. Copley, but I'd like to know why you've taken such a personal interest in me—and what this co-conspirator is doing here," I said, jerking my head in Bentley's direction.

"All fair questions. But please call me Jim. To answer the first question, Robert brought you to my attention as soon as he found out that you were being transferred back to New York. Said you were very talented, and under-appreciated at Reuters."

I looked at Bentley. "You never gave *me* that impression."

"Well, you don't take compliments very well, do you?" he replied. "You would've thought I was trying to pick you up or something."

I opened my mouth, and instantly shut it again. He was right. I decided it was time to taste the scotch.

Copley gave us both an amused look before continuing. "Robert called me again as soon as he found out that you were being let go. I offered to hire you on the spot and send you to Cuba as a Copley reporter, but Robert convinced me that you'd get better access if you weren't officially credentialed. And then, of course, you paid your own way despite my clandestine offer to fund your journey. Very admirable. And you did a superlative job, so I was delighted to bring you onto our staff."

This time I glared at Bentley. "You let me go risk my neck when I could've gone as a Copley reporter?"

"Would you have been able to do what you did if the G-2 knew you worked for Copley?"

We both knew that the answer was no, but I wasn't going to give him the satisfaction of hearing it from me. "And you let me think it was the CIA—"

"I told you, that was a mistaken assumption on your part," he said, looking positively smug. I could've kicked him, but decided that might not be the best move if I wanted to keep my job.

"And the 'State Department'?" I asked, directing my question to Mr. Copley. "Was that just another ploy?"

"It's more complicated than that, Miss O'Connor. You see, Copley Press has a very close relationship with certain departments within the government. President Eisenhower and I worked out an arrangement. When one of my reporters has material that might be of assistance in furthering a legitimate government objective, we encourage him — or in your case, her — to share it with the proper parties."

Thankfully I wasn't in mid-sip, or that expensive scotch would have been all over the glass coffee table. "And all this goes through you?" I asked Copley.

"When it's done properly. Robert was convinced that you would not participate in such a program voluntarily, but he also persuaded me that you were in a unique position to help with some very important objectives in Cuba. So I made a few phone calls."

My mind was reeling. "Are you saying that Copley reporters work as spies?"

"I wouldn't say that. It's a much less formal arrangement. All it involves is a reporter willing to perform his — or her — patriotic duty. And at the risk of sounding like I'm trying to use the 'everybody's doing it' defense, we are hardly alone in this. Journalists from every important American news organization — from the *New York Times*, to the television networks — occasionally supply the government with useful information. As I said, one is only doing one's patriotic duty. The Cold War is very real, and the prospect of nuclear annihilation is very real as well."

"But when I told those men that the CIA would help them, was I telling the truth?"

"Yes. But the agency hadn't been able to get one of theirs in to meet with the anti-Castro leaders. You succeeded where many had failed."

"A lot of good it did them."

"We could have let you go on believing that this was

uniquely a CIA initiative, but I felt that you deserved to know the truth. And I hope you appreciate the level of confidence I have in your ability to recognize how important it is for you to keep everything I've told you completely to yourself."

Who'd believe me? I thought to myself. *And if it's true that everybody else is doing this sort of thing, who would even publish the story?* "So did Bent—ah, Robert go to Reuters for 'international seasoning,' or because he could get a closer glimpse of what might be interesting to your friends in the government by working as Reuters' UN correspondent?"

"Both," they answered in unison. Bentley did the polite thing and let Copley finish answering my question.

"Robert is a fine journalist, but when he first applied for a transfer to Copley Press from the Illinois paper where he worked, I was a little concerned about his experience in the international sphere. His journalism experience. And it is true that Reuters, having been around a lot longer, has more caché than my company, although that's changing rapidly."

"Not if word gets out that your reporters spy for the US," I pointed out.

He furrowed his brows. "I think I've explained that no one actually serves as a spy, so I trust that you would never be the source of such unflattering misinformation."

This was my do-or-die moment. I could stay and play this game, or be pounding the pavement with a poor reference from Copley himself, which would make it very, very difficult for me to get a job doing anything other than writing obituaries. Or worse, a gossip column.

"While I may not like the 'accommodation' you've reached with the current administration, as far as I know you're not doing anything illegal—distasteful, perhaps, but not criminal. So no, I would never spill the beans, as long as I don't have to do any more spy work myself."

"Fair enough," Copley replied, completely unruffled. "Of course, if at any point you do decide that you have some worthwhile information to contribute…"

He left this invitation unfinished. I turned to Bentley. "And was our Mr. Pershing really with the State Department?"

"I'm afraid I'm not at liberty to answer that," he replied. "More scotch?"

I held out my glass. Bentley brought it over to the sideboard, where he refilled his as well.

"I went to Cuba willingly," I said as Bentley handed me my drink, "but the real reason I agreed to be the devil's messenger this last time was because I wanted to find someone and get him out of Cuba. A child, whose father is in the resistance."

"And did you succeed?" Copley asked.

"No. I'd like to try again, but I don't think I'll be able to return as a journalist."

"Why? What did happen, exactly? Our contact—"

"That would be Father Lopez?"

"Yes. He let us know that you'd been dropped off with the man who was to lead you to the rebels. When we heard that some of the leaders had been arrested, and we still had no word from you, we became extremely concerned," Copley said.

"For good reason." I told them everything that had

happened, leaving out some of Valdez' more colorful dialogue.

Bentley looked gratifyingly awe-struck. "You fought off two armed men?"

I answered with a sweetly sarcastic smile. "Don't you remember? I have certain skills that come in handy in such situations." Of course I'd been petrified the whole time, but I wasn't about to let him know that.

Mr. Copley leaned back in his chair, looking thoughtful. "Quite a remarkable story. Well, under those circumstances I certainly agree it's not practical for you to go back."

"Unless you could find some way to smuggle me in. Preferably with a fake ID."

"I'm afraid it's beyond my capacity to arrange a behind-the-scenes drop."

Bentley didn't try to hide his astonishment. "Why on *earth* would you go back now?"

"I told you. I promised Miriam Velasquez that I would get her son out of there. Can Father Lopez help me find them?"

Bentley and Copley exchanged glances. Copley answered the question. "I'm sorry to say he was arrested shortly after you left for the airport. Don't blame yourself. He was involved in a variety of anti-Castro activities."

The color must have drained right out of my face, because Bentley leapt up to go get me a glass of water. "I'm beginning to feel like some sort of jinx," I said after downing it.

"It wasn't your fault," Bentley said, with a gentleness I'd never seen him display before — to anyone.

"Robert's right. Father Lopez knew the risks he was taking. He's a brave man," Copley added.

"Is he a CIA agent?"

"I doubt it," Copley answered, his face inscrutable. "The man's a priest. But I wouldn't be in the position to know one way or another." I had a hunch he wasn't being entirely truthful, but didn't challenge his answer.

"However," he continued, "I may know someone else who can help you with respect to the child." He took a business card out of his breast pocket and handed it to me.

"Call this person. Father Bryan Walsh, director of the Catholic Welfare Bureau here in Miami. He's taken a great interest in the problems of Cuban refugees, particularly the children. Also, I should let you know that someone may be contacting you who would appreciate a thorough briefing about everything you saw and experienced in Cuba. Whether you cooperate or not is entirely up to you. There's no coercion involved. My employees are usually willing to share information when asked, because doing so is important to the national security of our country. But if you do not wish to do so, that is your choice."

I somehow refrained from telling him that I would sooner go back and have tea with Valdez than provide any more assistance to the CIA.

CHAPTER THIRTY-THREE

I decided to delay my return to New York until I could meet with Father Walsh, and let the color of my jaw return to normal. I could go home with a heavily bandaged arm and blame it on one too many pints followed by an embarrassing tumble down a flight of stairs, but Tim would be suspicious of an injured left arm combined with a swollen right jaw. So I asked the man at the front desk of the Eden Roc to recommend a cheap hotel that wasn't too disgusting.

He looked positively horrified. "But Madame's bill is paid for the next five days. Have we disappointed you in some way? Please let me know and I will do what I can to rectify the situation at once."

Five days in a luxury hotel on the ocean. Not too bad. I called Tim to let him know that I was fine and would be home within a week, asked about Ma, and hung up before he could start lecturing me.

Next I went to meet with Father Walsh. His office was in the kind of nondescript post-war building you'd expect in Miami: a sort of half-cement, half-glass shoebox. The very efficient matron at the front desk showed me right in.

With a surname like Walsh I was pretty sure he'd be from the Emerald Isle, and I wasn't disappointed. He had the round face and pointed chin of a leprechaun, and although not much was left of his brogue (having been raised in the States) I did hear a hint of it as he spoke.

He greeted me warmly, saying that Jim Copley had spoken highly of me.

"He contacted you?"

"Just to let me know you'd be in touch."

I didn't know how to take that. I should've been flattered, but I felt a little resentful that Copley had once again worked covertly on my behalf. "How kind of him. Did he tell you why I wanted to meet with you?"

"Yes. He mentioned that there's a child whose parents wish to get him out of Cuba while they help overthrow Castro. I'm hearing more about such requests every day. In fact, not long ago a woman in Key West went to the juvenile court to ask the State Juvenile Agency to find accommodation for her fourteen-year-old son while she returned to Cuba to work toward that same goal. How desperate these parents must be."

"Castro has lowered the draft age to fifteen."

"So I've been told. Who is it you're trying to help?"

I explained the situation to him, leaving out most of the gorier details. He looked very troubled by the time I'd finished.

"So apparently it's impossible for me to go back and get him," I said.

"That's understandable. Unfortunately, I'm only responsible for the children once they arrive. I have no way to help you search for a child who's still in Cuba."

I didn't try to hide my disappointment. "Well, would you please call me if you come up with anything?"

"Certainly. And keep up hope. God works in mysteri-ous ways."

"So I've been told." I gave him my number at the hotel, at the office, and at my mother's house. I thanked him for his time and departed.

I went back to the Eden Roc feeling so dejected I didn't even ring room service for a pick-me-up. I was lying on the bed, staring at the ceiling, trying to come up with a plan when the phone rang. It was Bentley.

"How did your meeting with Father Walsh go?"

"For Chrissake, are you following me?"

"Nothing of the kind. I just know you well enough to know that you'd be at his office before daybreak, and not leave until you had a chance to talk with him."

Right again, I thought. "He wasn't encouraging. Out of his line of business, you might say."

"That's tough. I'm sorry, Katherine."

"Maybe you could ask one of your friends in high places to send out a search party?"

"Unlikely. But wait—that does give me an idea. You're in possession of some pretty valuable information, or at least someone pretty high up thinks you are. So you might be able to—well, I won't say sell, because that's too pejorative—but you might be able to arrange a quid-pro-quo. Tell them they have to find a way to get the kid out in exchange for a briefing. Who knows, you might be able to find someone around there crazy enough to send you back."

"Bentley, that may be a brilliant idea—although I can never decide if you're trying to help me or send me to my doom."

"I'd never desire your demise. Having you around makes life so much more interesting." He hung up before I could reply.

"Wish I could say the same about you," I said to the receiver before replacing it.

* * * * *

My "debriefing officer" called late that afternoon.

"I'd like to speak with Katherine O'Connor," said a masculine voice when I picked up the phone.

"Speaking."

"This is Devon Marshall. I believe Jim Copley told you to expect my call."

"He did."

"Would you mind coming to my office so we can talk? It's important that we meet in a secure location.

"Just say when and where."

I agreed to meet him at ten o'clock the next morning. "Take a cab," he added, "we'll reimburse you."

When I jumped into a cab the next morning and gave the driver the address, he said, "Oh, yeah. The CIA house."

Wonderful, I thought to myself. That did not inspire confidence.

Devon Marshall met me at the door. He was bald and dumpy, with wobbly jowls and an attitude that practically preceded him into the room. After offering me a cup of coffee he led me into a chamber-like room containing a small table, two chairs, and a tape recorder.

"I'll talk, but I won't be recorded," I said as I took a

seat, "I don't want this interview coming back to haunt me."

He didn't look pleased, but he didn't argue. "As you wish."

"And I have another condition. A serious quid-pro-quo."

"What did you have in mind?"

"There's a child, the son of two people who are part of the resistance. They want him to come to America while they're fighting Castro. I promised I would bring him out with me, but things didn't turn out the way I'd planned."

"Do you know where he is?"

"I have a vague idea."

"We'll do what we can."

I rose. "That's not good enough. Sorry to have wasted your time."

His face folded into an exasperated grimace. "Oh, hold your horses. Let me see what I can find out. Wait here."

I sipped my coffee and waited. A few minutes later a tall blond gentleman entered the room. He looked more like a surfer than a spy.

"Miss O'Connor, I'm Ned Shackelby. I understand you're seeking some help in exchange for the information you have to offer."

"That's right. I want to be sent back to Cuba, with a fake ID, so I can hustle a particular child out of there."

"I'm afraid we can't oblige you. Chances are you're already on Castro's 'Most Wanted' list, and it would be irresponsible for us to send you back. And because you'd be in jeopardy, the child would be, too."

"Irresponsible. I see. Well, can you think of another option?"

"I do know the name of someone, an American who's lived in Cuba for quite some time, who's trying to find a way to get the children of resistance fighters out of Cuba. I'll pass along this child's name and information. I can't make any promises, but if anyone can find him, he can."

"And how will he get the boy out?"

"I'm not sure, but this gentleman is working on a way of getting many children out safely. And we're going to do what we can to help."

I mulled this over. It was the best solution I'd be able to come up with for the time being. If it didn't work, I'd find some way to go back myself.

"Okay. It's a deal. But do I have your word on this?" All I could think as this came out of my mouth was the scene in *Gone with the Wind* where Rhett Butler gives his word "as a gentleman" to a Union soldier, which meant he was lying through his teeth because he knew he was no gentleman.

Blondie smiled. "For what it's worth, yes." I found his forthright answer reassuring, and proceeded to tell him everything I'd seen with my own eyes, most of what had happened to me personally, and also added some militarily relevant details Nacho had shared with me.

"There are at least ten thousand troops currently deployed in the Escambray. They're armed with Czech machine guns, and several Soviet military advisors have been seen directing troop movements. Some of the Cuban forces are regular army, but most are members of the militia. They're poorly trained and trigger-happy, but there are a lot of them, with more arriving every day. The strategy seems to be to form circles around the areas of suspected infiltration and starve the anti-Castro forces out; as my friend Nacho said, there's a lot of water but not much food available in those mountains. They're also lining the major roads into the area and searching anyone who looks suspicious. There may be a plan afoot to move the opposition forces north, but there is so little co-ordination between the various rebel groups that it's hard to tell how successful that strategy will be."

By the looks of it, Shackelby was writing down every word I said. "Not a very optimistic picture," he commented when he'd finished. He asked a few follow-up questions. I gave him Emilio's name and his last known address, and Carlos' information as well. He escorted me to the door, where the same taxi was waiting for me.

"How'd it go?" the driver asked as I got in.

"It was heavenly. Those boys really know how to show a girl a good time."

"You're the first person I've heard say that," he said as we drove away.

* * * * *

It was another three days before I made it back to New York. Mr. Copley called twice to see how I was doing, and never even mentioned my CIA interview. The second time he called he told me to "take a few more days" and report to the head of the New York office when I felt up to it. "You can take whatever domestic beat you want," he said. "With things so up in the air about that boy, I imagine you want to stick close to home for a while. Don't worry. I'll have you in South America soon enough. That's what you wanted to do next, isn't it?" As much as I'd fantasized about it, I found that this sort of star treatment made me uncomfortable. But I wasn't about to turn him down.

Tim met me at the airport, and after quizzing me about how I'd hurt my arm—which was now in a small cast—he took me straight over to the hospital to visit Mom. (I could tell he didn't buy the stairway story, but he didn't push.)

"She's been a little more responsive," he said eagerly. "Two days ago a nurse thought she heard her murmur something, and just yesterday I saw her open her eyes for a few seconds."

After his encouraging report the sight of my mother prone in her hospital bed hit me pretty hard. The image of her I carried in my head had nothing to do with the pale, shrunken figure connected to a feeding tube. Sensing my disappointment, Tim squeezed my good hand and said, "Remember, there's still hope. And if—when—she comes out of it, why, they'll fix her up right as rain in no time." But I knew this wasn't true. Even if she woke up, there was no telling how much damage had been done. She could have trouble speaking, or be paralyzed on one side—or worse.

He left me after an hour or so, relieved, I'm sure, to have another person to help with the vigil, which he and Maureen had not been able to keep up for more than a few hours a day once he'd used up his vacation time and Maureen's husband had grown tired of staying with their kids. And a hospital is a depressing place. There's only so much a person can take, no matter how committed they are to the welfare of a loved one.

I sat for a while, read Ma part of the newspaper, found a station on the transistor radio Tim had brought that played her favorite music, and went out to see if I could dig up a cup of coffee. When I came back Ma's eyes were wide open, and full of terror. She saw me and started to gurgle.

"Hang on, Ma! I have to get a nurse!" I said, then dashed into the corridor, screaming like a maniac for help. The duty nurse came running. I sputtered something frantic and meaningless, but she understood enough to go to Ma's bedside. Ma looked at her, blinking, her face full of fear and confusion.

"It's alright, Mrs. O'Connor. I just have to remove this tube. It will be a little uncomfortable."

I had to close my eyes as the nurse started to pull the long tube out of my mother's nose. I'm not squeamish, but seeing my own mother in such agony was too much for me. I opened them when I heard her gasp for air.

"Mary Kate, what am I doing here? Why can't I move?" she sounded like she had a sore throat, but she spoke clearly, with just a trace of the garbled speech that so often follows a stroke.

"It's okay, Ma. You had — an incident. A little stroke, they think." I forced myself not to cry. I knew my tears would only scare her more.

"But I can't move!"

"That's normal," the nurse said soothingly, "it may take a little while for your brain to start communicating properly with the rest of your body."

"How long have I been here?" Ma asked me.

"A few days. Not too long," I lied. "Do you remember anything, anything at all?"

"I was sitting at the kitchen table. Now I'm here. What's been happening to me?"

I don't know what I'd expected her to say—maybe that she'd ask me about Emilio, or tell me that an angel had visited her while she slept. I went over to her and grasped her hand. Three of her fingers moved within mine. "You're going to be okay, Ma. It may take some time, but you're going to be right as rain."

CHAPTER THIRTY-FOUR

I t was the week before Thanksgiving. I was in my office cubicle, going over the list of things Ma wanted me to buy at the grocery store. She'd made a remarkable recovery. "Miraculous," was the phrase her doctor used, which only made me uncomfortable. Other than a slight limp, she really was "right as rain," in about a month.

Even so, Tim, Maureen, and I had insisted that we celebrate Thanksgiving at Maureen's house on Long Island, rather than at Ma's. She'd agreed readily enough. But looking at her list, I realized that Ma planned on making everything but the turkey, which wasn't exactly what we'd had in mind. I was wondering how to approach her about this when the phone rang.

"Is there a Miss Katherine O'Connor there?" a man's voice asked.

"Speaking."

"Miss O'Connor, this is Father Bryan Walsh. We met in Miami."

"Yes, of course." My heart started beating rapidly. *Don't hope for too much,* I told myself. "Have you heard anything?"

"Yes. That's why I'm calling. A gentleman has been in touch with me regarding temporary placements for young-sters who are in the same situation as the boy you mentioned during your visit. I'd rather not get more specific on the phone."

"I understand completely."

"It does seem promising. He's come up with a list of two hundred children—"

"*Two hundred?*"

"That's right. I don't know yet if your—ah, candidate —is on the list, but I should know within a few weeks. But we have to work out something with the State Department, so that these children can come in on a visa that would allow them to stay indefinitely. One hopes they will be reunited with their families very soon, but we've no guarantee that will happen, so we need for them to receive something longer than a tourist visa. Of course that's not really your concern—"

"May I call you back in a few minutes? I think I may know someone who can help."

"Really? How wonderful. I'll be in the office all morning."

I said goodbye and raced over to Bentley's cubicle. "I need your help," I said, ignoring the fact that he was on the phone himself.

He gave me that unique "can't you see that I'm on the phone?" look, and waved me away. I didn't budge. At last, he hung up.

"Where's the fire?"

"Do you still have that 'friend' at the so-called 'State Department'?"

"Oh, brother. Can we go somewhere a little more private to talk about this?"

"Where? The men's room?" Copley News Service was

331

headquartered in San Diego, and the New York office was tiny, housed in an unused corner of the *New York Times* building. We were all crammed in like a family of meerkats.

Bentley stood up. "Come on." I followed him out the main door and down the hall. He pulled out a key and unlocked an unmarked door that I'd always assumed was a broom closet. When he turned on the light I could see that it was a very compact conference room, with a small table, four chairs, a telephone, and a tape recorder.

"What's this? The Star Chamber?"

"Hardly. Just a place to hold private interviews."

"And you have the key."

"I asked for one. I'm sure you can get one, too."

"I certainly will. So, to repeat my question, are you still in touch with dear Mr. Pershing at the so-called State Department?"

"What's this about?"

"Father Walsh has been contacted by someone who wants to bring two hundred children of members of the Cuban resistance to Miami. Emilio Velasquez may be among them. But they need some kind of special visa to get them out."

"Did he tell you who he's working with?"

"No. I assume he doesn't want to endanger the man. And I can't ask Copley to help. He's in Costa Rica at that conference. But you must know someone who can pull some strings at State—or at some other specialized government agency. In fact, I'd be willing to bet that you have some acquaintances who'd be extremely effective at helping Father Walsh and his mysterious partner carry this off."

"I have no idea what would have given you that impression."

"Right. Other Copley reporters may cooperate with the CIA from time to time, but I think your relationship with the agency is a little more... shall I say, 'intimate.'"

"And you'd be wrong. But I may know someone at State who can help. A guy named Tracy Voorhees. He was in charge of the Hungarian refugee program in 'fifty-six. He'll know how to get it done."

"Did he go to Yale?"

"I'll let that pass."

"Sorry. Couldn't help myself. I really am grateful, though. Thank you."

"You're welcome. But one of these days I'm gonna call in all my chits."

"No problem. I always pay my debts."

CHAPTER THIRTY-FIVE

Raul hadn't celebrated Christmas since he was a young boy, so he was very surprised when Tito's present was delivered to him on Christmas morning. It was, of course, a cigar. The note read, "It's not too late to convert. Merry Christmas, Tito." Raul had a chuckle over his friend's choice of words. Convert to a cigar smoker? Convert to Christianity? Or convert to a whole new way of life?

He was in the courtyard, about to light the fat Cohiba, when another of the *Hispanic-Sovieticos* called out to him. "Raul, there's some kid here to see you. He looks too old to be your bastard, though."

Emilio, Raul thought as he tucked the cigar into his breast pocket. He hadn't seen the boy in months. *I should have bought him something for Christmas*, he thought ruefully.

Emilio was on the sidewalk in front of the house. Raul sensed right away the depth of the change that had taken place within him. He no longer exuded the captivating, care-free confidence that had so enchanted Raul when they met. *This is what war does to children*.

Emilio offered Raul his hand in a manner that was way too dignified for a child his age. "I'm glad you're here," he said. "Merry Christmas."

"Merry Christmas to you, my friend. It's been too long. Where have you been?"

"We were in Santa Clara, but we've been staying at Carlos' house for the past couple of weeks. His wife died, so he said we could stay with him because he had nothing left to lose if the *Fidelistas* found us there. Now my mom says I have to go to Miami. I was supposed to go with Miss Maria, but she got captured."

Raul felt his stomach tighten into a painful knot. "Captured? When?"

"When she tried to come get me. They just grabbed her. She's okay, though. Someone told my mom that she escaped."

Raul exhaled an enormous sigh of relief. "So now you and your mother are leaving?"

"No, just me. She'll come soon. That's what she says, anyway."

An inexplicable wave of panic swept over Raul as he digested this information. *But she won't come,* the abandoned boy inside him shouted. *Don't let her send you away!*

He looked down and discovered that his hands were shaking. Emilio was staring at him, wide-eyed. "Are you okay? You look like you're about to puke."

"Maybe I ate something that disagreed with me," Raul said, trying to sound unconcerned. "When are you leaving?"

"Tomorrow. But sometimes they just send you home from the airport for no reason. 'Nothing is worse than a moron with a pinch of authority,' that's what Carlos says. I hope there's a moron like that at the airport tomorrow, who sends me home."

"I hope so too, for your sake."

"But if not, I guess this is goodbye."

Raul stooped down and enveloped the boy in his arms. "It'll be alright," he whispered, and then felt like he'd just told the biggest lie of his life.

The boy stiffened and pulled away. "That's what grownups always say. And it never is. It's never alright."

Raul was incapable of giving Emilio any more false reassurance. *I can't let her do this to him.* "I'd like to come and meet your mother before you go," he said. "If she raised a son like you, she must be pretty special."

"You can come with me now, if you want."

"I'd love to."

They took a bus to get to Carlos' house. When they arrived Emilio opened the front door and shouted, "Mommy, I'm home. I brought a friend who wants to meet you."

An old man hobbled into the room. He held a pistol in one hand, and it was pointed right at Raul's chest. "Emilio, you little idiot, where have you been? And who the hell is this? You don't have the sense God gave a billy goat!"

"Look, I'm a friend of Emilio's. My name's Raul—"

Miriam appeared at the archway separating the small living room from the hallway. "It's okay, Carlos. I know who this is."

Emilio raced over to her. "Mommy, Carlos almost shot Raul."

"He's just trying to protect us. Where have you been? You should have been home hours ago. I've been worried sick."

"But I had to say goodbye to Raul."

Miriam gave Raul a wan smile. "He's told me about

you. You've been a very good friend to my son, at a time when his father could not be with us. Thank you."

Carlos lowered his pistol. "The next time someone unexpected comes into this house, I'm going to shoot first and ask questions later. With luck, it will be Fidel." He shot Miriam an aggravated glance, then shuffled away.

Raul moved closer to Miriam. Raw emotion flooded through him. "Don't send him away," he managed to get out as his voice cracked.

Emilio picked up on this with great enthusiasm. "You see? Raul understands, because he's a man. I need to stay here to protect you and the baby."

Miriam put her hand on her rounded belly. "I promise you, I will come for you after the baby is born."

"I know you think you're doing what's best for him, but believe me, it doesn't work out that way," Raul said, not bothering to comment on Miriam's pregnancy.

She looked down at Emilio, who was soaking up every word like a sponge. "Go to your room, Emilio."

"I don't have a room."

"Our room, then. Go. NOW."

The boy's eyes flickered from Raul to his mother, but he obeyed her command.

Miriam waited until they heard his door close before she lit into Raul.

"Don't you think this is already hard enough, for me, for him, for his father? What right do you have to come here and tell me what to do? And to say all that in front of him, as if he needed another reason to be afraid—"

"He should be afraid. Whatever you think you're saving him from, it won't be worse than living without the people he loves. He'll feel thrown away. Nothing will ever repair the hole in his heart."

The anger in Miriam's eyes melted away. She went to Raul and put her hands on his shoulders. "You were one of them, weren't you? The Lost Children of the War. Your parents sent you to Russia, didn't they? And you never saw them again?"

Raul felt his limbs begin to tremble. "That's why I know what I'm talking about. You're not saving him. You just think you are. He'll be alone—"

"No, he won't be. I will come for him."

"But you can't control that. You're sending him into a limbo from which he may never return. He'd be better off staying with you."

"Raul, your mother saved your life. Please let me save the life of my son."

Then they moved to the couch, where she held his head in her lap as he wept.

CHAPTER THIRTY-SIX

T he call came the day after Christmas. My heart was racing as I put down the receiver. I had to take several deep breaths before I went into the kitchen to tell my mother the news.

"Ma, he's here."

I didn't tell her who I was talking about, and she didn't ask for an explanation. She just said, "Good. His room is ready. Come and see if I missed anything."

Totally confused by this response, I followed her into the bedroom that my three brothers had shared as boys. She'd made the bed with new sheets, and covered it with the quilt she'd received as a wedding present. She'd even dug up some of the boys' old paraphernalia, like a baseball signed by some of the Yankees, a toy truck that had seen better days, and a couple of toy soldiers.

"How—when did you know?" I asked her after I recovered from my initial astonishment.

"I never knew. I had faith," she said.

If I'd been employing proper journalistic techniques, I would have reminded her that when I asked her for the *second* time if she remembered anything about what had happened while she was in a coma, she'd looked at me as if I were the nutty one, and then told me (again) that she didn't remember a single thing about the whole episode.

But something about the matter-of-fact calmness with which she'd just answered my question made me swallow all of my follow-up queries.

"What sort of things will he be wanting to eat?" she asked.

"Beans and rice. Roast chicken. Not too many vegetables. Ice cream."

"Do you suppose he might like to try a shepherd's pie?"

That had been my brother Jamie's favorite dish. "I'm sure he'd love it, Ma."

* * * * *

Father Walsh sent Emilio and two other children who'd arrived on the same flight to an order of nuns who ran a small Catholic elementary school. The school was closed for the holidays, so the sisters put four cots in a classroom and one of them, a young woman who spoke Spanish, slept with the children overnight. By the time I arrived, on the morning of December 27th, the two other kids had already been picked up by their relatives.

No one had told Emilio to expect me. I found him sitting at a table in the makeshift dorm, drawing pictures. The nun who was minding him smiled at me as I came into the room.

"Look who's here, Emilio. A friend of yours."

He looked up at me, and his face contained not a trace of his usual buoyancy. "I didn't know you were coming," he said.

"I told you I'd get you out of Cuba. I just couldn't do it

myself. But you're coming to New York, to live with me and my mother, until your mother comes for you."

"Is your mother a good cook?"

"The best," I said. His smile didn't dissipate the shadow in his eyes.

"My mom's having a baby. Do you think that's why she sent me away? Because I'd be too much trouble if she has to take care of a baby?"

"No, that's silly. My mom had five children. Mothers always have enough love for all of their children, and you're a good kid. She just wants you out of danger. Don't worry. She'll come."

"You don't know that," he said, so flatly that I didn't have the heart to contradict him. How could I argue with the truth?

"Sometimes you just have to have faith," I said.

His mood improved somewhat when we boarded the plane. It was bigger than the small craft that he'd flown in to come to Miami, and the flight attendants were very solicitous of the adorable little guy, even though they spoke no Spanish and he spoke almost no English. The pilot even let Emilio come up into the cockpit for a minute, where he gazed in utter fascination as the man pointed out the various controls. When he came back to his seat he said to me, "I'm going to be a pilot. So now I have to learn how to speak better English, even after I go back to Cuba."

Believe it or not, it was only then that it hit me: I would have to stay in New York and help my mother take care of Emilio, not just because of her health, but because the child was going to a place where he didn't speak the language. I'd been secretly hoping that after he arrived I could go back to doing international work. At least for the fore-seeable future, that would be impossible.

How can you think of yourself at a time like this? my con-science scolded. *Did you really think you could take him away from his mother and just drop him off with an old woman? Copley said you could work whatever beat you wanted until you had everything sorted out. You'll just have to tell him you need to work out of the New York office a little while longer.*

Emilio's mood picked up again when I pointed out the Statue of Liberty as we started our descent. The taxi ride into Manhattan was also pretty thrilling; he'd never seen anything to compare to the skyline of New York, other than in movies. But Emilio's awe at seeing the legendary skyscrapers of Manhattan was nothing compared to what I experienced when we arrived at my mother's house.

She met us at the door, bent down until her face was level with Emilio's, and said, "Welcome to our home. I'm Mrs. O'Connor, Miss Maria's mother." And she said this in Spanish — the accent was pure American, but the words were correct.

I was amazed. "Ma, when did you learn how to speak Spanish?"

She straightened up and gave me an almost scornful look. "And how do you suppose I'm to take care of a boy if I can't even ask him if he's hungry? There's a Spanish priest at the church now. I went to him and explained that I'd be taking in a Cuban boy, so he taught me how to say a few things. I can't say much, but you'll be here, in and out at least, and he'll learn some English from a tutor before we make him go back to school." She looked down at Emilio and asked, *"Tienes hambre?"*

"Very hungry," he answered in English, with the biggest smile I'd seen on his face since the day he'd shown me the magic shell.

"Good," my mother said, and led him to the kitchen.

CHAPTER THIRTY-SEVEN

Raul leapt out of bed when he heard the first explosive roar. He raced to a window and threw open the shutters. He could hear the plane's engine somewhere overhead, but when he looked outside he didn't see the fountains and flowers of the courtyard. He saw Guernica burning.

He staggered back into the room, eyes closed, trying to slow his breathing. When he looked out again the landscape was as it should be. But a second explosion sent another wave of terror through him and he dove under his bed, where he stayed until it sounded as if the bombing was over. Feeling sheepish, and grateful that he had a room to himself, he crawled out and went back to the window. The sound of gunfire was deafening. It was as if every man in Havana was shooting some kind of weapon.

The door to his bedroom flew open. "It's finally happened," an ebullient colleague shouted, "the *yanquis* have attacked!"

"How do you know it's the Americans?"

"Who the hell else could it be? The Dutch?" the man replied, and dashed away to continue delivery of his glad tidings.

Since early January, Castro had been warning that an American attack was imminent. His dire predictions had driven the population mad with fear. Thousands of men and women joined the militia. Massive anti-aircraft guns, freshly delivered from the Soviet Union, were set up along the Malecón, the long boulevard along Havana's northern coast. Soldiers drilled in the streets, and women hoarded canned goods, despite the fact that by doing so they risked imprisonment.

Did Castro stand a chance? Even with the wonderful new Soviet armaments that he'd shown off during the parade celebrating the second anniversary of the Glorious Revolution, Raul wasn't sure Castro could defend the island against an all-out American assault. He'd only survive if the new president, Kennedy, decided to pull his punches — and Raul doubted the man was that stupid.

The first attack was over within a half an hour. The bombs had destroyed one ammunition depot, and put some holes in a few airport runways — hardly large-scale damage — but Havana dissolved into chaos. Roundups began within a few hours. Hundreds of G-2 agents and thousands of militia members burst into homes and offices across the city. They seized everyone who had the remotest tie to anyone who might be suspected of being anti-Castro.

Raul watched from the relative safety of a bookstore facing Havana's main thoroughfare as people were dragged away and shoved into buses and trucks. It was like watching the Nazis at work again.

The next day he met Tito for an afternoon coffee. His friend strolled into the café, cigar in hand, looking unusually glum. "There goes paradise," he said as he took a seat. "This place will be nothing but a sunnier version of the USSR in a few weeks, unless Kennedy kicks Castro's ass. And if he does that, we'll be back in Moscow in a month."

"I hear that the Americans are saying it wasn't them," Raul said.

"Is that right? And who do they think will believe that?"

Raul shrugged. "Any idea who they're arresting?"

"Whoever they want. Thousands upon thousands is what I hear. There's no place to put them all, so they're filling up the moat at Morro Castle with prisoners, shoving even more into La Cabaña, and packing them into theaters, schools—even churches is what I've been told. It's an ugly business."

Raul threw some change on the table. "I have to go. I forgot about something I had to do."

Tito raised a skeptical eyebrow. "This have anything to do with that little kid who used to hang around?"

"No. I haven't seen him in months. I just forgot to file a report, that's all."

"Whatever you say."

Many public buses had been requisitioned to transport prisoners, so Raul took a cab over to Carlos' house. The driver was ecstatic. "We're gonna kick those *yanquis'* butts," he kept saying over and over. Raul just smiled politely.

No one answered when he knocked on Carlos' door. Raul walked around to the back of the house to see if he could detect any signs of activity. The old man was sitting on a picnic chair in the miniscule back yard. He looked stunned.

"They took her," he said as Raul approached.

"Where?"

"I don't know. Maybe to the Blanquita, that big theater in Miramar. Someone came by this morning and said he'd heard there were some women being held there. There's only men in the La Cabaña moat, or so they say. Castro won't have to worry about executing them. Dysentery will do it."

He looked down at his gnarled hands. "I couldn't get out of bed fast enough to shoot the bastards. They broke down the door and grabbed her. Why would they take her now? Armando's dead, and she's about to have a baby. What harm could she do now?" The old man started to sob, not bothering to cover his face or wipe his tears. Raul handed him his own handkerchief.

"I'll find her," he said. Carlos did not respond.

Raul walked to the corner. He waited a few minutes, but no taxi drove by. So he started to walk. It took him over an hour to get to his quarters, where he changed into his USSR Civil Engineering uniform and picked up the official name badge he'd been issued when he was traveling around Cuba doing his surveys.

The Blanquita Theater was less than a mile away. The line of people seeking information about their loved ones stretched a good three blocks away from the massive building. Raul shoved his way through, intent on one thing. He was not going to let Emilio lose his mother.

When he made it to the front of the building he saw some policemen hooking a water cannon up to a fire hydrant, intending, no doubt, to clear away the crowd if they became too unruly. A few dozen militiamen prowled around the entrance, all armed with machine guns.

Two of them confronted Raul when he got close. "Back off. This is a secure area," one said.

Raul pulled out his passport and his badge. "I've been sent to make a report on the number of prisoners to Minister Kerlincov," he said sternly, making up a Russian name. "As you can see, I'm here working for the Soviets, who so generously provided those wonderful guns you're all carrying. If you won't let me by, I'll be forced to report you to Major Guevara."

"Oh, yes, sorry. Go on in."

No one else stopped him until he entered the theater itself. Dante's inferno had nothing on the scene that greeted him there. The theater was one of the largest in the world, able to seat 5,000 people, but the authorities had crammed thousands more than that into its cavernous interior. Men and women moaned, screamed, and prayed aloud, begging to be let out, protesting their innocence, pleading for water. The air conditioning wasn't func-tioning—or had been cut off—and the sanitary facilities were no longer working. It was nearly impossible to breathe. Raul reached for his handkerchief to cover his face, remembering too late that he'd given it to Carlos. On the stage, at the front of the room, two policemen held onto large German Shepherds, threatening to release the snarling animals should anyone try to attack the guards.

As Raul started down the aisle one of the militia men blocked his way. "What are you doing here?" he demanded.

Raul showed the man his badge and repeated his story.

Guevara's name worked like a magic elixir. "You'll want to see Valdez," he was told. "He's in the manager's office."

Raul left the theater, headed down the main hall, repeated his request twice, and was finally shown to the manager's office. It, at least, had a window and a fan. The man he assumed to be Valdez sat at his desk, looking over long lists of names. Raul introduced himself and explained his mission one more time.

"How am I supposed to know who we have in here?" Valdez said. "They've been carting people in since yesterday morning. I had to forbid any more prisoners from being brought in, or my men are going to pass out from the stench."

"Do you know how long you'll be holding them?"

"Until someone tells me to let them go. Some of them have been invited to go over to G-2 headquarters for a little private talk. Maybe when they're done with the ones they want to interrogate I'll be given the order to release the rest. Or they may be kept here until Castro figures out what the *yanquis* are up to. These are all counter-revolutionaries, you know."

Raul thanked him for this information then went back into the theater. This time the guards at the door let him through without a word. He made his way down to the stage, holding his badge in front of him like a shield, and walked up to the militia member wearing more stripes on his uniform than any of the others.

"There's been a mistake," he said after introducing himself, without mentioning his alleged mission. "There's a woman here who shouldn't have been picked up. She's my fiancée."

"I've heard that story a dozen times today," the officer said, although he glanced at Raul's ID again, looking a trifle worried.

"Trust me. I'm telling the truth. I'm not the only Russian in Cuba who intends to take a Cuban bride. But I have to find her. You see, she's expecting my child."

This had the desired effect. "I'm sorry to hear that, comrade. I did hear someone shouting about a pregnant woman back in that corner. There's more than one in here, though."

Raul didn't bother to thank him. He muscled his way through the morass of humanity until he reached the far right corner of the theater, where he spotted two women sitting on the floor, leaning over a body that was pressed up against the wall, presumably to keep other people from trampling it. When he got there one of the woman looked up at him.

"She lost the baby. A little girl. I wrapped the body in my sweater, but a soldier came and took it. He told her he would bring it to be buried, and hit her pretty good when she fought him to get the child back. Poor thing's likely been thrown in a trash heap by now. These men aren't human."

It was Miriam. He squeezed in next to her and lifted her up into his arms. She was unconscious but still breathing. "Come on," he whispered to her. "We're getting out of here."

* * * * *

Raul managed to get Miriam admitted to a small Catholic

hospital, one of the few that Castro had not yet nationalized. He stayed with her until he was sure that she would be well taken care of. She regained consciousness just long enough to squeeze his hand.

The real invasion began the next day, on the southern coast at an area known as the Bay of Pigs. This time Havana remained fairly tranquil. People went about their business, hoping that Castro would emerge victorious. Or that he wouldn't.

Raul had just left the house to attend a meeting when he heard a voice he'd hoped never to hear again.

"I hear you've been rescuing damsels in distress."

He turned around. It was indeed Tamara, Che's minion. She came up to him and put her arm playfully through his.

"Let's chat. I'll walk you to your meeting."

Raul felt sweat break out on his forehead. *What had she found out? Did she know where he'd taken Miriam?*

"It was very chivalrous of you to save that poor woman," Tamara said. "Unfortunately, she works for the wrong side, doesn't she? Che won't be too happy to hear about that. Of course, he doesn't have to know, if you can give me some information that would satisfy his curiosity regarding the Soviet plans for Cuba."

She's trying to impress Che, he thought. Raul had no reason to trust her. But telling her what she wanted to know might buy him some time — and perhaps for Miriam, as well.

"I just found out that there's a plan to build missile bases here. Large ones. Bases that could launch very signi-ficant payloads. I did the survey maps."

"And do you still have them?"

He shook his head.

"Well, it's delightful news, anyway. Exactly the kind of information it pays to know in advance." She dropped her arm. "If you continue to provide such valuable information, I'm sure Che would be happy to keep you around a little longer. Here's how to reach me." Then she handed him a scrap of paper, and walked away.

Raul stared after her. *You're completely screwed now,* he told himself. *Either your superiors discover that you've defied their orders and shared classified intelligence against their direct orders, or that bitch decides to report to the Powers that Be that you dropped Che's name in order to help a suspected counter-revolutionary escape. You're a dead man walking.*

CHAPTER THIRTY-EIGHT

"I have some more information for you. The woman I rescued has agreed to talk. She has some very valuable information regarding US intelligence contacts in Cuba. I think she could help you round up anyone who slipped through the net."

"And why are you so interested in bringing her in now when you went to such lengths to save her?"

"You made some faulty assumptions the last time we met. I saved her because I knew she had valuable intelligence. But if she'd died she wouldn't be of any use to either of us, would she? You didn't stick around long enough for me to explain my whole plan."

Raul could hear the excitement in Tamara's voice as she responded. "Bring her by G-2 headquarters in the morning."

"I can't. I don't know where she is. She left the hospital, and contacted me by telephone. She'll talk, but only if we agree to make sure Castro leaves her alone. She's a woman with nothing left to lose, so it might be difficult to force her to cooperate. If we meet her in a neutral location where she feels safe, we can get everything we want from her, *then* hand her over to G-2."

This suggestion was greeted by silence. *Come on... say you'll do it....*If Tamara's desire to present Che with another plum, one she'd picked herself, could override the dictates of her Stasi training, then his plan stood a chance of succeeding.

"Did she suggest a place?"

We're in. Raul told Tamara when and where Miriam wanted to meet with them. He'd chosen the place carefully: a small marina in Miramar, where several members of Castro's government kept their yachts anchored— luxury vessels "forfeited" when their owners proved to be traitors to the Revolution. He counted on the fact that Tamara's clout could get them access to the docks.

Six weeks had passed since the Bay of Pigs invasion. It was a rout. Castro captured over 2,000 prisoners of war, all Cuban nationals who'd been trained by the US to invade their homeland and overthrow him. Kennedy had admitted that his administration was behind the attack. But all this didn't interest Raul very much. His only goal was to get Miriam out of Cuba, and reunite her with her son.

They were scheduled to meet that night at eleven. As instructed. Tamara showed up ahead of time and told the guards to let Raul and his female guest through, no questions asked, which they did. Raul saw her on the dock, standing exactly where he'd told her to be. She waved to them as they approached, as if she were greeting old friends. When they were within a few feet of her Tamara offered her hand to Miriam.

"You've made the right decision," she said.

"That remains to be seen," Miriam answered.

"We'll talk more when we're on the boat," Raul said, and pulled out the gun Carlos had given him.

Tamara stared in disbelief at the pistol pointed at her chest. "What do you think you're doing?"

"Arranging a private conversation," Raul said, gesturing for her to go aboard the large, powerful cabin cruiser moored to their right. "Ladies first. Into the cabin, and don't make a sound."

Miriam moved as quietly as a cat around the boat. She untied all the mooring lines and then joined Raul in the cabin. Raul handed her the gun.

"Don't listen to a word she says, and if she moves, kill her."

He went to the bridge, looked underneath the wheel, opened the electrical panel beneath it, and proceeded to hotwire the engine. *Sometimes it pays to be an engineer,* he thought grimly.

He could hear the shouts of the guards as he brought the engines to life and pulled out of the marina. *We don't have much time.* He opened up the throttle, locked the wheel, and then went below deck, where he found two canisters of gasoline and a jug of water. He jogged to the back of the boat and tossed the items into the sturdy dinghy that was tied behind the larger craft. It was bouncing chaotically in the cabin cruiser's wake, but Raul managed to make all three throws count.

He went back into the cabin, where Miriam was still holding the gun on Tamara. "You're insane," the woman shouted, her face mottled with rage.

"It's time for you to stop talking." Raul hit her square on the jaw, and the petite woman toppled over, unconscious. He shoved her up the small ladder and out onto the deck, where he buckled her into a life vest. Then he threw her overboard.

He looked back toward the island. Two boats were already hot on their trail. They weren't gaining ground too rapidly, though. He'd picked this boat for a reason.

He went to the bridge and cut the lights, then went aft again, where he tossed his gun into the dinghy. He untied the line connecting the two vessels, wrapped it around his arm, and leapt into the water. The cabin cruiser sped on through the darkness.

Miriam broke to the surface a couple of yards away from him and swam to his side. She held onto him as he pulled them both to the dinghy, which was bobbing nearby. Raul used it to lift himself out of the water just far enough to get a decent view of the two boats pursuing them. One had stopped, presumably to rescue Tamara. The other was headed in their direction, but it soon blew past them, making a beeline toward the yacht in which they'd escaped. If they'd noticed the dinghy at all they must have assumed, as Raul intended them to, that he'd cut it free to gain more speed.

They stayed there, holding onto the side of the small boat, absolutely silent, until Raul was sure he could no longer hear the sound of an engine. Raul hauled himself up and in, helped Miriam aboard, and then started the outboard engine. He pulled a waterproof compass out of his pocket and took a reading. "Ninety miles in that direction," he said quietly.

"I'm ready," Miriam said.

* * * * *

Raul had calculated that it would take about fourteen hours to make it to Key West, if the Gulf of Mexico cooperated. Dawn broke around six o'clock, and he was relieved to see calm water surrounding them all the way to the horizon. Miriam had fallen asleep, using a life preserver as a pillow. It was the first time Raul had ever seen her face look worry-free.

They'd traveled for about eight hours when Raul heard the sound of an aircraft approaching. *Damn. I should have known they'd do that.* Given Tamara's relationship with Che, of course they'd send out planes to search for them, once it had been discovered that Raul and Miriam weren't on the cabin cruiser. He cut the engine and shook Miriam awake.

"Get underwater. Hurry."

She didn't ask any questions, just dove in after Raul and followed him under the boat. They could hear the plane coming closer. Raul pointed upwards and then he crept up, letting nothing but his face break free from the water. He took a breath and went back under. Miriam did the same. They had to repeat this drill several times before Raul was sure the plane had flown out of sight.

He gave Miriam the OK sign. They surfaced.

"Up you go," Raul said. She was a strong little thing, and pulled herself back in to the boat without any difficulty.

He'd just grabbed the gunnels himself when Miriam let out a piercing scream. Raul felt a grip like a vise around his right ankle. He looked down. A gray shark had clamped its jaws around his boot.

Without thinking, he kicked the shark's snout as hard as he could with his free foot. It released him, and Raul sprang into the boat like an Olympic gymnast while Miriam continued to scream.

The shark returned and thumped the side of the boat. Raul reached for the emergency oar and shoved it into the water, once again hitting the creature on the nose. It swam away, only to circle around and bump the craft again. This time Raul was ready and smacked it closer to the eye. It left and didn't return.

"Why didn't you shoot it?" Miriam asked, her voice still shrill.

"Blood in the water would just attract more. Help me off with this, will you?"

Having a task seemed to calm Miriam down. She untied the laces on Raul's thick leather boot and pulled it off. Blood seeped through a series of triangular puncture wounds running across his lower leg, and his ankle had turned purple. After glancing around to see if there was anything she could use to stop the bleeding, Miriam took off her blouse and ripped it into strips, which she tied tightly around the wound.

It was only then that the pain hit him. Small black dots obscured his vision. *Don't pass out.*

"Water," he said.

She handed him the jug. It helped a little. "Can you use a compass?" he asked.

Miriam looked panicked. "No."

Raul held the instrument out to her. "You see this needle? It's pointing north. Pull the cord on the motor to get it started. Use the rudder—that stick I've had my hand on—to steer. Keep going so that this needle continues to point north."

He fell back as the pain in his leg seized him again. A rushing sound filled his ears. *She will find me,* he thought as he stopped struggling against impending unconsciousness. *Her long red hair will fall across my face as she weeps for me, and I will taste the salt of her healing tears. My mermaid.*

EPILOGUE

S ometimes a story just doesn't end the way you think it's going to.

Emilio and I were on a plane within hours of receiving the call from the Catholic Welfare Bureau telling us that someone claiming to be his mother had been picked up by the Coast Guard. We found Miriam in the Dade County hospital, suffering from exposure and dehydration, but the look on her face when she saw Emilio let me know it wouldn't take long for her to get better.

When they'd pulled Raul out of the water he was barely alive. Shock, dehydration, loss of blood, a broken ankle, and a budding bacterial infection were among the many ailments he battled while the rest of us waited, hoped, and prayed (yes, prayed) for him to recover.

The first time I saw his eyelids flutter open I wasn't sure he recognized me. I touched his sunburned face, and then I heard him whisper, "My mermaid." That's when I started to cry.

As I poured tears onto his chest, he patted my head and said with a woozy smile, "If Hitler and Stalin couldn't kill me, what makes you think a stupid shark stood a chance?"

Raul had wisely ditched his passport before escaping,

so Miriam and I were able to confirm his claim that he was Cuban. I also tried to make sure that no information appeared in his file that might tempt someone from the "State Department" to come calling, and as far as I know, Bentley & Company never did discover that they'd missed out on that particular treasure trove of information.

As soon as Raul's condition had stabilized, Emilio, Miriam, and I headed back to New York, along with two more Cuban kids. My mother's short-term memory wasn't great, but she was as cheerful as I'd ever seen her. And although she now walked with a cane, she'd even put on some weight. And she no longer mentioned Jamie as if he were still alive.

Emilio was thrilled to have a foster brother and sister after being alone for so long. His English was coming along nicely, but he needed the company of other children who shared his language, his culture, and his experiences. He needed their company to help him recover. He'd found his mother, but would never see his father again, and would never meet the little sister his mother had lost.

I went back to Miami and stayed with Raul until he was ready to come home, too. But after I brought him to New York I didn't stick around for long. Ma, Miriam, and Emilio were taking great care of him, and I was itching to get back to doing what I loved — international reporting.

I'd already started focusing less on what would make the front page and more on the kind of investigative reporting that might, as my mother had told me, "Do some good for someone." While stuck in New York I worked on ways to keep Fidel's tyranny in the news, so that people wouldn't stop caring about Cuba's fate. After all, I'd had a taste of his hospitality myself. So I began interviewing Cuban refugees, and told their stories in every newspaper that subscribed to the Copley News Service.

After Raul was safely ensconced at my mother's, I made trips to two different Latin American countries, and tracked down the Castro-sponsored groups who were fomenting revolution there, so that the world would know that the Cuban dictator planned on bringing other countries into the communist fold.

When I came home it was obvious to everyone — except the two of them — that Raul and Miriam had fallen in love.

I won't say it didn't hurt, but watching Raul help the children with their homework while Miriam cooked dinner, with Ma shuffling around and offering advice, I understood why it made sense for Raul and Miriam to be together. After all, what kind of life could I offer him? I wasn't going to give up my career, so I would always be traveling, and I wasn't cut out for motherhood. But Raul, Miriam, Emilio, and my mother — it was easy to see that they were creating a family.

Miriam and Raul were married on Valentine's Day, 1962. I didn't make the wedding, although I did send them a card from Chile, wishing them well.

I guess the real surprise came four years later, when Ma passed away. She left her house to the Catholic Church, on the condition that it be used as a home for Cuban refugee children for five years — to be run by Miriam and Raul.

The program begun by Father Walsh and James Baker, head of the Ruston Academy, had exploded. Especially after the Bay of Pigs debacle, Cuban parents were desperate to get their children out of Cuba, to escape communist indoctrination and Castro's tyranny. Between 1960 and the end of 1962 over 14,000 unaccompanied children came to the United States from Cuba, through what was eventually dubbed "Operation Pedro Pan."

Some of the Pedro Pan children ended up with very good foster parents. Many others did not, as the system for placing them was soon overwhelmed by the number of children arriving every day. Some of them were reunited with their parents relatively soon; for others, it took years. Some never saw their parents again.

All of the kids who passed through Ma's house ultimately found their parents, except one. Miriam and Raul eventually adopted him. Oddly enough, his name was Luis. They also had a son of their own, whom they named Armando. My brother Tim was his godfather.

And as it turned out, Ma had learned a lesson from Dad's death. Unbeknownst to any of us, she'd bought a very generous life insurance policy, and had been diligently paying the premiums for over thirty years, even after her dementia began to steal her away from us. Tim, Maureen, and I were the beneficiaries, which helped take the sting out of Ma's decision to leave our family home to the church (although I don't think Maureen ever truly forgave her).

I never did find out if someone from the CIA had talked to Mom about Emilio before her stroke, and I didn't really want to know. I've devoted my whole life to asking questions.

I decided it was best for that one to remain unanswered.

AUTHOR'S NOTES ON
THE HISTORY BEHIND
THE CUBAN CONNECTION

M ary Katherine Anne O'Connor plays a supporting role in my two previous novels, *Silent Lies* and *Deceptive Intentions*.* I've always liked her (and her mother, who also appeared in my first two books). So I decided to give Katherine the chance to tell her own story. I based some of her journalistic adventures on anecdotes from the lives of the most successful female foreign correspondents of the 1950s and 1960s, including Martha Gellhorn, Georgie Anne Geyer, and Lisa Howard.

My main characters always interact with real historical figures, and Katherine is no exception. James Copley, of the Copley Press, did indeed run quasi-spy missions for the US. He was not alone. This "dual function" of well-respected journalists began during World War II and continued until 1976, when congressional hearings on the subject disclosed that hundreds of individuals, from all the major news organizations, both print and broadcast, were cooperating closely with the CIA and FBI. Those helping get information to the CIA included reporters, editors, and publishers. Some journalists were even on the CIA payroll while they worked their regular jobs, and this fact helped me create the character of Robert Bentley. Only after the

Church Committee reported its findings did it become unfashionable for journalists to share intelligence with the US spy services.

Raul's life also reflects actual historical events. During the Spanish Civil War, the Nazis bombed towns in northern Spain as a favor to Francisco Franco, head of the Spanish Fascist party. Hitler also authorized these raids as a test run for the new German air force, the Luftwaffe, to see how their planes could be used against civilian populations. Raul's home town, Guernica, was the first to be destroyed, leaving behind hundreds of civilian casualties. After that "success," many other places were bombed — wherever Franco needed help in defeating the Republican cause.

In response, the Spaniards fighting Franco sent thousands of their children, unaccompanied, to foreign countries to try and keep them safe. They were taken in by Britain, France, Norway, Sweden, Denmark, Belgium, Mexico, and the USSR. When Franco prevailed, and the Spanish Civil War ended, they were all sent home — except for those in the USSR and Mexico. Many Spanish socialists and communists fled to Mexico, and were reunited with their children.

But Stalin flatly refused to let the children in the USSR return to Spain; he didn't want to give Franco the opportunity to brainwash them into becoming little fascists. The child refugees lived well until the Nazis invaded, when their supposed sanctuary turned into a gruesome corner of hell; the entire Soviet population suffered horrible deprivations and enormous casualties during World War II, and the unprotected Spanish children were not spared.

After Stalin's death, most of the "Spanish Children of Russia" elected to stay in the USSR. When Castro took over Cuba his chief strategist, Che Guevara, went to Russia to ask for aid. (Che and Raul Castro were probably the only true communists among Castro's inner circle.) Once there, Che was told about the *Hispanic-Sovieticos*. He immediately requested that a group of them be sent to Cuba, as teachers, translators, and engineers — and to help sell communism to the Cuban public. Given Che's usual tyrannical method of operation, I believe it's also possible that he recruited a few of them to spy on their fellow Russians.

Then, when life under Castro became unbearable, Cuban parents began to send their children, unaccompanied, to the United States. This became the largest peacetime migration of unaccompanied children in history, with the nickname, "Operation Pedro Pan." The parallels between their experience and those of the "Spanish Children of Russia" struck me as both ironic and tragic. I imagined what it would have been like for one of those unwilling Spanish émigrés to see the same thing happening all over again in Cuba: another generation, another dictator, another exodus of children. This became the heart of Raul's story.

Haydée Tamara Bunke Bíder, Raul's nemesis, was also a real person. Better known as "Tania," in 1964 she joined Che in Bolivia, where they were both killed while attempting to inspire the Bolivian peasants to revolt. The Bolivians weren't very interested in revolution, however, and in his diary Che complained, "The inhabitants of this region have heads as impenetrable as rocks."

The circumstances surrounding Katherine's involvement with the group of men who engaged in a last-ditch effort to defeat Castro are also historically accurate. "Blackie" was a real person, although Armando and Nacho were fictional characters based on historical figures. Even without aid from the CIA, it took five years for Castro to put down their rebellion, even with the aid of Soviet armaments and military advisors. For years afterwards the Escambray Mountains continued to harbor small groups of anti-Castro rebels, until Castro finally engaged in a Soviet-style mass relocation of every person living in the area. He forced thousands of peasant families to leave their homes and move to what were essentially prison colonies on the far western corner of the island.

I visited Cuba in 2012. It's my impression that the vast majority of the Cuban people are biding their time, waiting for the Castro brothers to die so that they can take their country back. The Castro regime is a relentlessly repressive, two-tiered system, wherein members of the ruling elite live well, but most Cubans do not. Any attempt to foster opposition is still met with extreme brutality.

Government officials are paid in Cuban convertible pesos ("CUCs"). One CUC is worth about twenty-five Cuban pesos. The average Cuban earns around 350 Cuban pesos a month; a beer in a restaurant costs five CUCs, or 125 pesos. And only CUCs are accepted in stores that carry an enormous array of goods that are not available to the rest of the population. Visitors to Cuba must exchange their money for CUCs, so the most lucrative non-government jobs in Cuba are prostitute, cab driver, artist, and tour guide, because these positions enable people to earn CUCs from tourists.

It's true that Cuban doctors are well-trained, but the medical infrastructure is in terrible shape. The medical equipment is outdated, and electrical power is not always available. Many buildings—sometimes whole neighborhoods—are literally collapsing from decay and lack of maintenance. If you're not a member of the ruling elite, your family has not been allowed to buy a car since 1959. What small progress has been made toward economic freedom is designed to let a little steam out of the pressure cooker of angry resentment, but any privilege granted—like a permit to open a private restaurant—can be taken away at any time, for any reason. Hopefully when the Castros do pass away, the ruling elite will allow some real change to occur, and Cubans can regain their liberty.

About the Author

M.L. MALCOLM began her professional career as an attorney in Atlanta, Georgia, after graduating from Harvard Law School. However, after practicing law for five years, she determined that "she and the law were not meant for each other," and is now a self-described "recovering attorney."

She has won several awards for her fiction, including special recognition in the prestigious Lorian Hemingway International Short Story Competition, and a silver medal from *Fore-Word Magazine* for Best Historical Fiction Book of the Year. Her first novel, **Silent Lies**, was selected as both a "Next Great Read" and a "Recommended Book Club Read" by the American Booksellers Association. She was also chosen as an "Author to Watch" by Target Store's "Emerging Author" program.

M.L. Malcolm has also spoken to over one hundred private groups and book clubs in fifteen states (and she would love to visit or Skype with yours!) Her publications include two historical thrillers, **Silent Lies** (Longstreet Press: republished as **Heart of Lies** by Harper Collins) and **Deception Intentions** (A Good Read Publishing: republished as **Heart of Deception** by Harper Collins), "Chameleon in Berlin," *The Strand Mystery Magazine*

(2012), along with numerous articles in *The Common Denominator* (Washington, DC) and *The Sacramento Union* (Sacramento, CA).

M.L. has lived in New York, Florida, Boston, Atlanta, France, and Los Angeles. She currently resides in Washington, D.C. Over the years she's collected an impressive number of hats (some might say an excessive number) and yes, she does wear them.

Made in the USA
Lexington, KY
05 June 2015